Missouri

HOMEGROWN

Missouri
HOMEGROWN

a novel

JESSE JAMES KENNEDY

Perfect Crime Books

Printed in the United States of America.
Perfect Crime Books™ is a Registered Trademark.

Cover art elements: iStock, used by permission.

This book is a work of fiction. The characters, places, institutions and events are not meant to refer to actual persons or institutions.

Library of Congress Cataloging-in-Publication Data
Kennedy, Jesse James
Missouri Homegrown / Jesse James Kennedy

First Edition: March 2017

To Kathy and Nick

for encouraging me to write this

Chapter 1

The Mexican fled through the woods with the speed borne of panic. Tripping over an exposed root, he landed face down in the dirt. The pistol slipped from his fingers, cartwheeled a few feet from him and settled on a pile of leaves, the barrel pointing at him like an accusing finger. The sound of a snapping twig off to his right sent him scurrying for the gun on his hands and knees. He grabbed the pistol, rose to his knees and fired several times in the general direction the sound came from. One shot ripped bark from a close tree, the other two were lost in the deep woods.

"Here boy!"

He spun towards the voice and fired another shot at another target he couldn't see. He continued pulling the trigger till the last round had been fired and then continued to pull it some more.

Jay McCray stood up from behind the fallen tree he had been crouched behind. "Yeah, that clicking sound means you're out of bullets son."

The Mexican spun toward Jay McCray. This time he had a target. Pointing the gun right at Jay, he pulled the trigger several more times before accepting the uselessness of the endeavor.

He dropped the pistol, leapt to his feet and started running. He was twenty feet away glancing over his shoulder when he stepped onto the bear trap. The steel jaws bit him just below his left knee. His arms flailed as he tried to keep his balance, but gravity got the best of him and he landed on his butt. His eyes widened at the sight of the trap on his leg. The scream that burst from his lips was loud and long and subsided only when there was no breath left to power it.

Jack McCray popped out from behind a tree forty feet from his uncle. "God damn, I'll bet that hurt!"

As they approached, the Mexican's focus shifted back and forth between them and the 12-guage shotguns they carried. They stopped about ten feet from him.

"I'm Jay McCray."

"And I'm Jack McCray."

They raised their shotguns. "When you get to hell," said Jay, "you be sure to tell the devil we're the ones that did this to you." The shotguns exploded with a thunder that only the McCrays heard because when that sound reached the Mexican's ears, one of those ears lay several feet away in the mud along with bits of skull and shredded brain matter. Jack's blast (a slug) took off half the skull. Jay's blast (double ought) caught the upper left torso nearly severing the arm.

Jay pulled his elk-handled bowie knife from its scabbard and threw it, sticking it in the mud next to the corpse. "We'll worry about the bodies later. For now just cut off his nuts and the rest of their nuts too and bring them up to the house."

"The fuck you want their nuts for?" asked Jack.

"You'll see."

"Well, why I got to do all the nut cutting?"

"Cause I got to tend to this," Jay nodded toward his left shoulder where Jack noticed for the first time his uncle had been shot.

"When did you get hit?"

"It was the first one I kilt. He got a shot off as he went

2

down. Lucky shot. Ain't no biggie though. Bullet went right through. Nothing a couple of stitches and a whole lot of whiskey won't fix."

As Jay walked back to the house. Jack pulled the knife from the ground and began his grisly chore.

Chapter 2

"Please Senor! I don't ask for myself or my husband, but for my babies. He kills babies! I beg you, don't let him kill my babies."

Officer Melendez looked at the two children flanking the woman on her knees before him. The girl, he guessed her to be about four, wore only an oversized T-shirt that came down to her knees. The boy, vigorously sucking his thumb, looked even younger. Tears moistened their cheeks. When their mother fell into uncontrollable sobs, they did the same.

The children's father stared out the window. He turned to Melendez. "Please Senor, we should leave this place. They will expect us to come here, it's not safe. We must go!"

Melendez put his finger under the woman's chin and lifted her face upward until he was looking her in the eye. "It's O.K. You are safe now." He turned toward the man. "I need you to take your family back into my office—"

"No!" yelled the man. "We must leave, all of us, it's our only chance."

"Take your family back into my office," Melendez spoke

4

firmly. "If anyone wants to harm you, they'll have to go through us."

"They will! They will kill all of us!"

"Senor!" This time Melendez grabbed the man by the arm and pulled him toward the office. "The office, please!" Shaking his head, the man relented, ushering his wife and children back into the office. With the family secured in his office, Melendez turned his attention to the other three officers on duty. "Everyone over here please." In total there were only eight officers assigned to the small station, three for the first shift, three for the second shift, and two for the night shift. This being the first shift, he had three officers plus himself, which was still a meager front against the cartel.

Melendez wanted to be a lawman ever since he watched the American westerns when he was a child with his grandfather in Juarez, on the old black and white TV with the coat hanger antenna. He wanted to be like those blue-eyed gringos who stood against the odds, dealing out justice in the form of lead. After joining the force, he quickly found out that's not how it works. Not in Mexico. Probably not anywhere else, outside of a Hollywood studio, either. Officer Melendez was more honest than most law enforcement south of the border, which meant he only took bribes when he had to. He wasn't for sale. But he knew that some bribes you either took or you ended up at the bottom of a deep hole in the desert, and the next cop to take your place would take the bribe anyway. Bribes from the Diaz cartel were these kinds of bribes. But turning over a family to be slaughtered was unacceptable. So was running. He'd always known, on some level, that there would come a time he'd have to draw the line. That time had come.

When the three subordinate officers stood before him, he laid out the situation. There was a moment of silence as he scanned their faces. All three showed fear in their own way. Jorge, the oldest at 46, was unreadable. That's how Melendez knew he was scared. Ordinarily, he was easy to read; only when he was scared did he go all poker face. Juan, a five-year veteran, was easier to read, eyes opened freakishly wide, beads of sweat manifested on his forehead, and his body became shifty and jittery, a racehorse anxious to get out of the starting gate and run. Carina, the youngest with only six months on the force, overcompensated to cover her fear. Her eyes narrowed, her chest inflated, and her hand went to her revolver. It's not that she wouldn't back down, it's just that she wouldn't let herself be the first to do it. "Juan, I want you to call all the off-duty officers, tell them what's going on, and get them in here," said Melendez.

Juan shook his head. "There's no way they will come in. I mean, the Diaz cartel? It's suicide."

Melendez thought about this. It was one thing to stay if you were already here in the presence of other cops. But cowardice was a much more acceptable indulgence when others weren't present to witness it. "Just tell them to come in." He paused. "Don't tell them why."

"Senor, I can't. I just—" unable to finish his sentence, or maintain eye contact with his boss, Juan lowered his gaze to the floor. He pulled the badge from his chest and held it out.

"Just put it on the desk," said Melendez after a pause. "Your revolver too."

Juan placed the items on the desk. He started walking for the door, but halfway there broke into a run. There was no point feigning courage in front of people who would be dead in a couple of hours.

Melendez turned to the two deputies he had left. "I need to know if you guys are with me or not. If you want to leave, this is your chance." He turned first to Jorge, knowing what his answer would be.

Unlike Juan, Jorge looked him right in the eye. "Fuck you for asking me that."

He looked to Carina. "You don't have to stay."

She looked at Melendez, then Jorge, then took a long look at the door that Juan had just exited. Just when

Melendez was about to repeat himself, she turned back to him. "No, I'm with you, boss."

"O.K." said Melendez. "Carina, you call the other officers. Jorge, you get the shotguns out of the gun cabinet. Service revolvers aren't going to cut it in this situation."

Both deputies moved quickly to perform their tasks. Melendez went to the open window and looked out. He told himself the dust rising on the horizon could be anything. A passing semi perhaps. Some gringo tourists who passed Tijuana to see "the real Mexico." It could even be Juan racing for safety. But the dust was moving in the wrong direction to be Juan. And the cloud was too long to be a passing semi or stray gringos. He ran to a desk and opened several drawers before finding what he was looking for and returning to the window with a pair of binoculars. He could make out the source of the dust. Six, seven, no ten! Ten black Cadillacs racing toward the police station.

Turning from the window, he met Jorge, who was returning from the gun cabinet with a shotgun in each hand and one under his arm. Melendez grabbed the two from his hands. "You post yourself over there." He pointed to the window on the right side of the front wall, from which he just came. "Carina!" She turned to him, phone held to her ear. "No time for that now." She hung up the phone, and he tossed her a shotgun, which she caught. "Post yourself at that window." He pointed to a window on the left side of the front wall. Melendez went to the front door between the two windows where his deputies were posted. He opened the door and pumped the shotgun just as the Cadillacs screeched to a halt in front of the police station. Every door of every car opened, and men poured out. Melendez counted no less than five men per car. His mind betrayed him with the thought that it was his deputies' loyalty to him that would be their death sentence. He pushed the thought from his mind, welcoming the anger that replaced it.

All the men took up positions behind the Cadillacs, aiming assault rifles at the police station. All but one. One stood in front showing no fear of Melendez or the shotgun he held. Melendez recognized this man as Hector. No one knew his last name. Hector wore blue jeans, biker boots and, despite the fact that it was ninety degrees, a leather jacket. His outfit was inspired by the Fonz from *Happy Days*, a gringo TV show that helped him learn English. Stepping towards Melendez, he pulled the mirrored sunglasses from his face, revealing what would be the good looks of a Spanish aristocrat if not for the scar running straight down the right side of his face from brow to jaw. It ran right across his eye, which had turned a milky white from whatever trauma caused the wound. Hector was a top lieutenant in the Diaz cartel. His authority in the greater Tijuana area was far more respected than any law enforcement.

"Officer Melendez!" Hector wagged his finger at him. "You know who I'm here for, and you really should have called me immediately and told me that they were here. But, I forgive you. Just send them out. I will give you a nice fat envelope, and we can forget this ever happened."

"I don't think so." Melendez tried to sound confident. "You've gone too far this time. How about you and your crew leave now, and I won't have to arrest you all today."

Laughter erupted among Hector and his men. When the laughter subsided, Hector wagged his finger again. "You funny man! That was a good one. But I am tired, and it is hot. Give me what I came for or, I promise, this will not end well for you."

Knowing this was his last chance to back down, Melendez decided to push beyond the point of no return, denying himself the option of cowardice. He pointed his shotgun straight at Hector. "You have two minutes to vacate the premises, or I'll have no choice but to place you all under arrest."

Hector frowned. He glanced at the two barrels sticking out of the windows flanking Melendez. "I don't know how many of you are in that building!" he yelled. "But your idiot boss has decided to commit suicide. There is no reason the rest of you should lose your lives because he is a fool. Come out now, and you can be on your way with a fistful of cash. This is your last chance!"

There was no response. He shrugged his shoulders and walked behind one of the Cadillacs. He twirled his finger in the air and pointed at the police station, before squatting down behind the car. Words were mumbled. Three gunmen popped up from behind three different cars. They were not holding ordinary guns. On each of their shoulders sat what appeared to be some sort of rocket launcher.

Melendez ran back into the station. "Take cover!" he screamed before leaping over a desk. The three rockets slammed into the police station at the same time. The entire front of the building turned into shrapnel-like debris that flew into the station.

In the initial moments after the blast, all Melendez could hear was a high pitched ringing in his ears, and all he could see was the cloud of white dust that hung in the air. As the ringing subsided, he heard shouting. As the dust settled, moving shapes emerged. Feeling around for his shotgun, all he came up with was bits of rubble. Finally, he spotted his sidearm on the floor a few feet away and reached for it. Before his fingers could grasp it, a boot pinned his hand to the floor. The man standing over him pointed a Tech-9 at him. The man reached down, scooped up the sidearm and stuck it under his own belt. "Hey Hector! I got the captain over here!" he yelled.

When the dust dissipated, Melendez looked to where he had stationed Jorge. All that remained was half of the upper torso. He never could move too fast. He looked for Carina. A gunmen dragged her across the floor by her hair. Her nose was bleeding, and a large piece of her scalp was peeled back, but she was alive. At least for now.

The gunman who found Melendez bent over and patted him down. The only thing he found was handcuffs. He rolled Melendez over on his stomach and cuffed his hands behind his back. When the cuffs were secure, he pulled him up to his knees. Carina was also cuffed and put on her knees next to him. Other gunmen ushered the family out of the office and put them on their knees next to the officers. They didn't bother to cuff them. The father stared at the floor. Tears made wet trails down the cheeks of the children. The mother's eyes were closed, her hands clasped in front of her face, while she rocked forward and backward mumbling some undecipherable prayer.

Hector sat on the desk facing them. He pointed at the father. "You have insulted Senor Diaz. And now you talk to the police about us, after all we have done for you."

"Please Hector. I just panicked. I feared for my family. Surely you can understand that. Give me another chance, I beg you. One more chance, and you'll not be disappointed. I will do anything, anything! Please Senor."

Hector scratched his chin. "I don't know. You caused us a lot of trouble, showed us much disrespect."

The children silently sobbed into their mother's chest as she clutched them. She had ceased praying and looked back and forth between Hector and her husband. The man looked first into his wife's eyes then directly into Hector's. "I will do anything," he said one last time.

Hector shrugged his shoulders. "I can't make any promises. But, if you want to make amends, you could start by helping us clean up this mess you made."

"Whatever you want Senor." He stayed on his knees but scooted closer to Hector, hands clasped in front of his face just as his wife had done moments before. But he prayed to Hector not God. "Just tell me what I can do to make this right, and it will be done."

Hector nodded, snapped his fingers and held out his hand. One of his men pulled a machete from a scabbard on his belt and placed it handle first into Hector's palm. "These pigs have to go." Hector pointed the machete at Melendez and Carina. He flipped it in the air, catching the end of the blade and shoving the handle towards the man at his feet. "Give me their heads."

The man rose to his feet and took the machete. He walked over looking down at Melendez. "Forgive me. This is not what I wanted."

Melendez looked up at him. "You're a coward." He looked around at all the faces surrounding him. "You're all a bunch of fucking cowards!" He spit towards Hector.

"Are you going to allow him to disrespect us like that?" asked Hector.

The man grabbed Melendez's hair, yanked his head back and swung the machete into his neck. The second swing sliced into Melendez's esophagus, causing blood to bubble out as he had to breathe out of this new hole in his throat. The man swung the machete over and over again, determined to end it quickly. But chopping a man's head off with a dull machete is harder work than one might think. Carina tried to lunge at the man beheading her boss, but one of the gunmen kicked her from behind, knocking her face down on her stomach. There was nothing more she could do but close her eyes and hope it was over quickly. It wasn't.

By the time he finished off her boss and got a third of the way through her neck, he got winded and had to stop to catch his breath. When it was finally over, he picked her head up by the hair and set it next to the other one. "I told you Hector." He pointed the bloody machete at the blank staring faces of the severed heads. "Anything!"

"You did," said Hector. "You told us." He pulled a cigarette from behind his ear and lit it with a flip of his zippo. He took a long drag before exhaling in a series of smoke rings. "Now them." He nodded towards the man's cowering wife and children.

A moan escaped the woman's lips, and she squeezed her children tighter. The man's thought process played out in his facial expressions. First, raised eyebrows: did he really just say that; then eyes narrowed, jaw tightened: anger; then his gaze lowered to the floor, shoulders slumped: acceptance. He spun around with the machete. His swings were wild and powerful, not focusing on decapitation, like he did with the cops but just trying to end their lives as mercifully quick as possible while avoiding eye contact. If he made eye contact with one of his children, he was sure he wouldn't be able to finish.

When it was over, blood was everywhere. His shirt was soaked with it. It dripped from his face, hands and machete. A large pool of it slowly expanded from beneath the pile of assorted body parts that had been his family. The machete slipped from his fingers, splashing blood onto his pant leg. Now that the work was done, he let his mind absorb what had just happened. He fell to his knees, sobbing and covering his eyes.

Hector flipped his cigarette into the pool of blood where it extinguished with a hiss. He pulled the chrome-plated Desert Eagle fifty caliber pistol from its holster under his shoulder, pointed the barrel at the back of the weeping man's head and pulled the trigger. The hollow point went into the back of his head small and came out of the front of his face big. The man fell forward landing on top of the pile of body parts. Hector turned to the rest of the crew and twirled the barrel of his pistol in the air. "Let's blow this taco stand!"

Everyone scrambled for the door. By the time Hector was walking out, car doors were slamming as the men packed into the cars to leave. Two nervous men carrying a crate of C-4 explosives were going back into the building. Hector slipped into the backseat of the lead Cadillac from which he'd emerged. Paco, his right hand man, slipped behind the wheel and started the car. Glancing in the mirror, he saw the two men who had carried the C-4 into the building come running out. They jumped into the last car, and Paco drove away with the rest of the cars following. When they were about a quarter mile down the road, the building blew. Everyone, except Hector and Paco, turned their heads to witness the blast. Paco allowed his eyes to drift to the rearview mirror. Fire rolled out from every side as the remaining walls were reduced to rubble. A cloud of dust and smoke bloomed above where the police station once stood, and the landscape now void of the only visible building on the horizon was reclaimed by nature.

"So, Paco, you've been to America haven't you?" asked Hector.

Paco's rearview mirror gaze shifted from the aftermath of the blast to Hector's face. "Si Hector, many times."

A splash of someone's blood painted Hector's cheek. He lit another cigarette, held a lungful of smoke, and then exhaled it. "Tell me what you know about Missouri."

Chapter 3

"I want you to take the lead on this one Jill."

The corner of her mouth curled in to a half-grin. "Is the brass O.K. with that? It's a pretty big case. Kind of sensitive too."

"It's my call." Tom Franks was on the verge of retirement and Jill Murphy was the best agent he trained in his thirty years with the Bureau. "I wouldn't be giving you the reigns if I didn't know you were ready. I'll be with you every step of the way."

"It means a lot Tom, you putting this kind of confidence in me. I won't let you down."

"I know. Now let's do this."

They walked down the hall, the sound of their in-cadence footsteps bouncing off the walls and filling the otherwise quiet hallway. Jill considered the weight that was being put on her shoulders. This case could make or break the rest of her career. They entered a room on the left, where five agents were already sitting at a table. A projector sat on a stand in the middle of the room, pointed at a screen mounted on the wall. She sized up the agents. The first three were textbook F.B.I., neither excited nor lethargic, completely nondescript. The fourth, Agent Bushy, was bigger and younger than the rest, blond crewcut, wide eyes, and upright posture. He was eager. The fifth, Agent Brinks, was leaning back in his chair, loudly chewing gum, grinning while his eyes crawled over her body. He might be a problem. Being a female would be the first strike against her in his book, being his boss the second. Add to that the fact that she was half Asian. She could already hear the old familiar jokes. "Me so horny, love you long time." Wouldn't be the first time she dealt with his type, wouldn't be the last.

"Good morning gentlemen. I'm agent Murphy, this is agent Franks." She nodded at Franks who was leaning against the back wall. "The seven of us have been chosen to be the lead team on a case that's very important to the Bureau. Agent Franks, the lights." As Franks flipped the lights off, she picked up the remote and turned on the projector. A picture of a large man with dark blue eyes, black beard and a mess of wild black hair on top of a large head filled the screen. He wore an army issued camouflage jacket and blue jeans. "This is Jay McCray. Veteran of the 10th Mountain Division U.S. Army. Tours of duty in Panama and Desert Storm during which he earned two Purple Hearts and a Silver Star despite never attaining a rank above private due to repeated disciplinary demotions for misconduct. He was eventually kicked out of the Army after being arrested for smuggling hashish across the Canadian border to Ft. Drum where he was stationed. After the Army, he went to his home in rural southeast Missouri. Thanks to an old army connection he made in Panama, he began dealing cocaine with his younger brother, Jimbo McCray. They were fairly successful for a few years before they both landed in prison.

"This is Brian Hollister, a.k.a. 'Dutch,'" she said clicking the remote to show the picture of a muscular inmate whose grin revealed several missing teeth. Two lightning bolts and a swastika tattoo decorated his neck. "In the penitentiary, Dutch, who was an enforcer for the Aryan Brotherhood, took issue with a shamrock tattoo that Jay had on his forearm. The brotherhood considers the shamrock one of their symbols, as many of the founding members were Irish Bikers who had similar tattoos. Members of the Brotherhood are required to tell non-members who have the tattoo to cover it in the presence of other inmates or be dealt with. Jay McCray took the position that the shamrock belonged to the Irish and, as an Irishman, it was his birthright. He refused to cover it. When it was all said and done, Dutch was found dead, face down in a prison toilet. An autopsy would later reveal that he was drowned there. It was common knowledge among prison staff, the warden and the inmates that Jay McCray committed the murder. He spent several months in solitary, but there was never enough physical evidence to charge him with the murder. Eventually, the McCray brothers were released. Jimbo McCray started cooking meth and was back in prison within a year. Jay became a marijuana grower and has thus far eluded law enforcement. He produced a sizable crop of limited quality. Limited, that is, until his nephew joined the family business.

"Enter, Jack McCray, a.k.a. 'the Kid,' Jimbo's son and Jay's nephew." She clicked the remote, and the previous picture was replaced by the picture of a shirtless twenty-year-old. His head was shaved and a large shamrock tattoo covered the right side of his ribcage. A joint dangled from his lips as he flipped two middle fingers at the camera. "Jack McCray was a promising amateur m.m.a. fighter and was invited to turn pro in St. Louis but was turned away before his first fight for a failed drug test. Although 'the Kid' flunked out of high school, by all accounts he is nothing short of a genius when it comes to the cultivation of marijuana. He has the proverbial green thumb. Most growers can be grouped into one of two categories, outdoor or indoor. Both have their advantages. Outdoor growers are able to turn out much bigger harvests, while indoor growers turn out smaller harvests of much higher quality. This is pretty much true coast to coast, except in the case of the

McCrays. Since Jack joined the operation, the quality of their outdoor crop has gone through the roof, rivaling the best indoor crops. Their ability to sell indoor quality at outdoor prices has produced widespread demand for their product, reaching as far as the St. Louis and K.C. markets. This got the attention of the Diaz cartel, which has taken over the K.C. market and is well on their way to doing the same in St. Louis. The cartel's response was to send a dozen armed men to the McCrays' home to kill them."

"We know this because of this man." She pressed the remote and the picture of Jack McCray was replaced by a Mexican in a wife-beater, flashing gang signs, with a sock hat pulled down to his eyes. "Jesus Gutierrez, real name John Cruise. He's one of ours. Agent Cruise had been undercover in the Diaz cartel for a little over two years. He was among the dozen sent to hit the McCrays. We decided to allow the operation to continue to protect Agent Cruise's cover." She paused to gauge the agents' reaction to the fact that the F.B.I. had been willing to allow two murders to take place. None of them so much as blinked. Good. No crusaders. She continued, "Agent Cruise confirmed arriving in southeast Missouri, and that was the last we heard from him. The eleven cartel members with him also disappeared. Less than a week after their disappearance we intercepted a package sent to the residence of Juan Diaz, the head of the Diaz cartel in Tijuana. X-rays revealed that the package contained twelve pairs of human testicles. D.N.A. tests would later reveal that one of those pairs belonged to our missing agent. Of course there was no return address on the package, but it was sent from a county bordering the McCrays'."

"Wait a minute sweetheart," said Brinks. "You really expect us to buy that a couple of backwoods Missouri boys took out eleven cartel gunmen and an F.B.I. agent?"

"You ever heard of the James Gang, Agent Brinks?" He rolled his eyes. "The Younger Brothers? Quantrill's Raiders? They were all backwoods Missouri boys. The cartel runs the urban areas through intimidation and an endless supply of soldiers. But isolate a dozen of them in the remote backwoods of Missouri, where the McCrays have lived and hunted all their lives, where they know every tree and trail, add to that Jay McCray's combat experience. I'm not only telling you the McCrays took them out, I'm telling you they never had a chance. These guys killed one of our own. The cartel underestimated them. Let's not make the same mistake."

Chapter 4

Jack was on the side of the house making out with the neighbor girl Suzie from down the road. Suzie was a bit overweight, a bit butter faced, but possessed a world class pair of knockers. Jack slipped a hand up the front of her shirt and tweaked one of her silver dollar nipples. She was leaning against an old Cadillac that had been sitting in that spot on the side of the house since the engine blew back when Jack's grandfather owned it.

"Why don't we go inside," said Jack.

"Ain't Jay in there?"

"Yeah, so, we can go in my room."

"I don't think your uncle likes me very much."

"Don't take it personally baby. My uncle don't like nobody."

She shook her head. "I don't want to go in there."

"Whatever." The wheels turned in his head. Then his face lit up. "I got an idea. You ever fuck in a Cadillac?"

Sheriff Fuller and Deputy Larose pulled up in front of the McCray place. Larose got out first from the driver's side, the sheriff was a little slower pulling his considerable girth from the passenger seat. The frame of the car rose nearly an inch when the suspension was relieved of his weight. Larose started to walk toward the front door, carrying a manila folder.

"Why don't you wait by the car," said Fuller. Larose gave him a dirty look, but Fuller ignored him and walked on past. Larose watched him climb the porch steps, each one protesting his weight with a loud creaking sound. He knocked on the front door and entered when Jay told him to come in.

Jay was sitting at the kitchen table smoking a joint, flipping the ashes into the meager remains of his breakfast plate. He pointed to the chair across the table. "Have a seat." Fuller sat down dropping the folder on the table and Jay passed him the joint. He took a couple of hits, coughing as if something inside him were fighting to get out. "Looks like you're out of practice," said Jay taking the joint back.

Fuller pointed at the bottle of whiskey sitting on the table. "You mind?"

"Course not."

Fuller grabbed the bottle, unscrewed the cap and took a long swig. He lowered the bottle for a couple seconds then took another long swig. He put it on the table and slid it across without the cap. Jay took a healthy swig of his own and slid it back. Fuller took another double swig then put the cap back on.

"So you come all the way out here to get fucked up or you got something else on your mind?" Jay took another drag off the joint.

"You remember them Mexican boys you," he paused searching his already buzzing brain for the right words, "dealt with."

"I do."

"Well, I been poking around doing a little research and they seem like some pretty rough old boys. Then I get word over the weekend that a bunch of Mexicans moved into Grady's old bar. I think we might of done stuck our peckers in a hornets nest. They already been fucking with the locals."

"So why don't you arrest them?" Smoke poured out of Jay's mouth, as he spoke, in a dragon-like fashion.

"I don't got the manpower."

"Well I wouldn't worry too much. There was a dozen of em last time and it only took me and my nephew to," he put the joint out in the remains of some hash browns on the plate before him and smiled at Fuller, "deal with them."

"There are at least twice that many this time. Maybe three times as many. I'm not even sure. Now I can bring in the Feds on this but—"

"Fuck that!"

"Exactly. It serves us well to keep a limited police presence, but in a situation like this—" Fuller shrugged his shoulders. "I got you what intel I could dig up on them." He pushed the folder towards Jay.

Jay grabbed the bottle and took another swig. "Don't sweat it man. I'll figure it out when I'm not so stoned." He slid the bottle to Fuller.

Fuller picked up the bottle. "And when exactly is that?" He took another double swig.

"Is that all you came out here for?"

"Well," Fuller put the bottle down and capped it. "As long as I'm here."

"There it is!" Jay said smiling. He got up and left the room. When he came back, He threw a fat envelope stuffed with hundred dollar bills on the table. "I put a little extra in there for the Mexican situation. That make you feel any better?"

Fuller pulled the bills from the envelope and fanned them out like a winning poker hand. He looked at Jay with bloodshot eyes. "You know, it does."

"Fucking asshole," said Larose. He was pissed at being left outside. Fat ass was probably in there copping a buzz, he thought. He walked around the car kicking the dirt at first. That got old quick so he started throwing rocks into the woods. Then his boredom gave way to his nosey instincts and he walked around the house to see what he could see.

His eyes fell on the Caddy and its subtle bouncing motion. Smiling, he crept up on the vehicle until he was close enough to see through the window. Jack was on top so all he could see from the angle he had was Jack's bouncing ass. He cringed and craned his neck so he could at least see some titties.

"Jesus fucking Christ!" said Suzie spotting him over Jack's shoulder. "It's that pervo pig."

Jack glanced over his shoulder at Larose's grinning face. "Fuck off!" he yelled before turning back to Suzie. "Forget him," he said and tried to go back to humping.

"No Jack. Not with him watching, he creeps me out." She pushed him away.

He took a deep breath. "Fine." He climbed out of the Caddy, zipping up his pants.

"That there, is indecent exposure. I think I'm going to have to see some I.D. boy." Larose turned and winked at Suzie who was pulling her cut-off jean shorts back on.

"Is that what you think? Well, I think I'm gonna have to see how far I can shove your head up your ass." Jack stepped toward the deputy.

Larose lost his smile. "Is that so little man?" He also stepped forward and the two were face to face staring each other down.

"Ya'll gonna kiss or what?" said Jay.

"I thought I told you to wait by the car," said Fuller.

Larose turned to see them on the side of the house. The sight of Jack's giant uncle made him rethink the confrontation. He took a step back from Jack and put his hands up. "Just joking man. Just joking."

"Yeah?" said Jack. Now he smiled. "I wasn't."

Chapter 5

Julio Diaz was the nephew of Juan Diaz, the kingpin of the Diaz cartel. Julio's father, Juan's brother, came up with Juan in Tijuana. They went from a couple of small time smugglers and dealers selling to tourists, to the second biggest crime family in Tijuana. Inevitably they began to bump up against Vilobos and his three sons, who were the number one crime family in Tijuana. Vilobos was an old school gangster who ran the city with his three sons in the old school gangster way. That is to say, they extorted lesser criminals and legitimate businesses for "protection payments," and rarely had to get their own hands dirty with any illegal activities other than setting the occasional example by cracking the occasional skull or slitting the occasional throat of someone who couldn't make their payment.

The Diaz brothers were much more hands on and much more ambitious. It wasn't long before, even after making their payment to Vilobos, they were making more money with their smuggling than the Vilobos protection racket. Old man Vilobos could have lived with this, but his sons were bothered by the respect the Diaz brothers were getting on the street and wanted to rob and kill them. The old man gave them a lecture on the foolishness of killing the goose that lays the golden eggs. The lecture made no impact on them whatsoever. In the end, the father and the sons compromised by agreeing to let the Diaz boys live but doubling their protection payments.

The Diaz brothers saw no reason they should have to pay twice as much as everyone else and refused. They braced for the certain blowback which appeared to begin when Julio's father was gunned down in the street outside his home. Julio was a teenager at the time and his father's sole heir as his mother had passed away two years earlier from cancer. Julio and his uncle took a considerable portion of the amassed Diaz fortune and used it to hire every man they could find brave enough to raise a gun against Vilobos and his sons. Vilobos and his sons had gone so long without resistance that they were totally unprepared for a war. The Diaz gang wiped them out. They killed the old man, the sons and a third of the Vilobos soldiers. Another third ran and never returned to Tijuana, and the remaining third went on the Diaz payroll.

What Julio never knew was that his uncle had made a deal with Vilobos. If Vilobos killed Julio's father, Juan promised to split his brother's share of the business with him. After Vilobos fulfilled his end of the deal, Juan double-crossed him. He figured he'd use Vilobos to take out his brother so he could take his end of the business, then he would use Julio to take out Vilobos so he could take over his racket. What he had not counted on was Julio. After Julio helped take out Vilobos, he just naturally assumed he would inherit his father's end of the business. To make matters worse, most of the gunman in their newly formed army were Julio's friends and likely to be loyal to him if push came to shove. Juan decided to allow his nephew half the profits for the time being, but he did draw a firm line. Since Julio did not help build the business, he would get half the profits, but his uncle would be boss. Julio accepted this.

Bolstered by their victory over Vilobos, their confidence

and ambition grew. When Juan suggested they move into L.A., it was actually supposed to be a clever way to get rid of Julio. Why settle for a smuggling fee off the top, he reasoned with his nephew, when the real money is in distributing in the States. Instead of turning it over to some gringo, we should put our own soldiers in Los Angeles and take the profit for ourselves. Julio took the bait and jumped at the idea. So Juan sent Julio, and the soldiers most loyal to Julio, first to San Diego. He expected the black gangs and honkey bikers to chop them to pieces in no time and leave him sitting on the throne with no one near his equal. But Julio and his men proved more formidable than he expected. They recruited from the sizable Latino population already in California, slugged it out with the blacks and whites, took San Diego, moved north and got a foothold in East L.A., then took over that city. Then came San Jose, then San Francisco. Like dominos, city after city fell until the Diaz cartel was supplying the whole West Coast. Within a couple of years they were moving east. Whatever existing distribution networks they came across they either offered them a better deal and absorbed them or wiped them out and put in their own people. They spread eastward like an army of locusts consuming everything in their path, all the way into the Midwest, without a single hiccup. Until the McCrays.

After Julio moved into the States, Juan made a point of bringing in people who didn't know Julio and would be loyal only to him. Of all these new recruits, Hector was Juan's right hand, his sledgehammer. No one was sure where Hector came from, but he had worked for criminal organizations all over Mexico and Central America. He answered only to Juan and viewed Julio as just another employee. He would be the first person Julio dealt with since coming to the States who wasn't directly under his command.

Hector arrived in St. Louis around noon. As far as first impressions go, he was pretty disappointed. Almost everything he'd seen of America, up until that point, had been from the movies and television. The Miami from *Miami Vice*, Manhattan from *Seinfeld*, Los Angeles from *Charlie's Angels*. St. Louis looked nothing like these. Unremarkable was the most accurate word he could think of to describe it. It was a completely unremarkable city. And the people, everyone was so fat and slovenly. In the movies and television there practically was no such thing as an ugly American, even the supporting roles were played by beautiful people. Where were the Angelina Jolies, Megan Foxes and Pamela Andersons? Where were the Brad Pitts and George Clooneys? Where were the flashy *Miami Vice* type clothes and the flashy cars?

By the time Paco pulled the car up in front of the house, disillusionment had soured his mood. The house, like everything else he'd seen in this city, was nothing special. The cartel owned it outright. It was better than renting. No nosey landlords to worry about. Paco parked the car in front of the house and got out along with Hector. Hector stretched his arms and back and looked around. A fast food bag tumbled down the street and a group of young black men in sagging pants shot them hard looks from across the street.

"You want me stay and watch the car boss?" asked Paco.

Hector shook his head. "If these pendejos haven't instilled enough fear in the locals not to steal our car then we're in worse trouble than I thought."

The front door opened, and Julio came out along with Santiago, his top man, and another of his top lieutenants. They crossed to where Hector and Paco stood. "You must be Hector. I'm Julio." He extended his hand. Hector gave the hand a long look as if he didn't know what it was, then gave it the briefest of shakes. Julio motioned to the man on his right. "This is—"

"Let's go inside," interjected Hector. Without waiting, he pushed past Julio. Julio exchanged glances with Santiago before following.

Inside, Hector and Julio sat across from each other at the kitchen table. Julio's two lieutenants stood behind him. Paco stood behind Hector. Everyone else had cleared the room. "Let me just say," said Julio. "I have—"

"Let me ask you something," interrupted Hector as if Julio wasn't even speaking. "Of all the contraband we sell, which is the least lucrative? Is it the coke? Heroin? Methamphetamine?"

"No," said Julio. He could see where Hector was going with this. "The least lucrative would be the marijuana."

"The marijuana, I see." Hector leaned back in his chair and lit a cigarette. "And these men, the McCrays, are they coke, heroin or meth dealers?"

"No," said Julio.

"What do they do?"

"They grow marijuana."

Hector took a drag off his cigarette and exhaled, sending a thick wave of smoke rolling lazily in Julio's direction. "And where do these marijuana growers live? This city? Another city?"

"No." Of course Julio knew damn well that Hector already knew the answers to all these questions. He lit his own cigarette, resigning himself to the little show Hector was obviously determined to indulge.

"Where then?"

Julio shrugged his shoulders. "Down around the Ozark area. It's in the southern part of the state."

"And this 'southern part of the state,' is it a lucrative market, a place we need to be?" He ignored the ashtray right in front of him and flipped his cigarette ash onto the floor.

"It is not," said Julio exhaling smoke.

"And these people, these, how you say, heel-bee-lees—"

"I don't know if you could call them hillbillies exactly, the—"

"I said they are heel-bee-lees." He sat up tensing in his chair and stared at Julio.

Julio stared back for a few seconds then put his hands up. "Fine. Hillbillies they are then."

Hector leaned back again. "And these heel-bee-lees, have you killed them?"

Julio took a long drag off his cigarette and took his time exhaling. "You know we haven't," he finally answered.

"You haven't." He nodded his head while crushing out the butt on the kitchen table before flicking it on the floor. "So let me make sure I got this right. The reason that Senor Diaz and his family had to endure this atrocity, and a dozen of our men are dead, is so you could go to an area we don't need or want, due to a perceived threat to our least profitable enterprise. And the entire squad you sent was wiped out without even accomplishing their objective. In short, you were bested by a couple sister-fucking, inbred heel-bee-lees who don't have enough I.Q. points between them to tie their own shoes."

"Well," said Julio crushing his own cigarette out in the ashtray. "I'm afraid they're a little more formidable than you give them credit for. But let me assure you I—"

"*You* are going to do exactly what I tell you to do, so I can clean up this mess you've made. Then we'll have a long talk about whether or not you still deserve to represent you're uncle's interest on this side of the border. Till then, pick out a few people to take care of things here, and tell the rest of your soldiers that we all will be taking a little vacation."

Chapter 6

Buzz Spivey was a Vietnam vet and owner of the Buzzsaw, the most popular local bar and favored hangout spot of the McCrays. He'd brought a wife home from Vietnam and had three daughters with her. By the time the youngest turned four, the marriage had soured, and both Buzz and his wife began affairs, eventually divorcing. His wife quickly married a truck driver, moving with him and her three daughters to St. Louis. Years later, Buzz also would remarry and have two boys with his second wife. His ex-wife never pressed for child support, and he never pressed for visitation. The two older daughters only visited a couple of times, just long enough to confirm that they preferred the city and realize how lucky they were to have escaped this place. The youngest daughter, who learned to call her stepfather daddy, never returned.

When Jill began to make her plans concerning the McCrays, she assumed, because of the racial makeup of the region, that she would have to give the coveted role of undercover operative to one of the underlings. Agent Bushy was a natural with his Midwestern farm boy looks. But here was the perfect cover for her. A half Caucasian, half Asian female, close enough to her age, born and bred in the area but gone long enough that nobody would recognize her. Nobody would question a hometown girl coming back to go to work in her dad's bar as a waitress. Enough people would remember that little half-Asian girl well enough to validate her cover but not remember her vividly enough to hazard a guess at what she would look like today, outside of her ethnicity. The question was how to get Buzz to cooperate. She found the answer in his son Dennis Spivey.

Like his father, and countless other boys trapped in the middle of nowhere, he decided that joining the Army when he turned eighteen was his way out. Also like his father, and countless other boys from the middle of nowhere, he became a grunt and ended up in combat. In Vietnam, the Army had its numbers bolstered by the draft. If a soldier could keep his head down and survive his tour, he had a good chance of coming home. In Iraq there was no draft to provide the government with cannon fodder. This was circumvented by simply sending soldiers who enlisted back for a second, third, even a fourth tour. This led to an increased number of post-traumatic stress disorders and outright nervous breakdowns. Dennis became one of these mental casualties. While at home on leave, between deployments, he decided he had enough. His initial plan of escape consisted of a shotgun in the mouth. An hour passed as he sat there salivating on that barrel, trying to work up the nerve to pull the trigger. Finally, he gave up on that in favor of a handful of Vicodin and a bottle of tequila, after which he lay down for what he hoped would be the last time. He woke ten hours later in a pool of vomit, still hopelessly alive.

On the day he was supposed to ship out for yet another deployment, he took off walking west with nothing more than the clothes on his back, $23.28 in his wallet and a half a pack of Marlboro Lights. He didn't put his thumb in the air, but when he was offered a ride, he accepted. These rides usually didn't last long. The most he ever offered, in the way of conversation, was to mutter, "Fuck all the bullshit." Six months later he was arrested for vagrancy in California. He was living under a bridge, completely unrecognizable except for the fact that he was still wearing the same clothes. He'd grown a thick beard, his hair was long and dirty, his odor hit you several feet away as if thrown at you. The only comment the police could get from him was, "Fuck all the bullshit." Eventually, the police did figure out his identity and he was turned over to military custody.

The Army had no desire to draw attention to the broken men the war was producing. Their standard operating procedure for dealing with these cases was to offer them a general discharge and a lifetime supply of psych drugs, on Uncle Sam's dime, to keep the whole PTS thing (which they rarely admitted existed) numbed and sedated. All the vet had to do was keep quiet, not make a big deal out of his experiences. Most of them were more than willing to do that in order to be let out of the biggest mistake of their lives.

Fortunately for Jill, she caught the potential value of Dennis Spivey's status before his discharge. The Feds made some calls, pulled some strings and got the Army to put the brakes on his case, holding him in a military prison.

"Desertion during wartime is a very serious charge. We no longer execute people for such crimes, but the Army has been looking to make an example. Your son could be looking at a very lengthy prison sentence," said Agent Franks. "Lucky for you, you're in a position to help the government and, by extension, help your son. Play ball and I can get all charges dropped and a general discharge. Not only will he not have to serve a prison sentence, but the incident doesn't even have to go on his permanent record."

Buzz resented the idea of playing Judas to his people, but he bought the threats hook, line and sinker. He gave Jill a waitress job and introduced her as his daughter. She was in.

Chapter 7

Days after the sheriff's visit, Jay still hadn't come up with a plan to deal with the cartel. He did know that he couldn't be perceived as hiding. He had to make an appearance in public. When the McCrays' favorite cousin called to tell them she'd borrowed her daddy's pick-up and was heading to the Buzzsaw if they wanted to toss a few back, he knew it was time for that appearance.

Tracy was the McCrays' third cousin from their mother's side, the Kennedy side, but they all three were closer to her than any of their other cousins, many of whom they couldn't have picked out of a line-up. They viewed her as nothing less than a little sister. Jay and Jimbo's mother passed away over a decade ago, Jack's disappeared on the back of a Harley years ago, and they had not seen their aunt and three female first cousins since they were kids due to one of those backwoods family feuds that tend to span generations. And women they weren't related to were viewed either as sexual interests or irrelevant. Tracy alone provided that necessary feminine energy without which they would be little more than a pack of wolves. They were even kinder to each other in her presence, though she only saw herself as one of the boys. She wasn't movie star beautiful but she had that girl-next-door, tomboy cuteness that many men find more endearing than the plastic barbie-doll perfection of classic beauty. She had soft but lively green eyes, curly hair and that mischievous half-smile/smirk so common to the Irish, the one where you can't quite distinguish if they are laughing with you or at you but can't help being charmed either way. She was a bit on the skinny side, waifish even. But she was country girl tough, less interested in makeup, clothes and girly drinks than four-wheeling, shooting guns and slamming whiskey.

Fuller said the cartel were messing with locals so if she was going to be there, Jay didn't want her to be there alone. He explained his thinking to Jack.

"I agree," said Jack.

"We ain't gonna start no shit, we ain't gonna take no shit."

"I agree."

"Jack."

"Yeah?"

"We *ain't* starting no shit."

"Understood you the first time."

"When the time is right, we will make our move. Right now we're just showing our faces to make it clear we ain't sweatin them."

"I got it."

"We *ain't* starting no shit."

"What the fuck?!"

"Let me hear you say it."

"We-*ain't*-starting-no-shit. Now can we please go get drunk?"

"Let's go get drunk."

No sooner did they get to the bar and out of their cars when all the doors of several other cars in the parking lot opened and armed Mexicans poured out. Jay wondered how long they had been waiting for them. He and Jack both pulled their pistols. The situation seemed tense for everyone but Hector. He was the only one who didn't pull his weapon. All twenty men with him had their guns pointed at Jay and Jack who stood side by side pointing their pistols right back. Tracy, who was close by in the parking lot waiting for her cousins, grabbed the shotgun off the gun rack of her daddy's pick-up and took up position next to Jay.

Hector still made no attempt to go for his own gun and, in fact, acted like he didn't even notice the McCrays as he just stood calmly smoking a cigarette. Taking a big drag, he exhaled in a series of smoke-rings before finally looking at Jay. "Senor McCray, I presume?"

"Pleased to meet you." Jay aimed his pistol at Hector's face.

Hector looked around at his men then turned back to Jay. "I understand you heel-bee-lees don't care much for education. But I trust you have a sufficient enough grasp of basic arithmetic to see you're outnumbered, do you not?"

"I do," said Jay.

"And if I were to order my men to fire, you surely don't think you could win this particular confrontation, do you?" Hector took another casual drag off his cigarette.

"Naw, I don't think we could win, but I know for a fact that I could kill you dead before any of your boys get me."

"I see. And you are a very brave man to be willing to trade your life for mine. Very impressive. Very scary." Hector held his hands out and made them shake as if frightened. "But your family members backing you up there, are they so willing to forfeit their lives, I wonder?"

"Let's ask them." Jay kept his pistol and his eyes on Hector. "Trace, you ready to die?"

"Fucking A, Cuz, I'm with you, remember the mother-fucking Alamo!"

"What about you Jack?"

"Hell, I always knew I was going out like this sooner or later. Today is as good a day as any other."

Jay shrugged his shoulders. "Looks like we're willing. You willing?" Jay asked Hector.

Hector took one last drag off his cigarette before exhaling and crushing it out. "It is tempting. But I don't think I'm going to kill you today gringo. Soon. I promise you soon. But this," he waved his hand at all the guns pointed at Jay, "would be too quick and easy for you. You've earned a much more dramatic death than this. And I certainly don't want to kill your beautiful cousin before getting a chance to know her better." He winked at Tracy, who took her left hand off the shotgun long enough to flip him the middle finger. Hector turned away and walked to his car. The rest of the cartel backed up to their respective vehicles keeping their guns pointed at the McCrays. The McCrays returned the favor, not lowering their own weapons. Even as the armada of vehicles left the parking lot, everyone kept their weapons pointed until the cartel force was out of sight.

Jay, Jack and Tracy put their guns away and entered the bar together. Jay's eyes made the adjustment from the bright sunlight to the subdued illumination of the bar's interior. He noticed Sheriff Fuller and Deputy Larose sitting at the bar. Larose was just getting off duty and Fuller was just coming on as he preferred second shift due to a fondness for sleeping late. Larose was having his usual after work beer and Fuller was drinking because he was the boss and drank when he wanted to. Jay wondered if they were oblivious to what just went on outside or if they knew and just decided to play it neutral. Jack was the first to the bar. He ordered three double shots of Jameson, one each for himself, his uncle and his cousin.

"So how are things at the lollipop guild?" Larose asked Jack before bursting into laughter at his own joke.

Jack reached over and grabbed Larose's cigarette from the ashtray in front of him. He took a drag. "Fucking menthol!" He threw it into Larose's mug of beer.

"You little fuck!" Larose jumped up from his stool.

"I'm sorry, I thought you was done with that." Jack smiled,

Tracy laughed. Her and Jay had pulled up to the bar next to Jack.

Fuller squeezed between Jack and his deputy. "All right boys. We're all friends here."

"Friends is a strong word," said Jack.

"Maybe we best just let them go at it," said Jay. He knew Jack had some pent up aggression from the standoff and it would be better he relieve it with a fistfight than go off on some half-baked Mexican killing spree.

"You sure that's a good idea?" asked Fuller.

"I think so. I'm tired of hearing these two mutts barking at each other. Let's let em off their chains."

"Hold up now," said Larose. "I respect you Jay. That's why I held my temper for as long as I have. I ain't trying to piss you off by whuppin your nephew's ass and end up having you put me six feet under."

"Well," said Jay before slamming his shot of whiskey and turning to face Larose and Jack. "Let's get this straight right now. The two of you have it out. Right here, right now. When it's over, it's over. Everybody moves on. Nobody looks for payback, including me. That O.K. with you Jack?"

A smile stretched across his face. "That's the best fucking thing you could have told me. I ain't never gonna turn down a chance to stomp a pig, no strings attached."

Jay turned to Larose.

Larose nodded his head slowly. "Yeah, fuck it. Let's do this."

Larose unbuttoned his uniform top and Jack slammed his whiskey shot and pulled his T-shirt over the top of his head and tossed it on the bar. The room was filled with the sound of scooting chairs and tables as the bar's patrons, who had followed the confrontation in rapt silence, cleared the center of the floor for the impending combat. Jack warmed up by bouncing up and down on his toes and throwing crisp punch combinations into the air. Larose tried to do the same but his punches were slow and sloppy and even his attempts to bounce up and down looked awkward.

But as obvious as it was to everyone that Jack was the superior boxer, it was equally obvious that Larose had at least thirty pounds on him and three inches. Like most Midwestern boys, Larose was more of a wrestler than a boxer. He'd had a respectable record on his high school team. And thirty pounds was a lot in wrestling.

Jack came up to the bar next to his uncle. He pounded his fist on the bar twice. "Shot!"

"Make it three," said Jay.

Buzz set three shot glasses in front of them and filled them with whiskey. Jay slid one to Tracy who sat to the left of him and one to Jack on his right. They tossed back their shots then slammed the glasses on the bar. Jay looked at his nephew's reflection in the mirror behind the bar. "Don't get cute. Just take him out quick and easy. All business."

"Fuck that." Jack smiled at his uncle's reflection. "I'm gonna punish this prick."

The sound of scooting tables and chairs gave way to the excited murmur of a crowd anticipating violence. Predictions were discussed, odds were negotiated, and bets were made. Despite his smaller size, Jack was the early favorite.

The crowd's murmur petered out as Jack and Larose began to circle each other on the open floor. Jay stood at one side, the sheriff at the other. Jay folded his beefy arms in front of his chest as he studied the two combatants with the focus of a man studying a chessboard. Tracy got up on the bar to see above the heads of the other spectators. "Whup his ass Cuz!" she yelled.

Larose put his fists up to his chin attempting a classic boxing stance. Jack, on the other hand, didn't even look like a man about to fight. His arms hung limply at his sides, he stood flat footed, a shit-eating grin smeared across his face. Turning his head slightly to the right he stuck out his jaw. "Come on then," he said waving Larose in. "Let's see what you got." He stood there, hands down, jaw extended, easy target.

Larose wound up and let loose a big looping round house

haymaker which Jack easily dodged still not raising his hands. The force of the missed punch sent Larose stumbling and almost falling before he regained his balance and spun around to face Jack who had circled around behind him.

Jack, hands still down, stuck out his chin again. Without hesitation, Larose threw a left hook, this time focusing more on speed than power. Still, Jack easily dodged it. Larose tried to catch him by surprise by following the missed left hook with a right hook. Again, nothing but air.

Jack pretended to yawn. With hands still at his sides. He stuck out his chin again. Larose, pride stinging from the chuckles that rippled through the crowd the last time he missed, made his own attempt at bravado. He mimicked Jack dropping his hands and sticking out his own chin.

Jack leapt in, not with a looping hook like Larose threw, but with a straight right cross that landed solidly on the chin and sent Larose reeling backwards before landing on his ass with a thump. Jack grinned and gave him a thumbs up to tell him to get back to his feet.

"God damn it!" muttered Jay under his breath. He held the opinion that when you got a guy down you should not allow him to get back up.

Larose got back up. He was done trying to box with Jack. Instead of putting his fists up to his chin, he put them all the way up to his hairline, completely covering his face with his arms. He charged forward figuring he'd absorb Jack's punches with his arms till he got close enough to grab him and turn it into a wrestling match.

Jack, with no punches to dodge, stood his ground and planted his feet. When Larose got close enough, Jack landed a left hook to the body, easy to do with Larose's hands so high. This was one of his favorite punches ever since he saw a video of his hero Irish Mickey Ward score a knockout with it, the only body blow knockout he'd ever seen. Jack landed the punch on the right side of the body just below the ribcage. He dug his fist in far enough to hit the liver. The effects were immediate. Larose crumbled to the floor curling up in the fetal position. Jack turned his back on him walked over to one of the spectators and took a swig from the beer he was holding.

This was too much for Jay. "Quit fucking around!" he yelled. "End this!"

Larose was all but helpless on the floor. But Jack ignored his uncle and gave him time to recover. When he seemed to have his wits about him, Jack gave him the thumbs up again.

Larose was game. He punched the floor and rose on shaky legs. He charged Jack. He didn't hold his hands up at all this time focusing on just grabbing Jack. Jack landed a crisp jab cross combination as he came in, breaking his nose. But Larose ate the pain and pushed through, tackling Jack. Jack landed on his back with Larose on top of him.

"You're mine now you little fuck," said Larose as blood dripped from his broken nose onto Jack's face.

Jay shook his head, knowing the fight could have been over. But Jack didn't panic. He'd been in this position before. Bigger guys always wanted to put you on your back and sit on top of you. The old schoolyard bully move.

Larose knew this was his chance. He tried to rain down a couple of big punches but Jack moved his head from side to side and Larose only busted his knuckles on the hardwood floor. When he paused to shake his fist out, Jack reached up and shoved his thumb deep into Larose's eye. He tried to touch brain. Larose twisted his head to the side and pushed Jack's hand away. The pain in his eye angered him enough to go for broke. A blizzard of punches came down at Jack's face but he kept his cool. He couldn't dodge all the punches but he covered his face with his arms and blocked most of them. Soon, as Jack knew he would, Larose ran out of gas. Jack knew several submission holds that he could apply from his back and a moron like Larose would be particularly vulnerable to a triangle choke. But Jack didn't want to win this fight with some tricky Jujitsu choke. He wanted to hurt him. He reached up grabbed

Larose by the ears and pulled him till they were face to face, at which point he bit deeply into his cheek.

Larose screamed. He put both his hands on Jack's face and pushed with all his strength. After a few pain filled seconds, he managed to shove Jack's head away from his own and slam it into the floor. When he felt his face he realized that Jack came away with a good chunk of his cheek still in his mouth. Jack spit the chunk of flesh up into his face and Larose recoiled in horror. This momentary shock gave Jack the chance he needed to explode, shove Larose off him and get back to his feet.

Larose paid no attention to Jack. He seemed to have forgotten he was in a fight. He stayed on his knees clutching his bleeding cheek. Jack was satisfied enough to go ahead and end it. He closed the distance with three steps and kicked Larose under the chin with his steel-toed boot. Larose landed on his back. He was surely done at that point but Jack put an exclamation point on it. Standing over Larose, he brought his leg up so high his knee almost touched his own chin before bringing it down on Larose's face. Larose's world was suddenly nothing but shattered facial bones and internal bleeding. When Jack raised his foot again, Fuller stepped forward to put an end to it. But before he could stop it, he made eye contact with Jay who shook his head from side to side. Fuller stopped. Jack stomped again. And again. When he raised his leg again, Fuller gave a sharp look to Jay, and Jay pulled him off before he could deliver another stomp.

"All right boy, I think that ought to just about do it then," said Jay.

Jack tried to push past his uncle for another go but Jay held firm. Jack settled for looking around his uncle's massive girth so he could see his handy work. "How you like me now bitch?!" he yelled at Larose.

Larose's only response was to cough up a volcanic eruption of blood and broken teeth. The sheriff bent down over his busted up deputy. "This is bullshit!" Fuller yelled at Jay.

Jay shrugged his shoulders. "I guess he ought not have fucked with a McCray then."

"It was supposed to be a friendly fight," said the sheriff.

Jay laughed. "Ain't no such fucking thing."

Chapter 8

Jill's official cover was that she was staying at her father's. Buzz did, in fact, have a room set up for her and, if her cover required it, she could stay there. For the time being, she was staying in a motel a couple of hours down the highway with the other agents. It made for a long commute but cut down on the chance someone there might recognize her. After a long shift at the bar and the two hour drive, she was exhausted when she pulled up to the motel room. As she walked to her room, she passed Agent Brinks who was standing in the open doorway of the room he was sharing with Agent Bushy.

"Hey there Jill," said Brinks. "I see they're making you wear space shorts for your undercover work. You know, space shorts, cause your ass looks out of this world." Brinks laughed at his own joke as Jill, who had been hit on for the last eight hours by drunks, almost all of whom were slicker than Brinks, gave him no reaction at all and just walked on to her room. Brinks frowned. "Fucking lesbian." He turned to Bushy who was sitting in the room watching Sportscenter. "Hey Bushy. Why did the feminist cross the road?" Bushy shrugged his shoulders. "To suck my dick!"

Bushy giggled, but it was nothing compared to the booming laughter that overcame Brinks. "To suck my dick! Get it?"

Jill had an adjoining room with agent Franks. After changing into sweatpants, T-shirt and flip-flops, she opened the door on her side. The door on his side was already cracked open an inch, but she knocked anyway.

"Enter," he yelled.

She walked in and sat in the room's only chair, kicking off her flip-flops and putting her feet up on the bed. Franks stood at the sink. He took a bottle of orange juice dumped half of it out and refilled it from a bottle of Smirnoff. "Screwdriver?" he asked.

"Please," she said.

He tore the shrink-wrap off the two plastic cups provided by the motel and poured two screwdrivers. He handed one to Jill then flopped down on the bed. They both took a drink. "So how was your day?" he asked.

"Exhausting!" She took another drink and slumped back in the chair. "Waitressing is hard fucking work let me tell you."

"Anything eventful happen?"

Jill smiled. "I saw them."

"Which one?"

"Both of them."

Franks sat up. "You saw both of them? Together?"

"Yep. They came in to drink and fight. Jack McCray nearly beat a deputy to death right in the middle of the damn bar. The sheriff was there and didn't do anything about it. Dollars to donuts the McCrays got him on their payroll."

"Was there anyone with them?"

"A girl, young, pretty. Buzz said she was their cousin, Tracy something or another. I don't think she's a player."

"So if they were both there, why didn't you call us?"

"Well, here is where it gets juicy. Apparently, before they came into the bar, they got in a beef out in the parking lot. With Mexicans!"

"Oh yeah?"

"Oh yeah!" Reenergized she sat up, gulped down the last of her screwdriver, set the cup on the table and burped. "Excuse me. So, I'm thinking Mexicans in this neck of the woods, beefing with the McCrays can only mean one thing."

"Cartel."

"That's right. Cartel. You said this case was mine right?"

"I did." He swallowed the last of his screwdriver, shook the bottle again and poured what was left between both their cups.

"Thank you." She took a sip. "Well, I want to play this out. Wait till the cartel moves on the McCrays, then bust the McCrays, the cartel, maybe even a dirty sheriff to boot."

Franks nodded his head. "Ambitious. I'll approach the deputy. I'll tell him I'm investigating the cartel and any information would be appreciated. I'll drop it kind of casually that anyone who provides information that explains why the cartel may be here will get immunity for any illegal activity. If he knows about the McCrays killing the cartel squad, he might see it as a chance to get revenge on Jack and clear himself of any payouts he took."

"I learned from the best." She raised her cup in a toast. He tapped his cup to hers and they drank. "Listen Jill. For now let's not mention the cartel connection to the team. O.K.?"

"O.K. Why?"

"Let's just play this close to the vest."

"Oh shit! Don't tell me we got a leak."

"There is an outside possibility, just a possibility mind you, that someone in the bureau has been leaking information to the cartel."

"Fuck me!"

"Look, even if it's true, the odds that the leaker is someone on our team is pretty low. Still—" He shrugged his shoulders.

Jill nodded. "O.K. We keep a lid on this for now. In fact maybe we just keep the team out of the loop altogether until we need them. Probably better not to put it in the report either. Not till we need to."

"I agree," said Franks.

Chapter 9

Sheriff Fuller had about twenty minutes till Lucy came on duty. Lucy was a portly, homely forty-eight-year-old woman who was technically a deputy. Her sole job was to work the night-shift which consisted of mopping the floor, answering any calls (usually there were none) and making a pot of coffee for whoever came in on the morning shift. If something serious occurred that could not wait till morning, then she called the sheriff. But her deputy duties rarely included anything outside the station.

Fuller leaned back in his chair, which protested with a loud creak, and slipped off his boots which seemed to torture his feet more each day. When the door opened, he looked up expecting to see Lucy coming in early. Instead he saw one Mexican after another come through the door until a dozen of them filled the room. He pulled his .357 from its holster and cocked it under his desk.

Hector sat down in the chair in front of the sheriff's desk. "Do you know who we are?" he asked.

Fuller looked around at the hard unfriendly brown faces and then met Hector's gaze. "I'm guessing you're here to see if we need any yard work done."

"That's cute," said Hector. "But, you know who we are." He pulled out a cell phone pressed a button and showed the screen to Fuller.

On the screen Fuller watched a video of a woman tied to a chair. She had a ball-gag in her mouth and tears ran down her face. A man stood behind her, his head cut off from the top of the screen. The man reached over her shoulder with a chrome semi-automatic pistol and slid the barrel down her shirt. The woman squirmed but the man kept pushing the barrel farther down her shirt until the top button broke exposing her bra. The man bent over, resting his chin on her shoulder. The face that came into view was Hector's. The woman was Fullers wife. The video ended and Hector put the phone back in his pocket and smiled.

Fuller exploded across the table, grabbed Hector's shirt in his left hand, pulled him close and with his right hand stuck his revolver under Hector's chin.

All of Hector's men pulled their weapons and a few advanced on Fuller, but Hector put his hand up. "No one make a move!" He put his hand down and looked into Fullers eyes. "If I wished to, I could have one of my men drop you before you could pull that trigger. But I'm going to give you a chance to kill me. I'm curious as to what you will do." Hector raised his voice so everyone in the room could hear. "If he decides to kill me, I don't want anyone to try and stop him. After he kills me, kill him. Then go to where we are holding his wife. After you each take a turn raping her, soak her in gasoline and set her on fire. Before you flick that bic, make sure she knows that her husband could have saved her but declined to do so. After that, go to Mizzou University, go Tigers!" Hector pumped his fist in the air. "And find his daughter Missy. Don't kill her though. Take her back to Tijuana and put her to work in one of our whorehouses." Hector smiled. "A nineteen-year-old blue-eyed blond gringo girl should be very popular. Then go to 1518 Londell View Drive where his mother lives and shove this same .357 he's holding under my chin up her ass and keep pulling the trigger till it goes click." He lowered his voice again addressing Fuller. "So there you go Sheriff. If you can pull that trigger then you are a more ruthless man than I and it will be a worthy death by your hand. But I'm betting my life you're not. Your move Sheriff."

The sheriff surprised himself by seriously considering pulling the trigger. After this momentary consideration, he uncocked his pistol and leaned back in his chair, releasing Hector's shirt. The door swung open and Lucy entered carrying a brown lunch bag and a paperback novel. She froze when she saw the room full of Mexicans.

"Tell her to give us a few minutes," said Hector.

"Do me a favor hun," said Fuller. "Run down to the grocery store and grab us a can of coffee, we're getting low."

"We still had over a half-can last night," she answered.

"Lucy, please."

"Oh, sorry. Yes sir," she said getting the gist. She stepped toward the door, put her hand on the knob, then stopped. She looked around the room at the men, then back at her boss. Her hand went from the door-knob to butt of the .38 revolver that she'd only ever fired at beer bottles. "Everything O.K. Sheriff?"

"It's fine," replied Fuller. He was impressed that she was prepared to back him. "I just need to chat with these boys."

"Okey-dokey." She gave Hector a parting glare before leaving.

"O-key do-key," said Hector. "This is how it is going to work. At any time you can kill the McCrays. That will be the quickest way to reunite with your better half. Of course, I'll need proof. Their heads will do. If you lack the huevos for this then you can provide us the information and assistance we need to accomplish this task. But make no mistake. If you want your familia unharmed, then the McCrays have to die and you have to play a significant role in their expiration."

"Fuller slowly nodded his head, "I'll do whatever it takes to get my wife back. But understand this. If you—"

"Yeah, yeah," said Hector. "If I harm one hair on her head you'll kill me. Right?"

Fuller nodded, "That's right."

Hector shook his head. "You gringos. Always so dramatic. You get that from all those Hollywood movies you know? You all think your life is a Hollywood movie and you're the hero. But, I confess, I also love your Hollywood movies. So allow me to indulge in your over the top American dialogue. If I hurt your wife you will kill me. I believe you would try to make good on that threat. But it is a threat. Know that what I tell you is a fact. If you betray me to the white trash McCrays, I'll lay waste to you and your entire family. And even if myself and every man in this room die, there will be another hundred cartel soldiers here within days to fulfill that promise." Hector smiled. "Now have a nice day."

Chapter 10

Jimbo McCray stood in line waiting to empty his lunch tray into the trashcan and hand it to the dishwasher. So much of prison was waiting in line. Waiting in line to go to chow, waiting in line to come back from chow, waiting in line to go to the showers, etc., etc. When the prisoners finished eating they emptied the remains of their tray into the trashcan and handed them to the dishwasher before going back to their cell. While waiting, Jimbo noticed that C.O. Preston was standing by the trashcan and staring at him. Preston was a dick of a correctional officer who liked to think himself a tough guy. He made a point of fucking with the biggest, baddest guys in the joint and, eventually, gave most of them a beat down. As tough as he pretended to be, though, he never attempted the beat down part on his own. He always made sure he had at least a few other guards with him to tilt the odds decisively in his favor. Jimbo was his current tough guy target of choice. Several inmates had warned Jimbo not to take the bait when Preston fucked with him, don't give him the excuse to bring down the hammer.

When Jimbo reached the trashcan, he turned his tray upside down and emptied the remains. But before he could hand it to the dishwasher, Preston started in. "Let me see that tray, inmate."

Jimbo took a deep breath, turned over his tray and showed it to him.

"There is still food on that tray, inmate. Empty it again."

Jimbo turned the tray over and banged it on the edge of the trashcan. He showed it.

"Now, inmate, I know you're stupid, but you're not that stupid. Does that tray look empty to you?"

"It looks empty to me," said the dishwasher waiting for the tray.

"Shut the fuck up and mind your own business." Preston pointed at the dishwasher making a point of flexing his bicep as he did so. It was a move he practiced in the mirror at home. He always made sure, when on duty, that his sleeves were rolled up tightly around his arms to accentuate the bulge. After holding the flex for a few seconds, he felt his arm start to shake from the effort, so he abandoned it and turned his attention back to Jimbo. "Empty it again inmate and do it right this time, without the attitude."

Jimbo tapped the tray on the trashcan again. This time he held it up with both hands right in front of the guard's face. He glanced at the dishwasher, "Wanna see something cool?" Before Preston could say anything, Jimbo shoved the tray forward into his face, breaking both the tray and the guard's nose. Preston landed on his ass. Blood poured from his nose and cheers erupted from every inmate left in the cafeteria. Jimbo dropped the two broken pieces of tray. "Clean enough for you now boss?"

Preston touched his nose and looked at the blood on his hand. "Oh, you fucked up now inmate."

"Guess I might as well go ahead and fuck you up then." Jimbo took a quick step toward him as if about to attack.

Preston scurried toward the door, first on all fours then rose to his feet and ran towards it. When he got to the door and realized Jimbo wasn't chasing him, he stopped and pointed at

Jimbo, not bothering with the flex this time. "Mark my fucking words, inmate, you fucked up"

Again Jimbo put a foot forward, and the guard ran out the door. Jimbo made a beeline for the door at the other end of the cafeteria. A battle was coming and he preferred to fight it on the home turf of his cell. The inmates gave him a standing ovation as he left the cafeteria. He made haste to get to his cell. They would be coming soon. On the way, he grabbed a mop that someone left leaning against a wall. When he got to his cell he disconnected the wooden mop handle from the mop head and tossed the handle on his bed and the head in the corner. He grabbed his bottle of shampoo off the shelf, crossed the cell and grabbed his cellie's shampoo off his shelf. He started by the door, pouring the shampoo on the floor from one wall to the other. He backed up doing the same thing covering more and more of the floor until he was all the way back to his bunk. Then he climbed up on his bunk and poured the last of the shampoo on the floor. He put the end of the mop handle against the wall, pinned it there with his foot and pulled the handle till it broke. The splintered end of the wood came to a nice sharp point. He remained standing on his bunk and held the mop handle behind his back.

Preston was the first to show up at the door of his cell, quickly followed by five other guards. All of them wore body armor and face shields. The first two also carried two large transparent riot shields. "Lay face down on the floor, and put your hands behind your back, do it now!"

Jimbo flipped him the middle finger with his left hand while holding the mop handle behind his back with his right. "Fuck the police!" he said.

Preston smiled. "You're mine now asshole. Formation!" When he yelled, formation, the six guards squeezed together in two rows with the first two in each row raising the riot shields. When he yelled the second command, they charged through the door. Their momentum carried them to about the center of the room when their feet flew out from beneath them. They hit the floor hard, tried to get up and hit the floor again. They tried to grab each other to steady themselves, but since each man had the same slippery footing this just caused them to fall in pairs.

One of them grabbed Jimbo's bunk. With something secure to hold on to he managed to get to his knees. Holding on to the corner of the bunk, he looked up to see Jimbo, who was still standing on the bed, looking down at him. Jimbo put his foot under the facemask of the guard's helmet and flipped it off his head. He whipped the mop handle from behind his back and stabbed the guard in the eye with the sharp point. The guard grabbed the end of the makeshift spear, and his mouth came open like he was going to scream but no sound came out. Jimbo shoved the spear farther in, and the guard stopped struggling. His hand dropped and he went limp. Jimbo tried to pull the spear out but it was stuck. He put his foot on the guard's forehead and yanked. When the spear came out with a wet sucking sound, the guard fell over backwards onto the floor, and Jimbo realized he had just passed the point of no return.

The rest of the guards, having grasped the seriousness of the situation, gave up trying to get to their feet or even their hands and knees. Now they were on their bellies, crawling toward the door, resembling lizards scurrying across a frozen pond. Jimbo thought of frog gigging back home. He held the spear up high and brought it down hard, stabbing the helpless belly crawling guards. It was tricky because of the body armor. If he stabbed that armor too hard, he risked breaking the tip of his spear. Eventually, he figured out the best place was the arteries on the side of the neck, where the armor didn't cover. Stab and slash these arteries and they bleed out fairly quick. He took his time, moving from guard to guard. He started with the ones closest to the door, hooking them with the spear, pulling them close enough to grab an ankle, then pulling them close enough to stick them. On the second to last one, the sharp point at the end of the mop handle broke off in the guard's neck. So, for the last one, Jimbo jumped on his back and choked him to death.

After the last one stopped moving, Jimbo sat on his back for a minute catching his breath. He knew that whenever one of the walkie-talkies the guards wore was turned over sideways for more than a minute, a distress signal went out, so he didn't have much time. It took some major squirming on the slick floor, but he managed to get himself and one of the dead guards out of the cell and into the hallway. In a minute or two he was wearing the guard's uniform and riot gear, face shield and all. He bolted out the door and sprinted for the gatehouse. The first challenge was crossing the open yard in broad daylight without being spotted. If he made it to the gatehouse then he faced an even bigger challenge which was getting the guard inside to open the door. If the door was opened, then he could overpower the guard, take the keys to whatever vehicle he drove and leave out the front gate. If the guard didn't open the door, then it was all over and when the other guards saw what he did to their coworkers they would likely beat him to death. He reached the gatehouse without any whistles going off or guards chasing him. He pounded and kicked at the door maniacally.

"What the fuck?!" yelled a voice from inside.

"It's a riot!" Jimbo screamed. "They've taken the whole prison! They saw me come out here, they'll be here any minute, you've got to let me in!"

"No one called the riot code over the radio."

"There's no one left to call the riot code! They're raping the guards that are still alive, for God's sake you've got to let me in!"

There was a couple of seconds of silence then the voice responded. "I don't know. I can't break protocol without at least trying to verify this."

"There's no time! Oh Jesus! Here they come! They're going to rape me! Please, please don't let this happen to me!"

And then he heard it. The click of the lock. The door opened, he slipped in and the guard slammed and locked the door behind him. He turned to Jimbo who took off his face shield. "Who the fuck are you?" asked the guard.

Jimbo smiled. "Wanna see something cool?"

Chapter 11

Julio did a real estate search for something in the vicinity of the McCrays that they could use as a base of operations. They didn't want some house in the middle of the woods. Some former business, close to a main road, would fit the bill. Almost all the available buildings in that area, big enough to house the number of soldiers they intended to bring, were former churches or bars. By far, these were the two most popular businesses in rural Missouri. No matter how many dotted the landscape, new ones kept opening and closing. These new ones didn't do too well. The only thing these people were more loyal to than their family churches were their family bars. Julio settled on an abandon bar that was well priced because it had not yet been cleaned out. When they got there, the fact that it was not yet cleaned out turned out to be an advantage. The inside of the bar was a bit dusty, but it was full of tables and chairs, which came in handy, an oak bar with stools and, to the delight of the crew, the shelves behind the bar were still stocked with partial bottles of booze. Apparently, the owner had to leave in a hurry.

At all times, one man sat at a chair looking out the

window to keep watch. The guy, who was currently standing guard, stood up quickly turning his chair over backwards. "Hector! We got company! A pick-up truck. It looks like that big dude." All the men sprang to life moving to the window.

"Is he alone?" asked Hector.

"Looks like it, boss."

"All right then, everybody spread out and act cool. He didn't come here by himself to make a move. Stupid fuck probably thinks he can cut a deal. I'm curious as to what he thinks he can offer." Earlier Hector had a desk they found in the storeroom pulled out and set up in a corner by the window. He took a seat in the chair behind it.

The men dispersed around the bar, trying to look casual while eyeballing the front door. The man who had been on guard at the window opened the front door just as Jay was stepping up to it. "Good morning gringo sir. Welcome to our hacienda. Come on in." Jay stepped into the bar and the Mexican stopped him just inside the doorway. He attempted to pat him down but Jay put his hand on the man's face and shoved him stumbling backwards several feet. The Mexican ran up on Jay till they were nose to nose. "You want to die white boy!"

Jay didn't flinch. "All you boys, armed to the teeth, against just me. And you need to pat me down." Jay turned from the man in his face and looked directly at Hector. "Do I scare you that much?"

Hector gave him a hard look. "Let him through. We're all friends here. Have a seat." He pointed at the seat in front of his desk. Jay brushed past the man he was nose to nose with and sat down in the chair. "I'm guessing you want to make a deal?" said Hector.

Jay nodded. "You guess right."

Hector shook his head. "You really should have thought about making this deal before you disrespected Senor Diaz. You would have had a much better chance at a positive response. But because you are brave, I will show you the respect of hearing your offer before I kill you."

"I appreciate that," said Jay. "But, you should really do yourself a favor and accept the offer I'm about to make. And here it is. If you all leave right now, I'll let you live. And I don't mean by tomorrow or the end of the day. I mean right now, pack up and leave. This is the only offer I will make. There will be no negotiation."

There was a few seconds of stone silence before Hector burst into laughter. The rest of his men joined in and soon the whole room was giggling. Jay raised his voice to be heard above the laughter. "And if you don't leave now, then we'll start killing you today."

The laughter ended abruptly. Hector and Jay glared at each other. Hector had just enough time to realize that he should have insisted that Jay be patted down before Jay made his move. He moved fast for a big man. Good thing too. If the gunmen in the room had another second, one of them likely would have killed him. But Jay managed to yank the steel hand-grenade from his pocket, smash it into Hector's mouth, knocking him over and breaking several teeth, two of which he swallowed, and pull the pin before anyone could get a shot off. He held the grenade up for everyone to see. With his free hand he pulled another grenade from his pocket and pulled the pin with his teeth. Now he held up two grenades. Everyone else in the room, except Hector, who still lay on the floor, pointed their guns at him though no one dared fire, knowing a kill shot would guarantee the release of the grenades. Jay slowly moved backwards toward the front door. "This is as nice as I'm going to ask ya'll to leave. Ain't nothing here for you but death."

Hector stood up, swaying on unsteady legs, mouth full of blood, front teeth reduced to jagged remnants. He pulled his own pistol and pointed it at Jay.

When Jay reached the front door, he mule-kicked it open and stepped back in the door frame. He looked Hector in the eye. He quietly uttered one word, "Boom," before chucking the two grenades into the room and disappearing out the door.

Every man in the room dove for cover. Several behind the bar, some turned over tables and crouched behind them, some just dropped to the floor and covered their heads. Hector jumped up on his desk and dove through the glass window behind it. He turned his face away and broke the glass with his shoulder, but a large piece of it nearly severed his left ear before he landed head first on the pavement outside. Everyone waited for the blast that would send the shower of shrapnel that might end their lives. But it never came.

After an excruciatingly long twenty seconds, Julio peeked over the edge of the table he was hiding behind and spotted the two grenades lying in the middle of the floor. He came out from behind the table and approached them. With each step he grew more confident till he was standing over them and they still hadn't exploded. He picked one up and examined it. "They don't have charges, they're dummies!"

The men came out from behind their cover. Initial relief was followed by a wave of embarrassment which in turn gave way to anger. On the sill of the window that Hector had dived out, two hands appeared before Hector's face rose into view. His busted teeth were matched by his cut up face and an ear that hung at an odd angle due to the fact that it was only secured by a slight piece of skin. "Kill that puto!" He pointed toward the front door from which Jay had just escaped. The men scrambled for the door, weapons at the ready. They were eager to redeem themselves.

"No wait!" screamed Julio. But it was too late. They were already at the front door.

Across the street from the bar was a large barren field. Across that field, about 500 yards from the front door Jay had just exited, was the edge of the thick woods. Not ten feet back in those woods, Jack lay in the prone position on the cool, damp ground. The barrel of his .308 rested on a log in front of him, his eye centered the crosshairs of the powerful scope on that door. He saw his uncle come out running for his truck. He held the crosshairs on the front door. It wouldn't be long now. It was about a minute, give or take, when the door opened a second time, just as Jay said it would. They were lined up, all in a hurry to get outside and start shooting.

Hector would later assume that it was several snipers all firing at the same time. Seemed the most likely explanation with two dead and one severely wounded. But it was just Jack. And he only fired the single shot. The first man, who appeared in the doorway, flung the door open with his left hand and pointed his pistol with his right. Jack squeezed the trigger. It caught him on the left side of the body just below the chest. Right in the heart. He died instantly. The bullet passed through him, hardly slowing down at all. It had a slight downward trajectory. The second man got it high in the middle of his stomach, severing his spine, before exiting out his back. It took him almost an hour to die. The bullet still had plenty of power, though the man's spine altered its trajectory. It hit the third man in the groin area. He would live but never be the same again.

After that shot, the rest of the cartel dove for cover for the second time that day. By the time any of them worked up the nerve to try to go out again, this time using the back door, Jack had cut a quarter of a mile through the woods to a dirt road where Jay picked him up.

Chapter 12

Jimbo pulled the stolen Mazda behind J.T.'s convenience store and parked it where it couldn't be seen from the street. He'd dumped the guard's Jeep in a grocery store parking lot not far from the prison, then walked to a long term commuter parking lot where he stole the Mazda. He made the four hour drive home before it was even reported stolen. J.T.'s used to be a gas station/convenience store but they stopped selling gas years ago, and now the old time pumps out front where no more than decorations. It was just a small mom and pop shop that sold booze, cigs and groceries to country folks who didn't want to make the long trip to town. Jimbo walked around to the front door and pushed through it, causing the bell attached to the top to jingle. J.T. was behind the counter, cutting coupons out of a newspaper, and Johnnie Mueller, who Jimbo went to high school with, was in front of the counter eating from a box of powdered donuts.

"Well shit on a shingle!" said Johnny. "If it ain't Jimbo McCray! How you doing old boy?" He stuck his hand out.

"Out-fucking-standing." Jimbo shook his hand. "How bout you?"

"Hanging in there Jimbo, hanging in there."

Jimbo turned to J.T. "J.T., I need to charge a few things, I'll have my brother or my boy come pay for it tomorrow, couple days at the most."

"No sweat Jimbo, your credit's good. What do you need?"

"For starters, I ain't had real whiskey in years. How bout you pass me a fifth of that Beam." J.T. handed him a bottle from the liquor shelves behind him. Jimbo took the cap off and took a long swig. He rotated his hips and moaned in an orgasmic fashion. "God damn! That sure does beat the hell out prison hooch, I'm here to tell you." He offered the bottle to Johnny, who wiped the powdered sugar from his mouth with his arm, took a swig and handed it back. He then offered it to J.T. who set his scissors down, took a swig, and then handed it back. Jimbo took one more long swig then put the cap back on. He grabbed a clear plastic container of beef jerky off the counter, unscrewed the cap and took out two pieces. He put the pieces together and ripped a bite off both at the same time. "Can I get a carton of Camels too?" he asked with a mouthful of jerky. J.T. put a carton of Camels on the counter. Jimbo bit off another mouthful of jerky. "So what's new fellas? Fill me in. It's been a long time. What did I miss?" J.T. and Johnny looked at each other. "What?" asked Jimbo.

"You talked to your brother lately?" asked Johnny.

As they filled Jimbo in on the situation between the McCrays and the cartel, which was the hottest gossip on the country grapevine, four of those cartel members pulled up out front. Three of them tried to get gas from the defunct gas pumps, the fourth sat in the car finishing his beer. The three getting gas flipped the lever several times, squeezed the handle and, when that didn't work, tried kicking the side of the pump, which, surprisingly, didn't work either. The one in the car climbed out, chugged the last of his beer then tossed the empty bottle over his shoulder. "I'm going to take a piss," he said walking toward the storre.

"Tell them the pump isn't working," yelled one of the others.

"Get more beer," yelled another.

He entered the store, ringing the little bell in the process. "El bano?"

The three men stared at him.

"El bano?!"

"I think that's Mexican talk for where's the pisser," said Jimbo. He looked at the Mexican. "It's back in the corner." The Mexican stared blankly. "Back in the el-corner-o," He pointed toward the bathroom. The Mexican grunted and headed toward the bathroom. Jimbo took another swig of whiskey and put the bottle on the counter. "Well I think I'll go take a piss myself.

Johnny and J.T. glanced at each other. "I think I'm gonna hit it," said Johnny scooping up his box of donuts and heading for the door.

"Take it easy," said J.T. He picked up his paper and reached for the counter, his hand pausing. "Where the fuck did I put those scissors?"

When Jimbo entered the bathroom, the man was standing at the urinal completely oblivious of him. Jimbo quietly moved toward him till he was standing right behind him. When he went to flush the urinal, Jimbo slipped his left arm around his head and covered his mouth, then stabbed him repeatedly in the right side of the neck with the scissors. On the third stab he hit the artery. Blood began to spurt. After bleeding out the guards with a broken mop handle, doing it with the scissors was cake. When he felt the body go limp, he dragged it into a toilet stall and sat it on the toilet. He pulled the pistol out of the man's shoulder holster and tucked it into the back of his pants. He stepped out of the stall and went over to the mirror. There was blood on his face, neck, hand and the shoulder of his shirt. He washed up and turned his shirt inside out. He left the bathroom and headed for the front door. "I'll be right back for the whiskey and smokes," he said.

The Mexicans were arguing in Spanish about how to get the

defunct pump to give gas. "It's a little tricky," said Jimbo. "Let me give you a hand." He walked over, pulled the nozzle out of the tank, put it back in, flipped the handle up, then back down, and then smacked the side of the pump. "Hmmm. What did you guys do to it?"

"Nothing, it's a piece of shit!"

"Oh well." Jimbo hung the pump handle back up. "Let me ask you something, is this car stolen?"

The men glared at him then one of them stepped toward him. "Fuck you white boy."

"I didn't mean no offense man. I'm just saying, am I going to have to worry about some cop running the plates when I'm driving it down the road."

"What the fuck did you just say to me?"

"Never mind." Jimbo smiled. "Hey, you guys wanna see something cool?"

Chapter 13

Julio swallowed the last swallow from the last bottle of tequila in the defunct bar that had become their home. He tossed the bottle over his shoulder, hearing the clank clank as it landed on the floor, stubbornly refusing to give him the satisfaction of shattering, which was the entire point of throwing it. "More tequila!" he screamed at the handful of men around him.

"There is no more tequila, amigo," said one of the men.

"Mescal then."

"We are literally in the middle of gringo land. I doubt most of these barbarians even know what mescal is."

"Fuck!" Julio threw an ashtray at the mirror behind the bar which, already having been shattered by Hector, robbed him once again of the satisfying music of breaking glass. He stood up quickly, turning over the barstool he had been sitting on. He stumbled halfway to the front door before turning around. "Keys!" he yelled.

The men exchanged glances. "Keys to what?" asked one brave soul.

"The keys to Fort Knox. What the fuck do you think? The keys to a fucking car."

"What car?"

"What the fuck do I care what car? Any car that will carry me out of this shithole to more tequila."

"I can go get you more tequila," said the brave soul.

"If I wanted you to get me tequila, I would tell you to get me tequila. Now someone give me some keys!" Julio heard the echo of Hector's egotism in his own voice and started to hate himself a little bit.

The man he was talking to relented and tossed him a set of keys. "That's to the old Buick on the side of the building. At least take a few men with you."

"Fuck off!"

"Hector said nobody should go—"

Julio shot him a glare.

He put his hands up. "Sorry."

Julio plowed through the front door. Outside, he stood still for a moment, allowing the cool night air to caress his face. He stumbled to the old American car on the side of the building and fell into the driver's seat. He rolled down the driver and passenger windows. The night air was his only friend, so far today, and he didn't want to be separated from it. Miles down the road, he realized he had no idea where he was going. In St. Louis, K.C., or any of the other American cities he'd lived in, he could set out in any direction, on foot, and within blocks come to multiple venues to purchase alcohol. But out here you could drive miles without seeing anything man-made at all. He decided to just stick to the road he was on and not get off on any side roads. That way, if he didn't find anything, he could just turn around and follow it back. He was so enjoying the combination of tequila buzz and cool Midwestern night that he'd almost forgot what he was on the road for. Then he saw the lights up the road. He decided to pull into whatever it was. If it was a place where he could get booze, he would. If it wasn't, he would turn around and head back.

Pulling into the packed parking lot, he ignored the timid

voice in the back of his head saying this is a bad idea. Wherever you went in America, the parking lots of popular bars were all the same. Neon lit beer signs, the seductive sound of laughter, shouting and music getting loud every time the door opens, muffled whenever it closed, but always steady. He walked through the door like he owned the place.

All eyes were on him. Jack McCray sat with a couple of girls at the back of the bar. Jack pulled his pistol from his belt and chambered a round under the table. Jay sat at the bar. Julio walked over and sat on the stool next to him. "Shot of Cuervo!" he said to Buzz. Buzz's eyes shifted to Jay. Jay nodded his head. Buzz poured the shot and set it in front of Julio. Julio turned to Jay. "Buy you a shot?"

"Wouldn't turn it down," said Jay.

"You drink tequila?"

"From time to time."

"Shot of Cuervo for mi amigo!" Buzz filled a shot glass and put it in front of Jay. "I must confess something to you amigo," Julio said while staring at his shot glass. "This predicament we find ourselves in, it's all my fault. Truth be told, the cartel is not really interested in your backwoods, children of the corn hellhole. I was over ambitious." He turned and looked at Jay. "I sent those men who came to kill you. I am sorry about that."

"You should apologize to their families," Jay deadpanned.

"Yeah, you did a real number on them. That was truly impressive. And that dog and pony show you put on at the bar, wow, you got balls. No denying that." Julio turned back to his shot glass. "But see that's where you sealed your fate. Those men, they were the first wave of an incoming tide. I know you Midwesterners don't know much about the ocean, so let me educate you. The first wave of an incoming tide is the smallest and weakest. You broke that wave to be sure. Me, Hector and all the men we brought with us, we are the next wave. Bigger and stronger than the first wave. Let's say you could kill every one of us, which, let's face it, is a tall order in itself. A bigger wave will follow. And a bigger one after that. Be careful not to become so focused on the wave, that you fail to see the ocean behind it."

Jay nodded his head thoughtfully. "Well Pedro—"

"My name is Julio."

"Sorry, well Julio." Jay raised his shot glass, Julio raised his, they clinked glasses and downed their shots. Jay put his glass on the bar and continued, "You ever hear of the I.R.A.?"

"The Irish Republican Army. Not everyone with brown skin is completely ignorant, Irishman."

"No, I didn't expect they were. Anyway, let me tell you something you probably don't know about the I.R.A. Most of those guys know they can never defeat the British Army. But what they also know is that if they never stop fighting, then they are never defeated."

Julio nodded his head, weighing Jay's words. "I'll drink to that Irishman. Two more bartender!" Buzz poured two more shots, they clinked glasses and downed their shots.

A slight hiss escaped Jay's lips. "You got to admit this stuff is about as tasty as dirty gym socks."

Julio laughed. "I don't drink it for its taste, I drink it for its medicinal benefits." They both laughed. Julio ordered two more shots. When the shots were poured, Julio continued, "I understand a lot of the more respectable gringos look down on us violent mongrels streaming across the border, soiling their red, white and blue utopia with our violent gangster ways. But when your people came over from Ireland did they not take over the gangster underworld, the only foothold available to them? Did the Jews and Italians not do the same? And when the Anglos came over from England, did they not jack the entire country from the Indians, slaughtering any that got in their way? They were the biggest gangsters of them all. Make no mistake Irishman, what we are doing in your cities and your hometown, the violence, the crime, it's not the Mexican way. It's the American way."

Jay stared at his shot glass. "Well Pedro . . . sorry." He turned to Julio. "Well, Julio, I'll drink to that." He raised his glass. And they swallowed their shots.

Julio stood up. "Well, I should be on my way then." He looked at Jay. "You know, if you left, just disappeared, I doubt we would put much effort into finding you."

"That's a really generous offer, Pedro. I'll make you the same."

Julio nodded. "Well then, till next time. I doubt our next meeting will be so friendly." Jay nodded at him and Julio headed for the door.

Before he had even reached it, Jack was up and following him. As he passed by, Jay grabbed his arm. Jack looked at him and Jay shook his head. "Not now."

Jack looked back at Julio, who was just going out the door, then turned back to his uncle. "What the fuck are you talking about? He's alone, it's a perfect time."

Jay let go of his arm and patted the stool next to him. "Come on, it's bad luck to kill a man who's just bought you a drink. That's ancient Irish wisdom I'm laying on you there boy. Now, let's do a shot of Jameson."

Jack took one last longing look at the front door, shrugged his shoulders and sat on the stool. "Whatever. I think you're getting soft in your old age."

"Buzz, how bout a couple shots of Jameson for me and my overzealous nephew here."

"Sure you don't want tequila instead," sneered Jack.

"Fuck you."

"And don't think I don't know you pulled that ancient Irish wisdom bullshit straight out of your ass."

Chapter 14

Shultz's specialty was tracking down prison escapees, and he'd earned enough success in this endeavor that he was the hands-down choice of the Feds when Jimbo McCray made his escape. He was told that a detachment of Feds were already in the area investigating the McCrays for crimes unrelated to Jimbo McCray. He didn't know many of the details but was given Franks name and the motel he was staying at as a contact. He decided to pay Franks a courtesy call to touch base and see if Franks could give him any helpful information. "I'm not here to step on your toes," said Shultz standing in Franks's motel room. "I'm just here to let you know what I'm doing and see if there is any way we can help each other."

"I can appreciate that," said Franks. Shultz didn't give Franks the impression that he would be anything other than a complication. He looked to Franks to be more soldier than cop. His weathered face was a map of wrinkles and aged skin crowned with grey hair that didn't look like it had known any other color in at least a decade, worn in an old school military buzz cut. But he had the lean hard body of a much younger man, and the confidence he projected gave him an air of formidability that made Franks nervous.

"If I might ask," continued Shultz, "do you have an undercover working the area?"

"We do," answered Franks. He broke eye contact with Shultz and looked down at his hands. He wished they were holding one of his screwdriver cocktails so he could take a big drink and try to cut the tension, but he didn't think that would be received well from this hard-ass, by-the-book dinosaur.

When Franks didn't expand on his answer, Shultz pushed. "I would like to interview the undercover agent if possible."

"Yeah, well, this is absolutely not a reflection on you, but we are going to keep the agent's identity on a strict need to know basis for the time being. But I would be happy to relay any questions you have, as well as instruct said officer to keep an eye and an ear open for anything relating to Jimbo McCray, and relay any information on that subject to you ASAP."

"O.K." Shultz took a deep breath and nodded his head slowly. "Well if there is anything I can do to help you with your investigation, don't hesitate to ask."

"Will do." Franks rose to his feet and extended his hand.

Shultz shook the hand affably enough, but when the shake was over he held the hand till Franks looked him in the eye. "You know," said Shultz, "I know I come off like a guy who's all cuddles and kittens, but I do have a hard side. I hope I don't have to show it to you."

"I don't intend to give you any reason to," said Franks. Shultz gave him a single nod, let go of his hand and left the motel room. As soon as the door closed, Franks went right for the vodka.

Chapter 15

As their truck approached the house, Jay and Jack noticed the front door was open.

"Fuck," said Jack pulling his pistol and chambering a round.

"I see it." Jay shut off the engine and let the truck quietly coast till it came to a stop. He grabbed the twelve-gauge from the gun rack behind him, pumped it, and they both exited the truck leaving the doors open so as not to betray their presence with sound of them slamming. "Stay low and don't start shooting till you got a kill shot or they see us," said Jay.

Crouched low, they advanced toward the house. Jay knew this was reckless. If it was an ambush, they would be watching. But, if it was an ambush, why did they leave the front door open? Either way, he wasn't in the mood to run from his own house and part of him reveled at the prospect of the plotting and planning being over. At least for now he could just give himself over to the fight.

A shape moved in the darkness of the house. As the shape moved toward the doorway, Jay and Jack raised their weapons. Out of the shadows and into the sunshine illuminating the porch stepped Jimbo McCray. Holding what was left of a bottle of whiskey, he tipped it up to his lips and drained the last of it before tossing it toward a rusty trashcan in the yard, which he missed.

"What?" Jimbo asked walking down the porch steps. "You gonna shoot me? That be a hell of a welcome home."

"I'll be god damned." Jay lowered his shotgun.

"No fucking way!" Jack tucked his pistol into his belt and ran toward his dad. They embraced, Jimbo momentarily picking his son up off the ground.

"Damn, you get bigger boy?"

"Fucking A," said Jack shoving his dad.

"What, you think you're ready to take on your old man now?" Jimbo shoved him back.

"Done been ready for a while old man."

"Well then let's see what you got boy." He grabbed Jack in a headlock and they went to the ground wrestling for position playfully, but still competitively.

Jay lit a cigarette and watched with interest. It took longer than ever before but Jimbo eventually ended up on top. "So I'm guessing you didn't get early parole," said Jay.

They got up from the ground, Jimbo breathing harder than Jack. "Well," he paused to suck in some oxygen, "I took advantage of this special, 'whup a guard's ass and get out early' program."

"Oh, that's great. And you come here cause," Jay let out a bitter laugh, "there ain't no way the Feds will think to look for you here, right?"

Jimbo shook his head and asked his son, "I been gone so long I can't remember, was he always this much of a pussy?" He turned back to his brother. "Don't sweat it bro. Just stopped by to get some weed, whiskey, food and a tent and I'll be off to hide in the woods. You know can't nobody find me out there if I don't want to be found. I'm starving now, matter of fact. What you got to eat?"

Jay flicked his cigarette butt out into the grass. "Some deer chili in the fridge. Guess I could fry up some taters. Could be I still got some whiskey you ain't drank up yet. And you know we always got buds to smoke. So let's smoke, drink and eat, then you get your nutty ass out in the woods. And don't call me a pussy again."

"Speaking of you being a pussy," said Jimbo. "I heard you done let the beaners move in and take over. I go away for a couple of years and you surrender everything to the god damned beaners?"

Jay spit into the grass. "Beaners ain't took over shit. I'm handling it."

"Speaking of handling beaners," Jimbo smiled at his brother and son, "ya'll wanna see something cool?"

Jay and Jack followed him to the backyard and there they were. The three Mexicans that Jimbo had run into at the store. They hung upside down from the same tree that generations of McCrays had hung and gutted countless deer. Their hands were tied behind their backs and tape had been put over their mouths.

"Motherfucker!" said Jay. "The fucking Feds could be on their way here right now looking for your dumb ass and I got three beaners hanging from a tree in my back yard. You can take off and hide in the woods, but how the fuck am I supposed to explain this?"

"Oh for fuck's sake, calm down Sally," said Jimbo. "Here." He yanked the pistol he had taken from the Mexican from his belt and popped off three shots, putting a round dead center in the forehead of each of the hanging men. The first two died instantly, the last one spasmed violently for a good ten seconds before going stiff and swaying gently back and forth. "There. Now me and my boy will go bury these fucks out in the woods and you heat up that deer chili and fry up the taters. Sound like a plan?"

Chapter 16

Fuller sat in his squad car trying to suck some courage out of a bourbon flask. It was a different Mexican that called him this time. He hated the other one. This one wasn't really any better, but he did seem like it was all business to him where as the other one seemed to get a sick pleasure out of it all. But, nevertheless, this one was insistent. He wanted results now. One McCray, dead or alive, by the end of the day or Fuller got one of his wife's fingers in the mailbox the next morning. Every day after was another finger.

Dead or alive. As if he could simply slap a pair of cuffs on one of the McCrays and deliver them up. Dead was the only choice and not much of one. He tried to come up with a plan. He could go out to the McCrays' place and hope one of them was there alone. Trying to get the jump on one was terrifying enough, more than one was beyond unthinkable. If one of them was alone, he could make small talk. None of them would expect him to make a move. He would have that in his favor. At some point, if he was lucky, they would turn their back on him. It worked for Bob Ford. But Bob Ford only had to kill Jesse James, not a McCray. If more than one of the McCrays were home, or if there was only one and he never turned his back? His mind drew a blank. Overall it was a pretty sorry ass plan. But what choice did he have?

He took another pull from the flask, tossed it on the passenger seat and started the car. He sat there for a minute enjoying the warmth of sun on his face. He let his mind race around for an escape from his situation, a rat scurrying down one dead end of a maze after another for an exit that would not be found. He shifted the cruiser into drive and headed for the McCrays. He drove slowly. It was a half hour drive normally, and he was determined to stretch every extra second he could. What if he drove straight into a tree? Surely if he were in critical condition in a hospital they would understand, would wait to make good on their threats, give him a chance to recover. But he wasn't sure. He couldn't risk it.

He drove even slower as he neared his destination, but all too soon he was pulling up in front of the McCrays'. To make matters worse, Jay was sitting on the porch steps. He had planned to sit in the cruiser a few minutes to work up his nerve. Now that was out. His stomach turned itself inside out. For one terrifying moment he was sure he was going to spew up the bourbon, but then it settled. His muscles didn't want to move, but he couldn't keep sitting there. Jay was watching. Couldn't let him get suspicious. He opened the door and got out. His legs were shaky. He put his hands on top of the cruiser to steady himself.

"Morning," said Jay.

Fuller closed the door and smiled. "How do?"

"To what do I owe this pleasure?"

"Oh, it's just a slow day. I thought maybe we should touch base on the Mexican problem, and I was kind of thinking I was in the mood for a little," he held his thumb and pointing finger to his lips as if hitting a joint.

"Sheriff Fuller wants to cop a buzz? In the middle of the day no less. We truly must be in the final days of Sodom and Gomorrah. Well, far be it from me to prevent the descent of a law officer into the pits of refer madness." Jay stood up. "Shall we step inside?"

"Works for me." Fuller followed Jay up the steps. He hadn't even ascertained if anyone else was home, but standing on those steps, staring at Jay's back, with Jay completely oblivious, he was sure that if he didn't make a move now, he never would. He pulled his revolver from its holster and pointed it at Jay's back. The gun was shaking and felt unusually heavy. He braced it with his other hand.

"You know if you're going to be coming out here for free weed, the least you could do is bring a bottle of—" As Jay reached for the screen door, he saw the reflection of Fuller pointing his revolver at him in the glass. He threw himself to the side just as the bullet whizzed past and went through the door. Jay jumped over the porch railing, landed flat on his back and rolled under the porch, pulling the pistol from the small of his back where it was tucked under her belt. Fuller ran over to the railing leaned over and aimed his pistol. When he didn't see Jay, he knew he must be under the porch. He backed up but was too late. Jay fired up through the gap between the boards. The bullet went up through the bottom of Fuller's belly, tore through his insides and exited out his upper back. Fuller dropped his pistol and stumbled backwards until his back hit the house, then he slid down to his butt. Jay rolled out from under the porch. He popped up pointing his gun at the sheriff. He climbed the steps keeping him in the guns sights. Fuller's eyes went to his revolver sitting a few feet away. Jay saw it and kicked it well out of his reach, then lowered his own weapon.

"Ambulance." Fuller coughed, blood spewing from his mouth, painting the front of his uniform red. "I need an ambulance."

"I don't guess I'll be calling you an ambulance Sheriff." Jay kneeled down in front of him.

"Why not?"

"Cause you tried to kill me."

"Oh yeah." He managed a laugh. "There is that." He closed

his eyes and went silent. Just as Jay was figuring him for dead, he opened them again. "You know I ain't had a cigarette in over ten years? Old lady made me quit. She always worried about me." His eyes closed again and he smiled. Jay knew he was thinking about her. After a few seconds they opened again. "I sure could go for a cigarette now."

Jay pulled out a pack of Camels. He took two cigarettes out and lit them both at the same time. He handed one over and kept the other. Fuller took a deep drag. When he pulled it away from his lips, the butt, as well as the tips of his fingers, was covered with blood. He held the smoke for a few seconds then exhaled. "God damned if that ain't even better than I remember." He coughed again but it was slight with little blood.

"So how much did they give you to turn on me?" asked Jay. "There ain't no reason to lie. Nothing you say will change the outcome of what is going to happen here."

"No money. They got my wife. They showed me a video. That prick, Hector, he had a gun. He was touching her with it. He also said they'd go after my daughter if I didn't play ball."

Jay nodded his head and took a drag off his cigarette. "Well, I can understand that. Man's got to at least try to take care of his family."

Fuller looked Jay in the eye. "Promise me, you'll save my family?"

"Sorry, man. Can't promise that. Most likely, they decided they would kill your wife no matter how all this turned out."

Fuller nodded his head. "One thing about you Jay, you don't sugarcoat. Lots of folks would just tell a dying man what he wanted to hear. Not you."

"I'll tell you this though. Your daughter will be O.K. If you had betrayed them, they probably would have made good on their threats. But once they figure out that you died trying to kill me, there'll be no reason to expose themselves by going after her. So, you did the right thing by her. I'll make sure her college is paid for and she has plenty of money to live on. I'll keep tabs on her, give her help when she needs it. I will do that for you."

"Thank you Jay. I appreciate that. I know when you say it, you mean it." He took another drag off his cigarette and looked around at the trees, the sky then at Jay. "Know what the odd thing about dying is?"

"What's that?" Jay was genuinely curious.

"I ain't never felt more alive. The color of the trees and grass, the sound of the birds, the feel of the breeze, it's all so— so—" His eyes opened wider and his breath sped up, then stopped. His head slumped to the side. His eyes stayed open, but Jay knew they saw no more of this world.

Chapter 17

It had been a while since it had rained. The normal, jungle like humidity that was typical of a Midwestern summer gave way to a dry baking heat more similar to a desert. Jack decided the plants were due for a visit and a watering. Making sure that plants, which were that deep in the woods, got plenty of water was a problem that various growers dealt with in various ways. The McCrays' solution centered on the long meandering creek that wound its way through their stretch of woods. All of their plants were within a quarter mile of that creek, most of them considerably closer. So Jack only needed to carry an empty water container with him and tote the water from the creek to the plant. The chore of watering all the plants would take all day. It didn't need to, but Jack liked to take time to sit with each plant. There were all kinds of books and websites that broke down the cultivation of marijuana to an exact science. Jack ignored all of them. He just spent time with each plant, and the plant let him know what it needed. He operated on pure instinct.

When he came to the first plant, he took the backpack off his back and dropped it on the ground. The backpack contained an empty gallon milk jug, a spray bottle, a canteen of drinking water for himself, a portable CD player with speakers, a pair of scissors, some deer jerky, and a pint of whiskey. He laid out the CD player and speakers and pressed play. Metallica's "Four Horsemen" blasted from the speakers. Jack held a firm belief that plants grew better with music and grew bigger and more potent with Metal than any other genre. He took the empty jug and spray bottle down to the creek and filled them. When he returned to the plant, he poured out the jug all around the base, making sure to soak the roots. After that, he walked around the plant, spraying the leaves and branches. With that done, he lay down, using the backpack as a pillow, gazing up at the six foot plant. He took a swig from the whiskey bottle, pulled a joint from his cigarette pack, and lit it. He held the smoke in his lungs and cleared his mind of everything except the sight of the plant in front of him and the vibrations of Metallica in his eardrum. He took another swig of whiskey. After finishing the joint, he did some minor pruning of dead leaves, packed up and headed to the next plant.

As a rule, they spread their plants out. This made maintenance and harvest more labor intensive but eased worries of a D.E.A. chopper or plane passing overhead and spotting anything. A single plant in a small clearing was much more difficult to spot than many plants in a big clearing. There was also the issue of thieves. Spreading out the plants made them more difficult to steal. Aside from distance between plants, there were other things to consider when choosing locations. First, one needed to look down at the soil. When growing in the woods, you had to make sure to find a spot that wasn't crisscrossed with the roots of wild indigenous plants that would suck the nutrients from the soil. Then one needed to look up. The plant would need sunlight, so it needed to be in a spot that was clear of overhead branches and foliage. But not too big of an overhead clearing. D.E.A. choppers looked for big clearings in the woods. The smaller the clearing, the harder to spot. When visiting the plants, Jack made a point of taking different routes each time. This was to make sure he didn't wear a path into the ground. If there was a path connecting the plants, then thieves who found one would have the equivalent of a map to the rest.

After about fifteen minutes, Jack came to the next plant. It was even bigger than the first. The way that it swayed in the breeze made it appear as if it was waving to Jack, and he felt as if it was as happy to see him as he was it. He repeated his process; water, shot of whiskey, this time he smoked a cigarette, and the song he jammed to was "Am I Evil." And so his day went. Plant after plant. He took his time, and by the time he started for home, the sun hung low in the sky and the shadows stretched long. It was full on dark by the time he got home and discovered he needed to dispose of yet another dead body.

Chapter 18

As far as criminal enterprise in the Show Me State went, growing weed was, at best, a distant second to the manufacture of methamphetamine. Decades ago men sat out in the Missouri woods making moonshine. Their sons took over those hiding spots and grew weed. Now a new generation took their turn, in some of the very same spots, cooking meth. The evolution of the backwoods outlaw. For the cartel, the meth heads were an opportunity.

Of all the places in the United States they had been to, nowhere had making allies been more difficult than here, the southeastern woods of Missouri, where the flat farmland rose up and formed the foothills of the Ozark Mountains. In the cities they had the playbook down. Start with the Latinos. Appeal to their ethnic loyalties. That gave them a foothold. Then look to the surrounding neighborhoods. Go to the top dogs, the gang leaders, try to incorporate them. Offer to be their distributer. Let them keep their turf and peddle your product. If they refused, then you slug it out, street by street, block to block, until their turf becomes yours. But, out here, there were no gang leaders. No gangs. Even the criminal element were just an assortment of individuals, and none of them wanted anything to do with the cartel. Turf wasn't a question of streets. Streets were just something they drove on. Turf was their property, which was mostly woods. Everybody wants money, but many of these people seemed to take a perverse pride in their poverty, turning their noses up at anyone who had too much money in some type of reverse snobbery. Potential allies were difficult to find.

This is where the meth heads came in. From Mexico to the Midwest, meth heads were all the same. They could always be bought. Not because they were money hungry, but because of their all-consuming, never-ending hunger for the meth. Their race, their culture, where they were from, none of that mattered. They were as desperate as heroin addicts, but heroin addicts were useless for anything more than prostitution, since they spent most of their time passed out, or nearly passed out, and the times they weren't high, they were dope sick. But meth heads were alert. Full of energy, they were capable of huge amounts of focus and work, as well as impressive bursts of violence that could be useful if properly harnessed. They could be functional soldiers, if they could hold onto a thread of sanity. And while North America had long ago surpassed Mexico in the cultivation of quality marijuana, the small time Missouri meth cook couldn't compare to the quality churned out by the Mexican super-factories.

Zoomey and Goose were two typical Missouri meth-heads. Zoomey and Goose were nicknames, of course, but they had carried these nicknames for so long that they were the only names anyone knew them by. Zoomey's nickname came from his love for speed. Goose's nickname came from his teenage years. Nobody was sure of its exact origin, but there were rumors of him once having drunken sexual relations with a goose. Zoomey and Goose weren't related, though they might as well have been. They met in the seventh grade when Zoomey told Goose he had a half pack of Marlboros, two *Hustler* mags and a pint of Mad Dog

20/20 in his locker. They skipped the rest of the day, sitting in the woods behind the school, drinking, smoking and debating the merits of a nice ass vs. a nice rack.

After that, they were partners in crime. They shoplifted, did some minor burglaries, smoked pot, tried to sell it. Zoomey got a girl pregnant not long after dropping out of high school. He rented a small mobile home for him, his baby and her mama. Goose moved into the spare room. They both got jobs as roofers to pay the rent and utilities. The old lady's food stamps kept them fed, and they still had enough money left over to stay drunk and stoned. Then they discovered meth. A guy at work turned them on to a couple of lines, and they never looked back. Less than two months later, they tried their luck with cooking. They started turning out low grade batches that proved much cheaper than buying it. With a little experience, they were turning out enough to stay wired and still have plenty left over to sell. They decided it was a much better deal than roofing for a living, so they quit their jobs and took it up full time. After an explosion left Zoomey with a scarred face, his girlfriend split with the kid. With them gone, Zoomey and Goose's life spiraled down to the point that they only lived to use, cook and sell meth. They would go days without eating or sleeping. Once, it only occurred to them to get food when Goose passed out walking down the porch steps, and they realized that neither had eaten a bite of food in nearly a week. Time gets slippery when you're on a binge. The only socializing they did was with their customers and "shoppers," who went around buying cold medicine so they could extract the pseudo.

Whenever they were heavy on product, and light on cash, they would take a break from cooking, hit the bars and sell what they could. One night when Zoomey was working the Buzzsaw, Goose headed for Uncle Jesse's, the second most popular bar in their neck of the woods. That's where he met Hector. "So how much do you have?" Hector asked.

Goose's eyes narrowed. "Enough." The question, coupled

with the fact that he didn't know Hector, fueled the natural paranoia that every successful dope dealer cultivates. He had just about decided that Hector must be a cop, or a ripoff artist, when the waitress put the bottle of beer he ordered in front of him.

"Let me get that for you," said Hector. He pulled out a ham hock size wad of hundred-dollar bills. "All I have is hundreds. Can you break one?" he asked the waitress. "You know what, never mind. Just keep the change." He peeled off a hundred-dollar bill and handed it to her.

Her eyes widened at the sight of it. "Thank you very much sir." She walked off putting extra effort into the swing of her ass.

"Now where were we?" Hector turned back to Goose, whose eyes were still glued to the wad of bills. "Oh yeah, how much do you have?"

Goose forcibly tore his eyes from the wad of bills and looked at Hector. "About an ounce."

"I'll take it all."

"Don't you want to know the price?"

"No need. I know you'll be fair. Would you like to know how I know you will be fair?"

"I would."

"Because I can tell you're a smart enough man to tell that if you're straight up with me and don't try to fuck with me, you're going to make a lot of money with me. More than you ever would without me. You wouldn't throw away an opportunity like that to cheat me out of a few extra bucks per gram, would you?"

Ten minutes later they were out in Goose's car. Goose held a lighter under a piece of aluminum foil full of meth while Hector held a straw above it, inhaling the chemical tasting smoke. It was garbage, of course. But he wasn't buying it for the high, he was buying it to establish a connection. And it worked. Half an hour later, Goose pulled out of the parking lot with a pocket full of money, and

Hector had his cell number. Goose thought he had a lucrative new customer. Hector had other plans.

Two days later, Hector called Goose and said he wanted to meet and talk business. Goose and Zoomey invited him out to their trailer, an unusual move, but for a big fish like Hector they decided it was worth it. They imagined Hector putting in a standing order for all the product they could cook. No more cruising the bars, only dealing with one customer. When Hector pulled up to their trailer, they were sitting out front in lawn chairs, trying not to look too anxious. "How do?" Goose said as Hector got out of his car.

"Senor Goose, how does it hang my friend?" Hector sat on a picnic table directly in front of them.

"May I introduce my associate Zoomey, Zoomey this is Hector."

"Senor Zoomey," Hector nodded at Zoomey, who nodded back.

"So," Goose rubbed his hands together. "What can we do for you? We got almost two ounces cooked, but we figure if you give us a week, we can—"

"Oh, I don't want any more of that god-awful stuff," interrupted Hector. "It's really terrible."

Zoomey and Goose exchanged glances. "Jesus Christ!" said Zoomey after a baffled moment of silence. He focused his anger at Goose, who had vouched for Hector. "What the fuck is this bullshit?"

"Let me show you something." Hector reached into his jacket pocket. Both Zoomey and Goose sat up in their chairs. "it's cool man," said Hector pulling out a bag of powder. He tossed it to Zoomey. "Give that a try."

Zoomey gave Hector a long hard stare before examining the contents of the baggy. The meth was pure white, not piss yellow like their stuff. Zoomey looked at Goose and jerked his head toward the trailer. Goose got up, went inside and came back out with a piece of foil and a straw. When he sat down, Zoomey tossed him the baggy and he did a hit. He exhaled the smoke and fell back in his chair. "Wow!" was all he said. Zoomey snatched the foil and straw from him, did his own hit and reacted in much the same way.

"I ain't never smoked no shit like that," said Goose.

"It was so clean. It almost didn't have no taste at all." Zoomey held out the foil and straw toward Hector.

Hector waved his hand. "No thanks. It's my gift to you." He lit a cigarette.

Goose took the foil and straw, did another hit then passed it back to Zoomey. "You said you wanted to talk business. If you don't want to buy our stuff, then what? You want us to sell your stuff for you?"

Hector lazily blew a few smoke rings and shrugged his shoulders. "You can sell it, smoke it or feed it to your dog for kicks. I don't care. I just want to give it to you."

Zoomey and Goose exchanged glances again. "You want to give it to us?" asked Zoomey.

"Correct!" Hector smiled.

"O.K." Zoomey took another hit and passed it back to Goose. "How much do you want to give us?"

"A five gallon bucket full."

Goose paused just as he was about to take a hit. Again he exchanged glances with Zoomey. This time, smiles bloomed across their faces as their meth fueled brains tried to compute how much meth would fit into a five gallon bucket. Neither was sure, but they both knew it was a lot. "You're going to give us a five gallon bucket full of this bomb-ass meth?"

"A five gallon bucket and a wad of cash. Or, maybe, two five gallon buckets and two wads of cash," said Hector.

Zoomey nodded his head slowly. "So cut to it then." His smile was gone. "What do we have to do?"

Hector flicked his cigarette away. "You guys heard of the McCrays?"

Chapter 19

The soft thud of raindrops against the van's roof combined with the gentle swoosh of the rubber windshield wipers to induce a hypnotic mood that had Jack spacing out as he stared at the lit-up windows of the old bar that had become the cartel's headquarters. His dad took a swig from the whiskey bottle. Shaking himself out of his trance, Jack looked over at Jimbo. A bolt of lightning ripped through the night sky, momentarily lighting up the van's interior as well as his dads face. Looking at the glassy-eyed intensity with which his dad stared at the building, he knew mayhem was on the horizon. Jimbo passed him the bottle and he took a swig.

"Where did you get the van?" asked Jimbo.

"Swiped it from that Baptist church behind the hardware store."

"Stole it from a church?"

Jack shrugged his shoulders.

Jimbo laughed. "I like that. That shit's all a racket anyway." He took the bottle back and took another swig.

Jack nodded his head and glanced at the three dead Mexicans in the back of the van. When they reached the woods, where they were supposed to bury them, Jimbo said, "Fuck all that noise. I got plans for these boys." They covered them with leaves, smoked a joint and went back to the house, neither of them telling Jay of Jimbo's plan. The plan consisted of some metal pipes, zip ties, shitload of fireworks, a bungee cord, a stolen van, these three dead bodies and Jack's pickup truck parked discreetly on a service road less than a half mile away.

"All right. Let's do this," said Jimbo. He took one more swig from the whiskey bottle and put the cap back on. He punched the dome light, shattering it, so it wouldn't light up when they opened the doors. They got out of the van and walked around to the back. When they opened the back door the smell of the dead bodies hit them in a way that it hadn't, for some reason, when they were sitting in the van.

"Fuck me!" said Jack.

"Just breathe out of your mouth." Jimbo grabbed one of the bodies and pulled it out. He held it under the arms, and Jack grabbed it by the feet. They carried it around and sat it in the front seat. They seat belted him in, but he still kept slumping forward against the steering wheel. "Give me your belt." said Jimbo. Jack took off his belt and handed it over. Jimbo belted the corpse's neck to the headrest. After settling the slumping issue, he zip-tied the corpse's hands to the steering wheel. They put another corpse in the passenger seat, this time using a pair of jumper cables that they found in the van to tie the passenger corpse's neck to the headrest. Jimbo stepped back to admire his handiwork. The rain intensified. He took the bungee cord, hooked one end under the seat and the other end to the bottom of the steering wheel, insuring the van would stay on a straight path. Then he prepared his surprise.

Jimbo pointed towards the grass where several chunks of concrete, plasterboard and other construction trash had been dumped by some contractor who saw a vacant lot as an opportunity to save money on a dumpster. "Grab me that big concrete block, the biggest one." As Jack went over to grab it, Jimbo looked through the windshield to make sure the van was aimed at the building. When Jack returned with the block, Jimbo started the ignition and shifted the van into drive. The van moved forward slowly. Jimbo picked up the block and tossed it on the gas pedal. The van lunged forward, the momentum slamming the driver's side door, as the van sped for the building.

"Well," said Jimbo. "Let's get the fuck out of here." They broke into a sprint, heading for the truck parked down the road.

The man sitting on guard duty by the window was there just to keep up the routine. The fact that it was a pitch-black moonless night, combined with the steady rain beating against the window, blurred everything on the other side more than a few feet away to the point of invisibility. The man leaned back in his chair smoking a cigarette. An S.K.S. Chinese assault rifle layd across his lap. Watching the waves of rain sliding down the glass, and listening to the relentless drumbeat of the downpour, lulled him into the same semi-hypnotic state Jack had experienced outside. By the time his mind identified the threat of the van speeding straight at him, he barely had time to jump out of the way. It crashed through the front of the bar, sending bricks and glass flying everywhere. All over the room, men pulled their weapons and fired at the two figures in the front seats. The man, who had been on guard, tried to belly-crawl over the broken glass to retrieve the rifle that fell off his lap when he dove for cover. When a couple of bullets whizzed too close, he froze and covered his head, opting to wait out the firefight as opposed to active participation.

When the gunfire did subside, everyone in the room kept their weapons aimed at the two bodies in the front seats. Hector was hunched behind his desk, aiming his pistol over the top. Julio moved forward slowly. He kept his pistol aimed as well. He knew the two in the front seats were dead but wasn't sure about anybody that might be in the back of the van. The only sound was the crunching of glass below his feet and the steady sound of the rain, which no longer had the barrier of a wall to dull it. Julio made it to the driver's side door. He opened it and quickly fired several shots over the shoulder of the dead driver in case there was anyone left alive in the back. When nothing moved or fired back, he risked a look. He saw the third dead body in the back. He popped a couple rounds in it to make sure it was dead. Assured that it was, he lowered his gun and took a deep breath. "All clear!" he said. The other men lowered their weapons and gathered around Julio. Julio looked at the corpse in the driver's seat, noticing the belt around its neck. He put the barrel of his pistol under its chin and turned its head toward him so he could get a better view of the face.

"It's Carlos!" said a voice behind him. Several men made the sign of the cross. Julio made his way around to the passenger side and got a look at that face. "This one's Roberto. I'm betting the one in the back is Diego." The three had been missing for a while.

"Get that fucking van out of here!" yelled Hector who still kept his distance. "Toss the bodies in the back of it for now and pull it behind the building. When it stops raining, bury them out in the woods." A couple of guys opened the driver's door, and a couple opened the passenger's door. They fumbled with the ties around the necks, eventually getting them off, causing the bodies to slump forward. They took off the seatbelts, cut the zip ties and carried the dead men, one at a time, to the back of the van and tossed them in. When they closed the van doors, one of the soldiers stepped out into the rain, bent over and puked from the smell of the corpses.

"Get your ass back in here!" yelled Julio. "Whoever did this could still be out there."

The men came back into the building. The one that had puked, walked on unsteady legs over to a barstool and sat down. The one with the stronger stomach climbed into the driver's seat to see if he could pull the van around back till they were given further instructions. The key was already turned forward, but the engine had died. He turned the key backwards then forwards again. Nothing happened. He tried it again. Nothing. "It won't start!"

"Try putting it in park," said Julio.

He slid it into park and tried again. Still nothing. He shook his head at Julio.

"Fuck," said Julio. "All right, everybody get over here. We're going to have to push this thing—"

That's when the pipe bombs went off. They were sitting between the two front seats, covered by a jacket. The blast was loud. Everyone outside the van ducked for cover. The man in the driver's seat calmly got out of the van, closed the driver's door and stood there staring into the van.

"You O.K.?" asked Julio. Could he possibly be unharmed after a blast like that, he wondered.

When the man turned, Julio got his answer. The right side of his face, including the eye, was gone. He could see every contour of the man's skull and jawbone on that side. The man took two steps toward Julio and fell flat on what was left of his face. His body began to shake and spasm. Julio ran to him, knelt down at his side and rolled him over. Everyone gathered around them. Hector was the last there, but the circle parted to let him up front. The one good eye looked up at Julio. Julio was sure he saw life in it.

"He's still alive," said Julio. "We have to at least try to get him to a hospital." He looked up at Hector.

Hector slowly nodded his head. Just as Julio was about to give orders for someone to bring a car around, to take him to a hospital, Hector pointed his pistol at the man's head and fired. His body stopped shaking. He went limp.

Julio stood up. "What the fuck Hector? He was one of us!"

Hector looked around. Everyone was staring at him. "What?" He shrugged his shoulders. "He was suffering. We're at least fifty miles from a hospital if not further. I put him out of his misery."

Chapter 20

They moved through the woods silently and efficiently. Every nerve firing on every piston, thanks to the primo meth, and their senses further sharpened in the way doing something dangerous at night naturally sharpens the senses. Zoomey stopped. Goose stopped behind him. Zoomey pointed to the ground. Goose saw the steel bear trap. He nodded. They side-stepped the trap and continued on. It was just after three o'clock in the morning when they found themselves at the edge of the wood line by the McCray property. They hunkered down for what they knew would be a long wait.

They had no intention of making a move any time soon. The lights were out in the McCray house, and they had no way of knowing who was in there. In their greed, they fantasized that both of the McCrays would be there. Each one was worth "a five gallon bucket of meth and a wad of cash." Neither of them had managed to figure out how much meth or cash that was but figured it would afford them the opportunity to do nothing but smoke all day without worrying about cooking, selling, or paying bills, for a long time. Still, two McCrays were a tall order. Even their meth-riddled brains would have registered some relief if it turned out only one was home. One five gallon bucket and wad of cash would still go a long way.

They fired up the foil. They knew they wouldn't likely see anything till morning. They talked in whispers and smoked. The sun rose and still nothing stirred in the McCray house. All the windows were covered with closed curtains. Nothing could be seen inside the house. Though they convinced themselves that they saw shadows passing across the curtains, they knew that the lack of sleep that accompanied meth binges could just as easily be creating the shifting shadows. It was later in the day, when the sun was low and the shadows long, that they got their only confirmation that anyone was in the house. The front door opened and Jay's sasquatch-like body filled the door frame. He looked to the left, to the right, then spit and disappeared back into the house, closing the door. Neither of them even had time to grab their rifles and center their crosshairs on him.

It was surprising enough for Jay to hermit up like that. There was no way both of them could be in there. He must be home alone. Their original plan, if Jay was home alone, was to wait for him to come outside and shoot him from a safe distance. But what if he didn't come out at all? It was certainly possible. They didn't have enough meth to last another day and night. So it was decided. They would go in that night. They would wait till an hour after the last light in the house went out. Then they would go in, burglar style.

They smoked and waited. As the darkness swallowed the light and the witching hour grew larger and more ominous on the horizon, their fantasies of an easy future became threatened by a growing fear of the uncertain violence that approached like a hungry predator. Neither spoke it aloud, but both began to doubt their ability to accomplish that which only a day before seemed an easy chore. They went from smoking every half hour, to every fifteen minutes, to continuously passing the foil back and forth, determined to fill their personal deficits in courage and strength with chemicals.

It was one-thirty in the morning when the last light in the McCray house went out. They decided to play it safe, give it two hours instead of one, and make sure he was in that deep REM sleep. The two hours passed fast. They knew, if they put it off again, they would end up not doing at all. It was now or never.

Jay sat at the kitchen table, staring at the door. Each morning he decided this would be the day he brainstormed till he came up with a plan to deal with the cartel. And each evening he found himself sitting alone not one step closer to a solution. He'd run through the file that Fuller brought him several times over, as if he'd find some new piece of info he hadn't seen before, something that would give him an edge. It was interesting reading. A general history of the cartel in the States, locations of various headquarters and crack houses, but nothing that would help him here and now.

He stared at the bottle of whiskey sitting in front of him. Except for one joint in the morning, he decided he wouldn't drink or smoke until he had a solution. It didn't work. Fuck it. He grabbed the bottle, unscrewed the lid and took a long swig. He lowered the bottle, took a deep breath then had another swig. He put the bottle down and lit the joint he had rolled to celebrate with when the lightbulb went off over his head and he had his brilliant master plan in hand. The whiskey and weed would soon pleasantly sedate him, but at that moment he felt completely defeated. Not only had he been unable to come up with a plan, but he was too weak to abstain from his vices for a single day. And if the Mexicans making a move wasn't enough pressure, there was also Jimbo to factor in. If he didn't come up with a plan soon, Jimbo would make a move on his own.

The weed started kicking in. His thoughts got blurry like he was seeing them through fogged up glass. Blurry, but also more honest. As much anxiety as Jimbo's presence brought,

Jay was, of course, glad he was here. He finished the joint and took another shot of whiskey. Tomorrow. He'd figure it all out tomorrow. He got up, walked into the living room and pulled all the cushions off the sofa. He went in his bedroom and opened the closet door. It was one of those big walk-in closets. He threw the cushions on the floor. There wasn't much else in the closet. His twelve-gauge leaned against the wall, a rolled-up sleeping bag sat in the corner and a dozen or so shirts dangled from hangers. He grabbed the sleeping bag, unrolled it and stuffed in all the shirts. He then went into all the other rooms, grabbed all the pillows he could find and stuffed them into the sleeping bag as well. When the bag was fairly full, he went to the kitchen, grabbed the bottle of whiskey, turned the light off and headed back to his room.

Goose shoved the flat edge of the paint scraper under the window. Once he got it through, he worked it over to the latch. They had both been proficient at popping these kinds of windows open back in their burglary days, but they were out of practice. It took a painfully long ten minutes but the latch finally clicked. Goose eased the window up and stuck his head through. The kitchen was dark. But the night was moonless so their eyes were already well adjusted. He saw no movement, heard no sound. He climbed through the window. Zoomey passed him the two rifles. It occurred to Zoomey that shotguns would have been better for this situation, but he hadn't put nearly as much planning into how to do it as he had put into what he would do with all that meth and cash. The little planning he had done involved shooting from a long distance that he could run from if needed.

Once the rifles were inside, Zoomey followed. Goose handed him back one of the rifles. They slowly started to move. When they got to the hallway, they raised their rifles, fingers on triggers, ready for someone to jump out. From their burglary days, they learned that when you walk down a hallway, you walked on the edge by the wall because then the floor was less likely to creak. They each took a side. Each time they came to a door, whichever one was on that side would gently turn the handle, open the door and look in. They looked in one empty room after another, progressing slowly down the hall. At last there was only one room left. There could be no doubt. It was the one.

Goose looked at Zoomey. Zoomey nodded his head. Goose opened the door and they rushed through, aiming their rifles at the prone form lying in the bed. They pulled their triggers. With each bullet that landed, they stepped closer, confidence growing, until they were only a few feet from the bed. They continued firing until they were both out of ammo. The echoes of the shots rang in their ears and the smell of gunpowder filled their nostrils.

"Wooooooooohooooooo!" yelled Goose.

"That's right!" yelled Zoomey. "Taking care of business, bitches!" They high fived each other. Zoomey pulled the blanket back and they saw the sleeping bag. He unzipped the bag. Nothing but pillows and shirts. They had just enough time to look at each other and register the confusion on each other's face.

Jay lay on the floor of the walk-in closet. He'd left the closet door open, knowing if any of Hector's men came for him it wouldn't occur to them to look toward the closet when they saw the bed. He aimed the twelve-gauge at the center of Goose's back and pulled the trigger. The double ought ripped into his back and blasted out of his chest, painting the wall with bits and pieces of various organs and soaking the mattress with blood. Goose fell forward, bounced off the bed and landed on the floor. Zoomey spun around pointing his rifle at Jay. Jay took his time pointing his shotgun at Zoomey's chest. Remembering he was out of ammo, Zoomey threw the rifle on the floor and put his hands up. "Wait!" he said.

Jay pulled the trigger.

Chapter 21

Jimbo woke in the small hours of the night. His mind, in those first few seconds of consciousness, was still in prison. The cool night air, the feel of his sleeping bag, the sound of the crickets all struck him as out of place and he sat up in a panic. The adrenaline kick-started the sleepy pistons in his brain and he looked around, saw his snoring son and remembered. A heroin rush of relief flooded over him at the realization that he wasn't in prison. He lay back down, closed his eyes and waited for sleep to reclaim him. He did what so many men do in those solitary moments they're alone with their thoughts. He flipped through the mental rolodex of women he'd known till he settled on one.

Her name was Lisa. Blonde hair, baby blue eyes, blowjob lips. She possessed an upper-class sluttiness and lived high enough on the social scale that you would never expect her to cross paths with the likes of Jimbo McCray.

Jimbo was on a meth binge the night he met her. He drank at alcoholic levels when he wasn't speeding, and when he was riding the meth train, the amounts of alcohol he could consume were legendary. Unlike most meth heads, who would hunker down somewhere when they were on a binge, Jimbo tended to be susceptible to wanderlust. He travelled far and wide. Once he made it to California. On the night he met Lisa he just made it to a nightclub in downtown St. Louis. To him the nightclub was a little too uppity. To Lisa it was a seedy step or two down. She went there that night wired on grad A uncut Peruvian blow, with every intention of debasing herself that night in some deliciously scandalous way that would shame her daddy if he ever found out. She was thinking some inner-city hood rat would do, preferably black. But when she met Jimbo, she knew this handsome, tough-looking piece of white trash, with his bloodshot Viking blue eyes, was all the right kind of wrong. When he beat the shit out of the bouncer and they had to run out of the nightclub before the cops got there, she was hooked.

They spent three days fucking in a hotel room she paid for with her daddy's credit card. They snorted up all of her coke and all of his meth, then she got another eight ball. When they were done with that, they collapsed into a coma-like sleep for the better part of a day and a half. When they awoke, Jimbo decided he'd had enough of the city. He wanted to go home. When she said she wanted to go with him, he actually laughed out loud.

"Well fuck you then," she said. "It's your loss anyway asshole."

"Calm down baby." He regained his composure. "It's just that I live in the woods. No offense, but you wouldn't last two weeks out there. Ain't no clubs or Starbucks. A few gas stations, a church or two and half a dozen redneck bars."

She shrugged her shoulders. "I'm tougher than I look."

He decided it would be sporting to see how long she could last. Besides, it would be cool to show her off while she lasted. And, in fact, she impressed him with how well she adapted to life among the lower class. His son was immediately smitten with her. She even won over his older, grouchy, introverted brother, bonding with him over an equally cynical view of the world, not to mention she was the only woman he'd ever met outside their cousin that could go whiskey shot for whiskey shot with the McCray boys. Whatever she missed from her old life, she did a good job of hiding it. Occasionally, she recoiled from the alien looking bugs that would fly or crawl in her direction and was no fan of the small country mice that would scurry across the floor, but, overall, she was tougher than she looked. She lasted a little over a month and showed no signs of giving up until that infamous morning.

She woke early after a healthy normal night of sleep, something she got a lot of since leaving the coke behind in favor of the bomb-ass weed these country boys grew. She pulled the tray of buds out from under the sofa and carried it to the kitchen table where she rolled a fatty. She took big hits, holding them with her eyes closed, while getting all Zen and becoming one with the silence of the early morning household. After a few hits she put the joint out. The munchies kicked in. Breakfast was another thing she rediscovered since leaving the coke behind. The thought of greasy bacon and runny eggs would have made her retch back when breakfast was a line and a cigarette. But after a wake and bake her stomach growled. Cooking was going too far though. A real country breakfast would have to wait till one of the boys got up and cooked it. Till then cereal would have to do.

She dumped the cereal in a bowl and absent mindedly poured the milk while her mind floated around on the random disjointed thoughts produced by the pot buzz. Her hunger grew even more ravenous at the sight of food. She inhaled the first bite. She had already swallowed before her mind registered that there was something strange about the way those Lucky Charms crunched, the way they slid down her throat. It was too soft to be a marshmallow when she first bit down, then too crunchy to be cereal. When she swallowed, it was too big to be either. She looked down. That was when the trauma began.

Splashing around in the milk and cereal were six, plump, drowning baby pinky mice. The horrifying realization that she had just eaten one of the baby rodents spread through her mind like an oil slick until it became her only thought. She began to shriek. It was a genuine terrified scream, the likes of which put the artificial screams of horror movies to shame. She rose from her seat backing up till the wall stopped her. Jay, Jack and Jimbo all came running. Jay had his shotgun, half expecting to find a man in a ski-mask, holding a machete. When he couldn't figure out what the threat was, he glanced at his brother, who only shrugged his shoulders.

"What the fuck is wrong with you!" shouted Jay, unable to endure the screams any longer.

Her screams softened to sobs but she was still unable to speak. She raised a trembling hand and pointed toward the cereal bowl. The three McCrays gathered around and peered down into it. Five of the mice had already drowned and floated to the top. One had just enough life to kick its leg a couple of times before succumbing to the milk filling its lungs.

"Sick!" said Jack.

They heard the screen door slam as Lisa ran out. They never saw or heard from her again.

This spurred what came to be known as the great rodent roundup. They considered traps or poison. But the infestation was too great. It would have taken too long. They tried using baseball bats to kill the offending mice, but, between the broken furniture from when they missed and the bloody mess from the ones they did kill, they abandoned this method as well. So they took inventory of the tools at their disposal and devised a plan. Their weapons of choice consisted of a hockey stick, a baseball glove and a tennis racquet.

The plan went like this: they would move a major piece of furniture, like the sofa. Dozens of mice would go scurrying in all directions. Jay would scoop one up with the hockey stick and flip it in the air. Jack would swoop in and catch it in the baseball glove. He would toss it out to the porch where Jimbo would swat it far out into the yard with the tennis racquet. This method proved not only efficient but surprisingly fun.

By the time they were done, they had become skilled in their respective hockey stick, baseball glove, tennis racquet positions and wished they had switched it up to keep it interesting. They toyed with the idea of making it an organized sport. Even went so far as to argue about potential rules. Tracy came over and they recounted the whole morning while passing around joints and the whiskey bottle. She laughed as if she had been there. Jimbo felt a slight melancholy knowing his time with Lisa was over, but the feeling of relief and excitement at being free again softened the melancholy.

As he drifted back to sleep, he had one of those epiphanies you have in that hazy space between consciousness and unconsciousness, the kind that, no matter how profound or deep, you have no chance of remembering. Sitting there on that porch watching the sun set, passing around the smoke and drink, laughing with his son, brother and cousin, the people he felt were family, not just relatives but family, was the most content evening he could remember. They were close to broke. Bills were piled up. There were days of great wealth from dealing still to come, days much more memorable and exciting but no day since or before that he felt that content warmth where he had no desire to be anywhere else or do anything else.

Chapter 22

Popeye was a champion fighting pitbull in his younger years. Many fight dog breeders would have used him as a stud after a bite to his upper leg left him with a permanent limp that impaired his fighting prowess. And his owner, Travis Lancaster, did stud him out to a couple of interested parties, and Popeye fathered a dozen puppies. But Travis trained and fought pits, he didn't breed them. He found Popeye more useful as a bait dog for younger pits. Popeye's mouth would be taped shut, and he would be thrown in with one of the younger pits, so they could work on their technique and gain confidence without risk of injury.

Of course, the number of sparring sessions a bait dog can survive are fairly limited. Popeye lasted over twice as long as any bait dog Travis had ever seen. But, finally, he had reached the end of his usefulness. His front right leg, having been further mangled in his last sparring session, made his limp worse. He was no longer agile enough to even be a bait dog. Travis decided to dispose of him in the dumpster behind the Buzzsaw, then he could go in, have a cold one and hit on a waitress or two. He walked behind the bar and lifted Popeye up into the dumpster. The dumpster was full. Popeye stood on top of the trash looking out over the top of the dumpster. He sniffed at the trash then, looked at his master.

"Sorry, old boy," said Travis. "End of the road for you." Popeye wagged his nub of a tail at the sound of his master's voice. Travis pulled the little .22 caliber automatic pistol from his back pocket and chambered a round. He put the barrel to the side of Popeye's head. Popeye started to turn to lick his master's hand, but before he could, Travis pulled the trigger. The firecracker popping sound of the .22 filled the night. Popeye's body tensed momentarily, before going limp and dropping flat on top of the garbage.

Travis twirled the little pistol on his finger, gunslinger style, before slipping it back into his pocket. He whistled a happy tune as he walked back around to the front of the bar, confident that no one heard the pop of the low caliber pistol over the blaring jukebox inside. He'd already forgotten Popeye as he rounded the front of the bar. He hoped the bartender with the big titties was working. He liked the way she leaned over the bar when she talked to him, her big knockers coming so close to escaping the low cut top. Then he heard it. The clicks of a dog's nails on pavement, the uneven clicks of a dog with a limp. He turned around. There he was. The left side of Popeye's head was matted with the blood that oozed out of the bullet hole. Blood also dripped from his mouth. When his master stopped and turned around, the dog stopped and looked up at him.

Travis shook his head. "Are you stupid or what?" Whatever sympathy he'd felt was gone. He wanted to be done with the animal. Once again, Popeye's nub of a tail wagged at the sound of his master's voice. Something inside Travis snapped. "You stupid mother fucker!" He ran up and kicked the dog in its side, the tip of his cowboy boot catching Popeye in the ribs, knocking him over onto his side against the wall of the bar. Travis began yelling, punctuating each word with a kick. "YOU," kick, "STUPID," kick, "MOTHER," kick, "FUCKER!" kick.

There is no telling how long this might have gone on had Jill not seen the incident out the window, set her tray of beers down and come bursting out the door. "What the fuck is your problem asshole!" she yelled.

Travis paused in the beating long enough to point a finger at Jill and yell back at her. "Mind your own fucking business bitch!" He returned to kicking the dog.

Popeye, no stranger to pain, took the beating without a whimper. Jill took one step toward him, intent on putting a stop to it, when Jay came out of the bar and slipped past her. He came up behind Travis, grabbed him by the back of the head and shoved his face into the brick wall. Travis's nose flattened into a mess of bloody smashed cartilage and his two front teeth broke. He spun around, slamming an elbow into Jay's face and pulling the .22 from his back pocket as he did. Jay grabbed the pistol and twisted it upwards and backwards, along with his Travis's finger. Travis grimaced as much from the sound as the pain of the digit breaking. The gun dropped to the sidewalk. Jay kicked it to the side. He slammed his knee into the man's balls. Travis put everything he had left into a right hook to Jay's face before the waves of pain rolled out from his testicles and drained his will to fight. Jay slapped a headlock on him and they stumbled into the parking lot. He felt the man going slack just as he felt his own legs hit the hood of a Camaro in the parking lot. He used the momentum of the fall to flip Travis over and toss him through the front windshield, which gave way immediately in a shower of broken glass. Jay rolled off the hood and turned towards Travis, but the man made no move to extricate himself from the front seats of the Camaro where he lay moaning.

A small crowd had gathered around the front door. When Travis went through the windshield, there were a few gasps and "Holy shit!" type comments. Then there was nothing but silence except for the moans from Travis whose face sprouted a dozen or so bits of broken glass. Jay turned to face the crowd. He was still pumped up on the adrenaline spike that accompanies sudden bursts of violence. Some of the people in the crowd looked at the ground, some at the night sky, and some at each other. None met Jay's eyes. Except for Jill. She looked him right in the eye with neither fear nor judgment. She subtly nodded her head at him. It was a slight gesture but communicated much. She turned her gaze from Jay to the dog. Popeye lay still, but Jill could see he was still breathing. She ran to the dog, dropped to her knees and stroked his fur. Jay squatted next to her.

"There's a hole in his head," said Jill. "This is more than a beating. I think the son of a bitch shot him." Jay scooped up the dog, carried him to his pick-up and set him in the back. Jill turned to one of the waitresses who had come out to see what all the commotion was about. "Tell my dad I had to leave early." She jumped in the back of Jay's truck and cradled Popeye's head in her lap.

As the buzz spread among the patrons, that there was a fight in the parking lot, they poured outside, only to be disappointed to find the violence was over. They moved over to the Camaro with the legs sticking out of the broken windshield. Travis moaned and groaned but barely moved. Nobody seemed particularly interested in helping him. When the owner of the car came out and joined the crowd, he grabbed his hair with both hands. "What the fuck man!" Despite his rage, common sense and self-control got the better of him, and he decided not to try and confront Jay who was just climbing into the cab of his truck. When he saw Jack McCray come out of the bar, he decided to appeal to him. "Jack, come on man, this ain't right. What the fuck did I ever do to you guys?" He pointed at his Camaro.

Jack looked at the smashed windshield, heard the groans of the man in the car and glanced at his uncle's tail lights as he pulled out of the parking lot. He put it all together and a smile spread across his face as he guessed at the previous events. "Take it easy," said Jack as he walked over to the Camaro. He pulled a wad of bills wrapped in a rubber band out of his pocket and tossed it to the car's owner. "That should be enough to pay for your windshield and the time and trouble of taking this poor fuck to the hospital." The car's owner pulled the rubber band off the wad and flipped through the bills. They were all hundreds. He nodded his head, the flames of his anger effectively doused. Jack reached in through the broken windshield and pulled Travis's wallet from his pocket. It was attached to his belt loop by a chain. Jack gave it a tug, breaking the belt loop. He pulled the driver's license out and tossed the wallet back into the car. "I don't know if he knows who we are," Jack said, turning back to the Camaro's owner. "But you make sure he knows who we are and that we know who he is." Jack held up the license for emphasis. "And if any pigs come around here fucking with my uncle over this incident, I'm gonna fuck with him. And I won't be nowhere near as gentle as my uncle was." He stuck the license in his pocket.

The Camaro's owner nodded his head. "I'll let him know," he said, opening the driver's side door. "Move over fuck head!" He gave Travis a shove as he got behind the wheel.

Chapter 23

Agent Bushy sat on the bed, pointing the remote control at the television and flipping through the myriad of stations from the first channel to the last for the fourth time in a row. Being picked for the advanced team in an investigation targeting the murderers of an F.B.I. agent was, by far, the biggest thing that had happened to him in his brief career with the F.B.I. Or at least that's what he thought at first. The research he did back in K.C. was supposed to be the boring part of the job with field work being the adrenaline pot of gold at the end of the rainbow. But, so far, the field had consisted of no more than sitting around a motel room with a few other agents watching television, playing cards and occasionally going into the bathroom to masturbate. They weren't even doing surveillance, which was boring enough but at least served a purpose. He came here with fantasies of shootouts with drug dealing cop killers, only to have those fantasies slowly give way to a growing suspicion that sitting in a cheap motel room may end up being the extent of this experience. He decided, if that turned out to be the case, he'd make up an alternative story to tell people about what he'd been doing during this time. Of course it wouldn't work with people in the Bureau, but he'd done a lot of bragging to friends and family members outside the agency about the big assignment he was going on. Agency rules prevented him from giving them any specifics, but he'd promised them more details when it was over. He used the empty hours in the motel to imagine the story he could tell his people later. He imagined describing how the bullets whizzed by his head as he charged forward, picked up a fallen agent, threw him over his shoulder and got him to safety. It was really embarrassing at the hospital later the way the agent's family fawned over him, calling him a hero. Why was none of this in the news? Well the investigation is ongoing, and the whole thing has to be kept covert. Did he kill anyone? Of course, all part of the job. How many? He thought about that. He couldn't inflate the number too much, had to keep it believable. Three was the max he could claim personally, two was probably safer. Fuck it, he thought, I killed three.

In the middle of his fantasies the door opened and Agent Brinks, the guy he was assigned to share a room with, came walking in and flopped down on the room's only chair. "Well," said Brinks, "Franks said we could leave this shithole as long as we go in the opposite direction of town. I checked, and there's a truck stop a few miles up the highway. You want to go grab a beer?"

"Fuck yeah!" Bushy jumped up from the bed and went to his suitcase to pick out clothes. After sitting in the motel room day after day, drinking a few brews at a truck stop was as exciting as a night out at the strip club. "You think we should ask the other guys if they want to come along?" asked Bushy.

"Fuck those dipshits. Besides, I wanted to talk to you, bounce some ideas off you."

"O.K.," said Bushy. He was actually tired of Brinks and would have preferred the other guys' company. He wondered why, if Brinks wanted to talk to him about something, he couldn't have done it during the long dead hours they'd spent in the motel room together. But, Brinks was a senior agent and could potentially be his boss someday or have something to say about his future career, promotions, etc. So it was worth staying on his good side. Besides he'd probably be a lot less annoying after a few beers.

On the way to the truck stop, Brinks flipped from one end of the radio dial to the other finding mostly talk radio and country music. He finally found a classic rock station and got about twenty seconds of a Rush song before it faded to static. "Fuck!" said Brinks flipping off the radio in frustration. "I don't know how these fucking people live like this. The Bureau should really hook us up with satellite radio when we are assigned out here in East Buttfuck Missouri or wherever the fuck we are. At least give us a CD player, you know what I mean?"

"Uh huh," said Bushy. "How much farther is this place?"

"GPS says it should be just around the corner on the right."

They rounded the corner, and there it was. A completely unremarkable truck stop. There was no bar, but the diner sold beer. They entered and found a booth. They waitress was a well past middle aged woman with granny glasses, orthopedic shoes and saggy skin. There were virtually no female customers, only burly truck drivers who rolled in off the highway, ate hardily, tipped well and rolled back out again. It wasn't what either of them would have hoped for in a night out, but at least they were out of the motel. They both ordered bacon cheeseburgers with a side of fries and drank Budweiser beer out of the bottle. The food was surprisingly delicious. Neither spoke while they ate as they lost themselves in the greasy joy that sat on their plates. When they finished their burgers, Brinks guzzled the last of his beer and leaned back rubbing his stomach, surprised at how much a full belly made this place, which seemed so disappointing at first, grow on him.

"Get you boys anything else?" asked the waitress taking their empty plates.

"Couple more brews," Brinks said shaking his empty beer bottle.

Bushy was looking at the menu again. "How is your pie here?"

"Officially, we are supposed to have the best apple in the Midwest," said the waitress. "But if you ask me, it's the peach cobbler that's truly blue ribbon."

Brinks rolled his eyes. "He doesn't want any pie, just a couple of beers, please."

"Don't tell me what I want." Bushy turned to the waitress, "Let me get a slice of that peach cobbler, with a scoop of vanilla ice cream on top."

"I thought we came here to drink?" said Brinks.

"I didn't say I don't want the beer. But the best desert I've had since we started this assignment is Hostess chocolate donuts from the gas station. Don't get me wrong, I love those things. But the food here is awesome. And I'm going to get my fill." He turned back to the waitress, "Slice of peach cobbler, scoop of vanilla, please ma'am."

"Beer and pie? You're going to make me puke you fat fuck!"

"Sir! Language! Please?" The waitress threw a fierce look at him through her granny glasses. It reminded Brinks of the terrifying grade school teachers that scolded him decades ago. Brinks held her judgmental gaze for a long beat before relenting.

"Sorry ma'am," he said throwing his hands up.

Order restored, she turned back to Bushy with a smile. "I'll be right back with your cobbler sweetie."

They sat in silence for the duration of Bushy's assault on the peach cobbler and the next round of beers. By the third beer Brinks's bravado, wounded by the mean waitress, began to recover, and halfway through the next round he got back to the purpose of this little fieldtrip. "So Bushy, don't you think this is kind of bullshit how they got us sidelined on this shit?"

Bushy considered this while taking a swig of beer. Finally he shrugged his shoulders. "I mean, it sucks, but while she's doing her preliminary undercover there is not a lot we can do."

"But that's just it Bushy," Brinks said sitting up in his chair. "Why do you think she's undercover and we're sitting on the bench?"

Bushy seemed to be ignoring Brinks, instead opting to focus his attention on peeling off the Budweiser label. "I don't know. This is my first assignment. She's got more experience than me."

"Well she ain't got more, fucking, experience than me!" Brinks slammed his fist down on the table making the Budweiser bottles dance. He looked around suddenly worried that the waitress may have heard him say the f-word. When he didn't see her, he continued, "This ain't about experience. Think about it. We are smack dab in Middle America, investigating white men in an area of almost all white men, and the lead investigator as well as the undercover spot is given to a Chinese bitch? We are second fiddle here because our skin is white, our eyes are round and we got dicks swinging between our legs. Wake up man! This is typical PC federal bullshit. She's a chick and a chink, she checks two boxes off their affirmative action checklist. You really can't see that?"

Bushy finished peeling off the label and set it down flat on the table. Then he looked up at Brinks realizing it was his turn to say something. "Yeah, I guess. Maybe."

"But mark my words," said Brinks. "There's one thing they can't ignore."

"What's that?" With no more label to occupy his attention, Bushy was finally getting interested.

"Results! You and me Bushy, we could go undercover in that redneck bar they drink at, what is it, the Hacksaw or something?"

"Buzzsaw."

"Right, the Buzzsaw! We get the younger one, Jack he's there all the time, to sell us some contraband, bust him, put some heat on him, maybe smack him around a little bit, get him to sign a confession implicating the uncle then, bam, we bust them both."

"They would fucking flip out on us if we went rogue and did that stuff on our own."

"Right there! Right there Bushy is why the white man is losing this country that he built. We let the PC police convince us that we have to wait around for permission. The brass isn't going to say anything if we hand them the McCrays on a silver platter. We got to take initiative Bushy!"

"Yeah, but what if we don't get the McCrays?"

"Bushy, these people are inbred, they walk around slack-jawed slobbering on themselves. You telling me you don't think a couple of top notch agents like us could outsmart any of these backward fucks any day of the god damned week?"

Bushy nodded his head. "We could. We could do this."

"God damned right Bushy. That's the can do attitude that put the white man on the map, that's manifest fucking destiny in the flesh! So I need to know now. Are you with on this or not?"

Agent Bushy swallowed the last of his beer and slammed the bottle down on the table. "Damn right I'm with you! Let's do this."

Chapter 24

Jay woke to hot breath on his face. He opened his eyes to see that he was nose to wet nose with the pitbull. It reached out a long tongue and started licking his face. Jay pushed the dog's head away and sat up. He was on the living room floor. The new waitress from last night was sleeping on the sofa right in front of him. He let his eyes slide down her body, lingering on her toned, bare legs. When his dick started to tingle and stiffen, he decided to tear himself away and go take his morning piss before it got too hard.

He stood over the toilet and closed his eyes enjoying that unique satisfaction that comes with the first morning piss after a night of drinking. When the stream petered out to nothing he washed his hands and looked at himself in the mirror. There was a slight red slash on the lower right corner of his lip where it split. He rubbed his tongue on it for no discernable reason other than to cause himself pain. There was a slight bruise under his left eye but it wasn't bad. He'd won the fight, decisively, and the wounds were far from the worst he'd carried away from indulging in an Irish conversation. Still, ten years ago he would have dominated the same fight, most likely without injury, and not even been breathing hard. Ten years from now, in the same fight . . . And why did he even do it? Was it to impress the waitress? He couldn't deny the thought might have been in his head, but he didn't think that was entirely it. Was it for the dog? Did he get in this fight for a dog? He'd certainly fought for less. He was overthinking but couldn't help it. Once he let his thinking get metaphorical, it wasn't hard to see. The dog was a former fighter that got respect. Now it was old. It served no more use. It got no more respect. How far off could that fate be for him? Maybe not far. But not today.

When he returned she was awake and petting the dog. "I think he's going to be alright," she said.

"He's a tough bastard," said Jay, genuinely impressed with the dog's resilience.

"He's a sweetheart." She kissed the dog on the head and stood up. "I've got to use your bathroom, freshen up."

"I'm gonna make some breakfast. Bacon and eggs or pancakes maybe?"

"Pancakes would be so awesome! Coffee?"

"I'll put a pot on."

"Cool. You better let the dog out to pee too." She headed for the bathroom. He watched her ass till she disappeared down the hallway.

The dog followed him to the door, limped out onto the lawn when he opened it and sniffed around furiously before finding an acceptable bush and lifting his leg. He actually seemed to smile as he watered the foliage. Jay scanned the wood line around the property for movement. Nothing. He studied the road. Same. The road could be more accurately described as a wide trail, and a rough one at that, with huge potholes bordering on craters that slowed the top driving speed to five or ten miles an hour. This would make it extremely difficult for either the cartel or the Feds to sneak up.

Satisfied there were no threats on the horizon, he propped open the door, went into the kitchen, put on a pot of coffee then went to his room. He found the smallest gun he had, a snub .38 revolver, loaded it and tucked it into his back pocket. Since the trouble started, and well before it if truth be told, he'd kept his .45 on him and a rifle or shotgun within reach. But he didn't want to freak out the waitress (he'd forgotten her name) and he didn't dare want to explain the situation to her. Going completely unarmed at that moment in time, however, was out of the question. A discreetly pocketed .38 was a reasonable compromise. When he returned to the kitchen, she was drinking coffee and making pancakes. "I would have done that," he said.

"I don't mind." She pulled a cup out of the cupboard. "How do you like your coffee?"

"Black." He sat down at the kitchen table. The weed tray was sitting there so he decided to roll one. She poured him a cup and put it in front of him while eyeing the weed. It was common knowledge at the Bureau that they would turn a blind eye to agents using drugs to maintain their cover during an undercover assignment. She hadn't smoked pot since college. Pot today was supposed to much better than then, and the McCray strain was supposed to be among the best today, so she wasn't going to pass up the opportunity to see what all the hoopla was about. She went back to the stove and flipped the pancakes. Jay finished rolling the joint and lit it. "You smoke?" he asked.

She turned to him smiling. "It's been awhile, but I don't mind if I do." She took the joint, put it to her lips and inhaled.

"Well, if it's been awhile, you may want to go easy on this stuff. Couple of hits ought to be plenty." He no sooner said the words and she started coughing. She handed him back the joint and turned back to the stove. After flipping the pancakes onto plates, she turned off the stove and tried another hit. She did better, managing to hold the hit without coughing. Grabbing the two plates of pancakes, she made her way around to the other side of the table, sat down and slid one of the plates over to him. "Thank you," he said, moving to put out the joint. "You good on this?"

"Maybe just one more hit." She held her hand out. He shrugged his shoulders and handed it to her. She took a big hit this time and leaned back in her chair. It was really kicking in now. Things somehow seemed more distant and more vivid at the same time. She exhaled the smoke and looked at the pancakes. "Wait, forks, I didn't—syrup too, do you, I mean where—hold on now—"

Jay laughed. "Don't sweat it, I got you." He took the joint from her and put it out before getting up, retrieving silverware, syrup and butter and bringing them back to the table.

Her pancakes were stacked three high. She strategically placed pats of butter between the first and second cake, the second and third and lastly on top. Originally she'd only agreed to breakfast as a premise to stay a little longer and see what intel she could get. But now the prospect of eating these pancakes overwhelmed her with excitement. But not until they were perfect. For the first time, she realized what artistry went into assembling the perfect stack of pancakes. First the butter. It wasn't just a matter of making sure it was spread evenly among the three cakes, but you had to make sure that it was melted to just the right consistency. Not completely melted to the point of liquid and not solid and still cold from the fridge, but somewhere in the middle. And then there was the syrup. When you poured the syrup over the top, you really had to soak it. When pancakes are in a stack, the ones on bottom don't get soaked, so you have to pour enough over the top so it pools up on the plate along the perimeter of the bottom cake. That way, when you got a dry piece from the middle, you could just dip it in there. When she got the cakes the way she wanted them, she cut into them with her fork. She looked at it. Perfect. The perfect combination of cake, syrup and butter. If a thousand world class chefs had a thousand attempts, they couldn't produce a more perfect forkful of food. She put it in her mouth. It was nothing less than an explosion of flavor, the sweetness of the syrup, the savoriness of the butter, the warmth of the cake all making love to each individual taste bud and producing something akin to an oral orgasm.

Popeye started barking outside. Jay sat upright in his chair. He didn't want to alarm, what's her name, but he couldn't ignore it. He got up and headed for the door, giving her a sidelong glance as he passed her. She didn't even seem aware that he was in the room, let alone that he'd left the table. Good. He slipped the .38 from his back pocket. Once he was out on the porch he saw Popeye was just in front of the porch and facing it, still barking. Was someone under the porch? He ran down the steps, squatted and pointed the .38. Nothing. He looked at Popeye. The dog would alternate between barking and a low growl but his gaze remained focused. Jay walked over stood behind the dog and followed his line of sight. He wasn't looking at something under the porch. He was looking at the corner post of the porch. What the fuck? He kneeled down by the side of the dog. "What's the matter boy?" Popeye shifted his gaze toward Jay for split second, wagged his nub of a tail, then turned his attention back to the post and growled. Jay shook his head and stood up.

"What the fuck is wrong with that mutt?" said a voice behind Jay. Jay didn't panic or go for his gun. There was no need. He recognized the voice. He turned to see his brother, his nephew and two girls he saw at the Buzzsaw last night. They were walking across the yard obviously having come out of the woods. Jack must have picked them up at the bar last night and brought them out to Jimbo's campsite. Jack carried his twelve gauge and Jimbo carried the .308. The shotgun would provide excellent short range defense for the campsite. The .308 was more of a long range offensive weapon. Jay thought that they would both be packing pistols somewhere as well. The girls were clearly not dressed for the woods. One wore a denim skirt and halter top. Her legs were filled with fresh cuts. The other was dressed slightly more casual in short shorts and a T-shirt. Her legs didn't fare too much better, but at least she wore cowboy boots. The other was barefoot carrying a pair of high heels in her hand. How in the hell she made it as deep into the woods as their camp must have been, Jay had no idea. Both of these local girls, he thought one was named Debbie, he couldn't remember the name of the other, would know who Jimbo was. Of course this was risky and stupid but there was no point getting mad about it. Jimbo was hard enough to reason with under the best of circumstances. Jay figured he had slightly less chance of convincing Jimbo not to get laid after being in prison for years, as he had of convincing the sun to stop rising in the east.

"I don't know," said Jay turning back to the dog. "That shot in the head had to hit his brain. I think it might have scrambled his eggs a bit. It's a wonder he's still alive."

"Is there something under the porch?" asked one of the girls. They gathered around Popeye.

"I think he's looking at the post," said Jay.

Jimbo bent over putting his hands on his knees. He looked from the dog to the post. "Get that post, boy! Get it!" he said pointing. Popeye leapt forward and sank his teeth into the wood. He growled and tried to shake the post, then just held on. Everybody laughed. "Well speaking of scrambled eggs, we're dying for breakfast. You better have bacon," Jimbo said climbing the porch steps. Jack and the girls were right behind him. Jay took one last look at Popeye, shrugged his shoulders and followed them.

Jill had relit the joint and was taking a hit over her now empty plate. "Hey Megan," said Jack remembering her from the bar last night. "Good shit, ain't it?"

Jay made a mental note to remember her name this time.

"You ain't lying," she said.

"This is my cousin Johnny," said Jay introducing Jimbo. There was nothing he could do about the two bimbos, who he didn't bother to introduce, but he could at least make it clear that this girl didn't need to know who Jimbo was. "Johnny, this is Megan Spivey, Buzz's daughter."

"Oh yeah. I think I remember you from when you was just a baby. You sure grew up pretty." He spotted the empty plate in front of her. "So what did you all have for breakfast?"

"Pancakes," said Jill. "They were so good. Soooo good!"

"Any left?" Jimbo asked Jay.

"Just what Jack's finishing off there." After taking a couple of hits of the joint, Jack had noticed Jay's half-finished pancakes, sat down and went to work.

"That's O.K.," said Jimbo. "I got a taste for bacon." He went to the fridge, pulled out all the bacon, some deer sausage and a carton of eggs, then threw some bread in the toaster. Everyone else took a seat at the kitchen table, and Jay rolled another joint while Jack finished his pancakes. Debbie and her friend went to the bathroom to try to freshen up as much as one can after a night of sex in the woods without the benefit of a shower and a change of clothes. When they returned to the table they sat on opposite sides of Jack and threw occasional dirty looks at Jill. She had a good ten years on both of them, but where they were chubby and soft, she was firm and lean. It wasn't that she was skinny in the way of a girl who doesn't want to be fat so she starves herself into thinness. She was toned. She had the supple athletic looking body of a high school volleyball player.

Jimbo rotated away from the stove, from time to time, for a hit off the joint. At one point he grabbed a bottle of beer from the fridge. "Me too," said Jack snapping his fingers. Jimbo tossed him one.

"Drinking already?" asked Debbie.

"It's just beer," said Jimbo. "Beer don't even count as drinking to a whiskey-swilling Irishman."

"You got anything non-alcoholic to drink, sides water?" asked Debbie's friend. "Your weed always gives me cottonmouth."

"Fresh pot of coffee," said Jay nodding toward the pot. "Cups in the cupboard above it."

Debbie and her friend got cups of coffee loaded with lots of sugar and milk. Jill got a second cup, poured Jay a second cup and one for Jimbo and Jack, then put another pot on. Jimbo finished cooking, put all the food on a couple of plates and put them in the middle of the table along with a stack of empty plates and a pile of silverware. Everyone helped themselves. Soon everyone had a plate and the room was filled with the sounds of knives and forks scraping plates as well as occasional moans of pleasure. Jill who had already put away a three-stack of pancakes had her hunger reignited by the second joint and was marveling over the perfection of bacon.

Jay sat at the end of the table where he could lean back, look through the window and see the road. The Feds hadn't come to search the house for Jimbo. But once they decided he wasn't hiding in the immediate vicinity of the prison, his hometown and family would be the next logical place to look. It wasn't smart for Jimbo to be here at all, but if they kept their eyes on the road, they should be able to see the Feds coming from far enough away that Jimbo would be able to get out the back and into the woods.

When Jay spotted movement on the road, he got up quickly and went to the window. Jimbo and Jack both sat up in their chairs. Jay returned to the table smiling. "Tracy is here." Jack relaxed and went back to his breakfast. Jimbo got up, walked over and stood behind the open door.

Tracy pulled up to the front of their house on her quad runner and shut off the engine. She skipped up the steps and walked through the doorway. "Knock knock," she said.

"Boo!" yelled Jimbo jumping out from behind the door. She jumped back at first, then, when she saw who it was, threw her arms around him. He picked her up, spinning her around. "Call me Cousin Johnny," he whispered in her ear. After a long hug they let each other go.

"God damn it's been too long Johnny. I missed you." They walked over to the table.

"Hope you're hungry," said Jay. "Johnny done cooked damn near every scrap of food in the house."

She grabbed a piece of bacon off his plate and took a bite. "Actually, I'm out of bud. Hoping you could hook me up with a morning buzz."

"Help yourself." Jay pointed to the weed tray sitting in the middle of the table next to the plate of scrambled eggs. "Papers are on the tray."

She took a juicy nugget from the tray. "It's cool. I got my pipe." She pulled a small penis-shaped pipe from the front pocket of her blue jean cutoffs, stuffed the nug into the bowl, walked over to the kitchen counter, hopped up on it and took a hit. "Oh yeah," she said exhaling smoke. "You know there is a crazy dog out there attacking your porch?"

"Yeah that's Popeye. He's got some issues," Jay said. He finished the last bite of his breakfast and stood up pulling his pack of cigarettes from his pocket. When he caught Jimbo's eye he subtly nodded toward the door. Jimbo returned the subtle nod, put a piece of deer sausage between two pieces of toast and headed for the front door.

Out on the porch Jay lit a cigarette and took turns looking back and forth between the road and Popeye, who still showed no sign of letting the porch post go. Jimbo sat on the steps and took a bite of his sandwich. As he swallowed, he wished he'd brought his beer. "Look," he said. "You don't even have to say it. I know I shouldn't be here. I just want to get a shower, eat some home cooked food, restock supplies and I'll be back out in the woods."

"It's cool man. But as long as you're here, you, me and Jack need to be keeping an eye on that road."

"No doubt, no doubt." Jimbo shoved the last bite of his sandwich into his mouth and stood up wiping his hands on his jeans. He stepped over next to Jay at the railing and tapped to fingers to his lips. Jimbo gave him a cigarette which he lit before taking a long drag. "So how bout that little fortune cookie in there? You get a piece of that?"

Jay shook his head. "She was just here to help with the dog."

"So, you going to try?"

Jay shrugged his shoulders. "Considering everything, now probably isn't the best time to bring any new people around here, know what I mean?"

"I do. And yet you brought her here anyway. Guess you were really worried about that dog, huh?" He paused waiting for Jay to respond. When he didn't, Jimbo continued, "So you think any more about our problem?"

Jay knew he was talking about the cartel. Of course he had thought about it, thought about it non-stop and still hadn't come up with anything close to a solution. "I have," he said.

When he lapsed back into silence, Jimbo prodded him, "And?"

"We can't beat them outright. There's too many, too well funded and too well armed."

"Is that so? Sounds like you ready to just wave the white flag then?"

"I didn't say that."

"What exactly are you saying then?"

"We can't beat them outright. But we don't have to. We just have to keep them from beating us. Hold out long enough so that the price they have to pay, to beat us, is so high that they decide it's not worth it." Jay knew this wasn't an actual plan. But he also knew there was something to it.

"Let me get a smoke," said Jack coming out onto the porch. Jay tossed him the pack.

Jimbo saw Jack's beer and went in to get his own. When he came out, the women, who had finished their breakfasts, drifted out with him. Jay brought out chairs, figuring it was just as well everybody hang out on the porch so as to make it easier to watch the road. He made a point of having Jimbo sit by the door so he could make a quick escape if need be. They smoked more dope. At one point Popeye decided that the post was no longer a threat and gave up on it. He climbed up on the porch and settled down between Tracy and Jill. Jack set up the washer pits and he, Jimbo and the women took turns pitching washers. Everybody but Jay started drinking beer. Jay eventually broke down and busted out the whiskey bottle. It was passed around by the men and Tracy. When they started running low on alcohol, Jack volunteered to make a run and suggested he pick up some meat, potatoes and corn on the cob so they could have a barbecue. Everyone agreed with this idea so he left with Debbie and returned with pork steaks, ribs, potatoes and corn on the cob.

Jay had the clever idea of setting up the empty beer bottles for some target practice. He wanted to be armed with more than the .38 if the cartel showed up, but he still didn't want to freak out the pretty new waitress. Target practice was the perfect excuse to keep the heavy artillery close at hand. They started with rifles and shotguns. Debbie, her friend and certainly Tracy were plenty familiar with rifles and shotguns, being lifelong country girls. But to Jay's surprise it was Megan (Jill), who supposedly moved to the city as a baby, that was the best shot of the women. When it came to the pistols, she was better than everyone except Jay himself. He even suspected she might have missed a couple bottles on purpose.

The day wore on. More dope was smoked, whiskey and beer drank, washers thrown and guns fired. Jack barbecued pork steaks and ribs. Debbie turned on Jay's stereo and put the speakers up in the open windows so they could hear it out on the front lawn. She danced with her friend to Lynyrd Skynyrd. Jill found an old baseball and was using it to play fetch with Popeye. It was a typical summer's day in the country. Except, Jay thought, for the fact that he had to watch the road for the gang of Mexicans that could come to murder them all at any minute, or the Federal agents that could show up for Jimbo.

It was the latter that would interrupt the day's good time. Jimbo was inside grabbing another round of beers. Jay was the first to see the black SUVs coming down the road. "Cops!" he yelled. He ran into the house where Jimbo was just on his way back outside with an armful of beers. "Go!" said Jay. He didn't need to say anymore. Jimbo put the beers on the table and ran out the back door. Jay watched him sprint across the backyard and disappear into the woods. He knew he was safe then. Jimbo could outrun most men in a straight up race, but in the woods he was faster than any man Jay knew with the exception of Jack whose smaller size gave him a rabbit like agility in maneuvering through the thicket.

Tracy, who'd followed Jay in, grabbed the weed tray. She found a sandwich baggy in a drawer and dumped the weed in it. "Is there any more?" she asked Jay.

"The roaches." Jay pointed to the ashtrays on the kitchen table. Tracy grabbed them and dumped them, cigarette butts and all, into the baggy before rolling it up and shoving it down the front of her shorts and into her underwear.

Jay turned off the stereo and they went outside. The Feds still had a way to go. They saw everyone outside and tried to speed up but the lead SUV a huge crater-like pothole causing the front of their car to scrape the ground and the agents to be thrown forward smashing into the steering wheel and dashboard. If they came back, they would learn from this, thought Jay. They would come at night when they couldn't be seen or park on the road a half mile back and come on foot through the woods. But there was nothing they could do now. They'd lost the element of surprise.

Debbie and her friend smoked cigarettes and drank their beers. They were bummed the party was over but otherwise unconcerned. They knew that if they kept their mouths shut, they had nothing to worry about. Jack and Tracy were family, Jay knew there was no worry there. It was only this new waitress he had to worry about. In the short time he'd known her, he'd already grown to like her, maybe a lot. But he had to admit to himself that he didn't know her enough to trust her and shouldn't have brought her here. She stood a few feet from the other girls with her arms crossed, face expressionless and unreadable. He walked over to her. "Don't say anything about Johnny. He was never here."

"O.K." she said.

"Please, not a word about him. No matter what they—"

"Jay," she interrupted. "It's cool. I got it. I won't say anything about Johnny. I mean it." She looked him in the eye and he believed her.

Jay turned around and lit a cigarette. The SUVs pulled up and the agents poured out. Most of them went up the porch and into the house, but Shultz strode right up to Jay. "Are you Jay McCray?" he asked.

"I am."

"This is a warrant to search your premises." He showed Jay a piece of paper. "Have you seen your brother?"

"My brother is in the pen."

"You know he escaped, and now I know you're a liar. Did he run out in the woods when he saw us coming?"

"I can't imagine it would be that easy for a hoodlum like my brother to elude some grade A officers of the law such as yourselves. Can you?"

"All right," he said raising his voice. "I need everyone lined up in front of the porch. "I'm going to need to talk to each one of you. I need you to have your I.D. out and ready to show me."

He started with Debbie and then her friend. They both said the same thing. "My daddy's a lawyer and he says I ain't supposed to talk to no cops without him being present." This was complete bullshit, of course. But Jimbo told them to say that, if the cops came. He figured the less they said the less chance they'd slip up. They stuck to the script. It worked. Next Shultz called over Jack.

"I'll tell you one thing," said Jack handing over his license. "I only got enough ribs and corn for us. So, if ya'll are gonna stay for supper, you'll have to settle for pork steaks and potatoes. Can you all eat pork, or is that like, I don't know, cannibalism or something?"

"You're Jack McCray. The fugitive's son." Shultz looked him up and down. "It appears the turd don't fall far from the asshole. Seen your daddy lately?"

"Isn't he in prison?"

It was clear he wasn't going to get anything from Jack, so he sent him back to the porch and called over Jill. "Are you from here originally?"

"I was born here. I left with my mom when my parents divorced. Now I'm back."

"What made you come back?"

"I was out of work. My dad owns the Buzzsaw. It's a bar not too far from here. He gave me a job as a server."

"How well do you know the McCrays?"

"Not very. They drink at my dad's bar."

"Do you know Jimbo McCray?"

"I don't."

"Have you seen this man?" He held up Jimbo McCray's mugshot.

"I haven't."

Shultz stared into her eyes. She stared back unflinchingly. He pulled a small notebook from his breast pocket. "What did you say the name and address of that bar was?" She told him, and he copied it down along with the name and address from her license. "I recommend you keep better company Miss Spivey." He gave her back her license. "You can go back over by your friends now."

Lastly he called over Jay. As Jay walked over, the other agents came out of the house. One of the agents looked at Shultz and shook his head. Jay knew that when he went inside, he'd find every drawer dumped out on the floor, all the clothes pulled from the closet and dumped on the floor, the mattress from the bed and the furniture all turned over. The house would be trashed. Things would be broken. They would not do these things because they had to. Obviously, if they are searching for a person, they know he's not hiding in a drawer. They would do these things because they could. "You may not like us coming here like this," said Shultz. "But believe it or not, this little social call is downright courteous compared to what it will be like if I have to come back here. Right now I'm only interested in bringing your brother in. I have no interest in you. But the longer I can't find him, the more I start to look at you, at your nephew, at your friends. The deeper I get into your business."

Jay nodded. "Well, I doubt Jimbo's going to be dumb enough to come back to his hometown where he knows it will be the first place you all look. But if he is that dumb, I'll be sure to let you know."

"Agent Pell!" yelled Shultz.

"Yes sir?" responded one of the agents.

"Make sure the fugitive isn't hiding in that tray of meat."

The agent smiled. "Yes sir!" He walked over to the barbecue pit. The cooked meat was in an aluminum pan covered with foil. The agent pulled the foil off the top and dumped the meat onto the ground. He then did the same with the tray of uncooked meat before kicking it around. "Doesn't appear the fugitive is here sir!"

Shultz looked at Jay. "Damn. I was sure he'd be hiding in there. Well, I hope I never see you again. But I suspect I will." He turned from Jay and headed for his car. "All right boys!" he yelled. "Mount up and move out!"

Chapter 25

Jill hadn't been much of a drinker before. But she found herself looking forward to downing her usual screwdrivers that she had during her debriefing, especially after a shift of waiting tables. Franks handed her her cocktail and sat down in the chair on the opposite side of the little motel table she was sitting at. "Anything new?" he asked.

She took a healthy gulp of her drink before answering. "I spent the night at their house."

"Really?"

"Yep."

"How did you manage that?"

"There was this dog at the Buzzsaw last night, and it got shot—"

"One of the McCrays shot a dog?"

"No, they didn't shoot the dog."

"The cartel shot the dog?"

"No, the cartel doesn't play a role in this report. May I finish?"

"Sorry." He leaned back in his chair and took a drink. "The floor is yours."

"O.K. So there was this dog at the bar last night and it

got shot. Who shot it isn't important. Jay got upset about the dog. It was kind of sweet really."

"He murdered twelve men and cut off their testicles," interjected Franks.

"I know, I know, I wasn't saying—whatever. Anyway, he was concerned about the dog and wanted to take it home to, you know, take care of it. So I feigned my own concern and went back to his place to help take care of the dog."

"Just to take care of the dog"

She gave him a dirty look. "I slept on the sofa. I ended up spending a good part of the next day there too."

"Did you see anything we can charge him with?"

"No. There was a little bit of marijuana but not enough to be worth charging him for. But, guess who showed up the next day."

"The cartel?"

"No, I didn't see or hear anything about the cartel." She held her finger up, in a wait a minute gesture, as she swallowed down the last of her screwdriver. She poured herself another and took a sip. "God that's good. Anyway, the next day, Jack showed up with two girls and his father."

"You saw Jimbo McCray?"

"Yep!"

"You're sure it was him?"

"They introduced him as their cousin Johnny, but, yeah, it was him. I'm sure of it."

"So am I to understand that you're hoping to cast a wide enough net to get the cop killers, the cartel, a dirty sheriff and an escaped convict?"

"Am I being greedy?"

"It's ambitious. There's a lot of moving parts, a lot that can go wrong."

"I figure if I hang around the McCrays long enough, sooner or later I'll witness the cartel make a move on them. That could be enough to get the cartel on attempted murder or murder if they succeed."

"Assuming you survive."

"Assuming that, of course. I suspect Jimbo will be popping in and out of the scene as he feels safe. I just have to make sure he's present when we make our move, that or find out where he's hiding. I'm pretty sure it's somewhere out in the woods probably not far from their house. The biggest issue so far is what do I bust Jay and Jack for? I haven't got shit to connect them to the murders. I don't even have enough to charge them with cultivation at this point. It's got to be something bigger than a bullshit possession charge. I need more time." She bit her lip for a few seconds then continued. "There is one other thing I have to tell you about." Her eyes dropped to the floor and she lapsed into silence.

"What is it Jill?" He sat up in his chair.

Still not making eye contact, she picked up her screwdriver and gulped till it was gone. She set down the empty cup and looked him in the eye. "Another group of Feds came, while I was there, with a search warrant for Jimbo McCray."

"And, of course, you didn't tell them who you were."

"Of course I didn't. And I didn't tell them Jimbo had been there. In fact, I straight up lied to them, said he wasn't there."

"Hmmm. O.K." He finished his screwdriver and poured them both another one.

"Well what the fuck was I supposed to do Franks? If I told them, yeah he was here, he just ran off in the woods, they would have went after him and my credibility with the McCrays would have been burned, and the entire case would be at a dead end, and after all that , Jimbo McCray probably would have got away anyhow." She sighed and took a drink. "So, how bad did I fuck up?"

He shrugged his shoulders. "Well, if Jimbo McCray isn't eventually captured and it comes out that you were that close to him and not only didn't do anything but lied to the lead investigator, it might not go good for you." He took a sip and continued. "On the other hand, if you hit the trifecta and get the killers, the cartel and the fugitive, I think all will be forgiven and you'll be untouchable. So, at this point, you might as well just go for it."

"I don't know. I'm thinking I should just bite the bullet and tell the agent everything, explain that I didn't want to blow my cover. He'll surely understand. I mean this is about the murder of one of our own, right?"

Franks nodded his head and scratched his chin. "Tell you what. Let me handle it. I'll find out who this agent is, talk to him and smooth it over. Keep him on ice. Buy you more time to work. Bottom line is, best case scenario, if you do get enough evidence to take all the parties involved down, we'll need more agents anyway. We'll offer to bring them on it. Like you said, these guys killed one of ours. How can he refuse to help?"

"Don't you think he is going to want to talk to me? Ask me about Jimbo?"

"Of course, but I don't know this guy or his team. If one of them is the leak, it would be better if they didn't know your identity."

"You're right." She took a drink. "You think you can handle this guy? He seemed like a real hard ass."

"Come on." He slammed the rest of his screwdriver before crushing the empty plastic cup in his hand. "Who do you think you're talking to?"

Chapter 26

Brinks and Bushy found a Walmart an hour down the highway where they decided to get their undercover civvies. Brinks chose their wardrobe insisting he had an instinct for this kind of work. He chose a pair of Wrangler jeans for each of them, flannel shirts, a camouflage cap for himself, a John Deere cap for Bushy, and each took a pair of cowboy boots. He also grabbed a matching pair of rebel flag belt buckles.

"Isn't that kind of faggy?" asked Bushy. "I mean the matching belt buckles."

"No!" Brinks shot back. "What's faggy about that? Is it faggy?" He took Bushy's belt buckle away from him and threw it back on the shelf and chose one with two six guns crossing in an x instead.

Bushy looked at the new belt buckle. "Why can't I have the rebel flag one?"

"The rebel flag buckle is mine," said Brinks.

"Why?"

"Because, it just looks right on me. I told you I got instincts about stuff like this."

"But why does it look right on you and not me?"

"God damn it!" yelled Brinks. "It just does! I can't explain it, now will you just focus."

Bushy threw the six gun belt buckle back onto the shelf. "I want the rebel flag belt buckle."

"Don't make me sorry I picked you for this Bushy."

"You heard what I said." Bushy crossed his arms.

"Do you understand what we're doing here? How serious this is?"

"Rebel flag belt buckle, or I walk."

Brinks stared into Bushy's eyes, Bushy didn't blink. "Fine!" Brinks said throwing him the rebel belt buckle. "Take the damn thing! Christ, it's like I'm working with my twelve-year-old spoiled nephew."

They made their way to the hardware department, where Brinks picked up a razor knife, then went to the checkout and purchased the items. Outside, Brinks used the razor knife to cut the sleeves off the flannel shirts. "These fucks love to show off their muscles," he said. They drove to a gas station where they changed in the bathroom. Brinks bought a pack of Marlboros and a can of Kodiak. He took one of the cigarettes from the pack and put it behind Bushy's ear, then put the pack in the front pocket of Bushy's flannel shirt. He put the can of Kodiak in his own back pocket. "Can you see the outline of the can in my pocket?"

"Yeah, I guess, but only if I look at your ass, I doubt any one's going to be looking at your ass."

"Please," said Brinks. "First off, you know any ladies in the joint are going to be looking at my ass. Second, most of these red state alpha males are just masking repressed homo instincts with their tough guy bullshit. A stud like me is eye candy to these freaks, trust me."

"If you say so. Are we good now?" asked Bushy.

"Almost. Follow me." Brinks led him to the front of the gas station where there was a row of gumball machines and prize machines that took quarters. He went to the last one shoved in four quarters and pulled the lever. A flat white piece of cardboard came out. Four more quarters, another piece of cardboard. "Temporary tattoos! They look just like the real thing," Brinks said opening the pieces of cardboard. One was an eagle, the other a snake. He handed the snake to Bushy. "Just lick it, and stick it on your arm."

Bushy looked at the snake tattoo then at the eagle. "How come you get the—"

"Don't fucking start," said Brinks.

"Well I'm just saying, you just automatically take what you want without a discussion, maybe I want the eagle."

"No! Fuck you! Fuck you! You got the rebel flag belt buckle, I'm taking the eagle tattoo!"

Again the stare down, but this time Brinks held firm. Finally, Bushy looked away shrugging his shoulders. "Fine, whatever, I really don't even care man, it would just be nice if you asked my opinion every once in a while, that's all."

"Jesus," said Brinks licking the eagle and sticking it on his bicep. "I swear to God, if I didn't need your help on this I would kick you right in your vagina."

Satisfied that they looked the part, they got back in their vehicle and headed for the Buzzsaw. "Let me do most of the talking. You just try to look like one of them, keep your mouth open, your eyes blank, you know like you got a slight case of the mental retardation," said Brinks. "Still, if you do have to talk, we should get our back stories straight so we don't contradict each other."

"We should tell them we're farm boys," suggested Bushy.

"I thought about that," said Brinks. "But we know fuck all about farming. Suppose some real farm boy started asking us questions we couldn't answer. It can't be anything white collar either or too technical. Something construction related or maybe a factory. Carpenters. We will be carpenters. That sound all right to you?"

Bushy scratched his chin. "Carpenters? Carpenters. I could be a carpenter. How about we frame houses?"

"There you go Bushy! Now you're thinking. We might just make an undercover man out of you yet. We are a couple of country boy carpenters stopping by the bar after a hard day framing houses to toss back a couple brews and score some Mary Jane."

"Scoring a little Mary Jane," said Bushy. "A little dubage, a little green, little wacky tobaccey."

"Like I said, Bushy, let me do the talking"

"You keep saying that, and you're going to piss me off. If you don't want me to say anything why don't I just stay in the car?"

"I'm not saying you can't say anything, but I can't sit by and let you blow this by going on about, 'wacky tobaccey.' You've got potential Bushy, but you need to put your ego in check here. You might just learn something."

"Yeah, O.K. Brinks, I'm going to trust you on this. I hope you know what the fuck you're talking about."

They parked outside the bar and sat in silence for about thirty seconds while their nerves gave birth to second thoughts as their plans approached the crossroads of becoming reality. "Man, I'm not so sure about this," said Bushy.

"Trust me Bushy, it's normal for a warrior to get jitters before battle. What separates the warrior from the coward is that the warrior defeats the jitters, and the coward is defeated by them. So which are you Bush-man? A warrior? Or a coward? Because it all comes down to what you do now, in this moment."

Bushy slowly nodded his head. "I'm a warrior."

"What"

"I'm a warrior!"

"I can't fucking hear you!"

"I said I'm a mother fucking warrior!" Bushy punched the dashboard.

"God damned right you are! Now let's go to war!"

"Let's go!"

They got out the car and slammed the doors. They half walked half strutted toward the bar. Brinks threw a few punches into the air and threw his head from side to side dodging imaginary counterpunches. Bushy clenched his fists and flexed his muscles. "Remember," said Brinks, "let me do most of—"

"Will you shut the fuck up with that bullshit already?"

"All right, be cool," said Brinks pushing through the door. Then they were inside. They stood there for a second letting their eyes adjust to the darkness. Brinks elbowed Bushy and pointed toward the bar. On the way over there Brinks made eye contact with a gray haired man standing by the Juke box. "Why don't you play some Lynyrd Skynyrd there old timer?"

The man scowled. "Why don't you play it your god damned self. And if you call me old timer again I'll stomp you into the fucking ground boy."

Brinks gave a nervous laugh. "Good one. You're alright old ti—. I mean you're alright man." The gray haired man's lip twitched and jaw tightened. Brinks turned from him and made haste to get to the bar with Bushy in tow.

"That was smooth," whispered Bushy as they sat on stools. "Sure glad I let you do the talking. I might have said something stupid and got us off to a bad start."

Brinks had just enough time to tell Bushy to shut up before the bartender was there. "Couple of drafts, whatever is most popular." The bartender nodded pulled out two frosted mugs and filled them with beer. He set them on coasters in front of the two agents, and Brinks handed him a ten and told him to keep the change. They looked the bar over. Not many people there. The gray haired man had finished his musical selection, which was not Lynyrd Skynyrd, and took a seat at the end of the bar. Brinks had no intention of trying to converse with him again. The only other man at the bar sat a few stools down on the other side. He had a long black ponytail and a blue jean jacket. He stared straight ahead while he did whiskey shots and smoked a cigarette. "That guy looks like a good place to start," said Brinks nodding toward the man.

"I thought the whole point was to buy from Jack McCray," said Bushy. "He's not even here."

"Exactly. He's not here. So, we try to establish contact with a local, with any luck he knows Jack McCray and can give us an introduction." Brinks looked back down the bar at the man with the ponytail. "O.K., I'm going in. Stay here, watch and learn." He took his beer and moved down the bar to the stool next to the man. "Barkeep, get my friend here a shot on me." He turned to the man and awkwardly put his hand on the man's shoulder, "I hate to drink alone." The man's head turned and he stared at the hand on his shoulder. "Make it a double," Brinks said to the bartender while taking his hand off the man's shoulder. The bartender poured the double shot, and the man thanked the bartender but not Brinks. When the bartender left, Brinks introduced himself. "Name's," he paused realizing he hadn't thought of an alias, "John," he held out his hand. The man neither took his hand nor returned the introduction so Brinks took his hand back. "Maybe you could help me with something," he said lowering his voice. "Buddy of mine, works on my crew, I'm a carpenter by the way, smoked a joint with me the other day, got to be the best damn herb I ever smoked. Anyway, he said he got it in this bar from a fella named Jack, Jack McCray. You wouldn't maybe be able to, you know, hook a guy up, would you?" The man slammed his double shot, stood up and left the bar without saying a word to or even acknowledging Brinks. Brinks picked up his beer and rejoined Bushy at the other end of the bar.

"So, how did it go?" asked Bushy.

Brinks shrugged. "Pretty good."

"Did he agree to give you an introduction to McCray?"

"It doesn't work like that Bushy. I laid the groundwork, established a rapport. He now thinks of me as a friend. Next time I'll ask about McCray."

"What's his name?"

"Whose name?"

"Your new friend?"

"His name, it doesn't—" He picked his beer up then slammed it back down. "God damn it! If all you're going to do is criticize then why *don't* you just wait in the car?"

"I didn't mean to criticize, I was just asking—"

"Well stop just asking, let me think a minute, figure out my next move."

Outside, Jack McCray was just pulling up in the parking lot. He'd traded a couple of fat buds for a fancy pool cue with a case and all. Even though he was supposed to be laying low till they figured out a way to deal with the cartel, he couldn't resist trying it out at the Buzzsaw for a couple of racks. As he made his way toward the bar he saw Otto, a drinking buddy and occasional customer coming out. "What do you say Otto?"

The man with the ponytail smiled and shook Jack's hand. "How's it going Jack? Just to give you a heads-up man, there's a couple of undercover pigs in there asking about you. They seem like real douche bags. I don't think you would have been fooled by them, but better safe than sorry. Know what I mean?"

"Good looking out brother. I appreciate it. Why don't you stop by the house later, I got some fresh buds drying, I'll hook you up."

"You know I will."

While Otto climbed on his Harley, Jack went into the bar. Bushy elbowed Brinks in the side and Brinks looked up to see Jack's reflection in the mirror behind the bar. Jack stepped up to the bar, right next to the two agents. "Let me get a double shot of Jameson, a Budweiser and some quarters for the pool table," he said to the bartender as he threw a twenty on the bar.

"Care for a game friend?" asked Brinks.

"Sure. Why don't you go rack?" Brinks and Bushy went over to the pool table as Jack waited for the drinks and his change. The bartender set the shot and beer bottle in front of him. Jack slammed the shot as the bartender turned back to the register to get his change. When he returned he put the quarters in Jack's hand, glanced at the two undercovers shooting pool and gave Jack a cautionary raised eyebrow. Jack winked, and the bartender relaxed into a smile.

Brinks shoved four quartiers into the coin slots and an avalanche of pool balls rolled down into the hollowed out space at the end of the table. Brinks set the plastic triangle on the table and started to place the balls inside of it. "Now remember, let—"

"Let you do all the talking, for fuck's sake, give it a rest already will you?" Bushy said from a stool sitting right next to the pool table.

"O.K., here he comes, shut up." Jack set his beer and pool cue case on the table Bushy was sitting at. He opened the case and assembled the cue.

"You know, they say you should never bet a man with his own cue," said Brinks. "But I'm the adventurist type. What do you say we go the next round of beers?"

Jack nodded his head. "Sounds good."

"Name is John by the way." Brinks held out his hand.

"Please to meet you John by the way. I'm Jack." Jack shook his hand.

"This is B—" Brinks just caught himself before he introduced Bushy by his real name, "Bob."

"John and Bob? Really? Haven't you guys ever done this before?"

Brinks and Bushy exchanged glances. "What do—" stammered Brinks. "I mean what are—"

"Forget it," said Jack. "Just fucking with you. Why don't you break?"

Brinks smiled. "Go ahead, Jack, be my guest."

"Oh no," said Jack. "You go ahead, *John*." He made air quotes around the name John. "I insist, you break!" Brinks stood in awkward silence before, once again, exchanging glances with Bushy. "Why do you keep looking at your girlfriend there?" Jack stepped up in Brinks personal space till they were nose to nose. "I told you to break. Now do it bitch!"

"What—what is—I mean, Jack—" Brinks stammered.

"John! I'm still fucking with you." Jack slapped him on the arm. "You guys really got to lighten up." He looked at Bushy who only nodded and took a big chug of beer.

"Good one," said Brinks. "Well I guess I'll break then."

They shot a game, which Jack won easily, then he played Bushy. Jack let Bushy win. He sensed that Brinks was the senior agent and wanted to fuck with the dynamic between them by giving Bushy confidence and fucking with Brinks's self-esteem. Other than that, Jack didn't fuck with them for the next hour and a half as the three of them shot pool and drank beer. The bar slowly filled with customers. Almost all of them noticed the strangers playing pool with Jack, and almost all of them figured they were undercover cops. Nobody thought Jack was fooled by them and they kept shooting subtle glances in their direction, wondering what mischief Jack was plotting. As Brinks got drunk he regained his confidence. "So Jack," he said stepping up next to Jack as Bushy eyed up an eight ball bank. "You wouldn't know where a fella could get a little something to smoke, would you?"

"See that?" Jack smiled. "I knew I liked you guys." Jack squinted his eyes and nodded his head slowly as if in deep contemplation. "I'll be honest, I usually don't take chances with dudes I just met, but you guys are just such regular guys, I feel like I can trust you. Yeah, damn it, I'm going to do it. I'm going to hook you guys up."

Brinks beamed. "Thanks Jack, I appreciate that. You won't be disappointed."

"Alright." Jack glanced around, stepped closer to Brinks, lowering his voice. "I don't want to do anything right here in the bar."

"Understandable," said Brinks.

"Meet me outside in front of the bar." Jack turned and walked away towards the bathroom.

Bushy, who had followed the whole conversation, jumped up from his seat. "Holy shit," he said. "It worked! You did it!"

Brinks smiled. "Candy from a baby, Bushy, candy from a baby. Let's go outside, and remember, keep it cool and let me do what I do. Safe bet there's going to be a big promotion in our future." He turned and headed for the front door with Bushy following. The beer-fueled confidence put a bounce in their step. They pushed out the front door and stood just off to the side. "Be ready," said Brinks. "As soon as he makes the sale, we take him down." He slapped Bushy on the arm. "You ready for this big boy?"

"Damn straight." Bushy had only now really believed this was about to happen and now found himself lost in visions of he and Brinks standing side by side as some F.B.I. bigshot pinned medals on their chests when Jack came out the front door.

Jack again glanced around and stepped close to the two agents. "You see any pigs out here?"

"No Jack, we looked around, coast is clear, ain't that right Bob?"

"That's right, coast is clear," said Bushy making a rare contribution to the conversation.

"Is that right Bob?" Jack looked around again. "Cause you know you can't just look around for squad cars right? I mean you got to watch out for the undercovers. Them undercovers are pretty fucking slick let me tell you. They could come walking in here right now and just blend the fuck in. They're masters of disguise, geniuses really. They walked in here, they wouldn't look like cops. They'd probably be wearing a John Deere cap, plaid shirts and jeans, probably even have a goofy belt buckle like the one you got on. Come to think of it, you guys kind of got a pork like smell about you." Jack sniffed the air around them and gave them a hard look. Then he cut the tension with a laugh. "I'm still just fucking with you!"

Just as Jack was fucking with Brinks and Bushy, Jill pulled up in the parking lot. It was her day off from the bar, but she figured she'd come in, do some social drinking and, if she was lucky, the McCrays might show up and she could spend some casual time with them and deepen her cover. She scanned the parking lot as was her habit when she arrived and spotted the two agents conversing with Jack McCray. "Cock sucking, ass licking, dipshit, fuck wads!" she said as she pulled out her cellphone and dialed Franks.

"What's up Jill?" He answered on the first ring. He knew she was going there and was expecting her to check in but not this soon.

"Franks, I just got to the Buzzsaw. Can you explain to me why I'm looking at Bushy and that ass clown Brinks talking to Jack McCray?"

"Fuck! They must have got the idea to go rogue, see if they could make an end run around us and wrap the thing up, make a name for themselves. I'm on my way, I'll bring them in."

"Sorry Franks, no time. I've got to deal with this now."

"Jill, what—"

She hung up the phone before he could answer and got out of the car.

"O.K.," said Jack. "Here's the deal. I got two different grades of smoke for you to pick from." He slid his hands in his jacket pockets. "In this pocket," he shook the left side of his jacket, "I got some good smooth shit. In this pocket," he shook the right side, "I got some really, really good shit that is stronger than the other stuff but it tastes just a bit harsher. They're both really good. Just comes down to your own personal preference."

"O.K., now we're talking," said Brinks who felt that his plan now had momentum of its own and that the victory and recognition that he deserved was inevitable. "How about you show me what you got?"

Jack shrugged his shoulders. "O.K. Check it out." He pulled his hands out of his pockets and turned them over.

In his left hand he held a pack of Camel lights and in his right hand a regular pack of Camels.

Brinks and Bushy stared at the two packs of cigarettes. They looked back in forth between the cigarette packs and Jack's face. "Jack? I don't, I mean what—"

"You said you wanted smoke didn't you?" Jack held the cigarettes up. "They got a machine inside, I can get these all day, or at least as long as the bar is open. And, word has it, there is a truck stop down the road where they supposedly sell this stuff by the carton, but you didn't hear that from me. So, which one do you want? I know, why don't we try one out of each pack then you can decide?"

Brinks looked at Jack, at the cigarettes, at Jack's face, turned around and looked at Bushy, no help there, and then back at Jack. Brinks looked like a man confronted with a complicated math equation that he had no idea how to begin to solve. "Come on Jack." He forced a smile. "Why you got to mess with us? I mean, come on. We just—"

That's when Jill stormed in catching them all by surprise. She came from behind Jack so it was easy to sneak up on him, Brinks and Bushy were harder because they were facing in her direction but she didn't want them to see her coming ahead of time because their faces may show surprised recognition that Jack might catch. She slouched down and used Jack as cover keeping his body between her and the other two agents. When she was right behind Jack she popped around him with the dexterity of an NFL running back and flew at the two agents. "Why don't you fucking pigs fuck off and go eat some donuts or write some tickets or something you fucks!" She punctuated the last word with a kick to Brinks's testicles that would be the most satisfying interaction with him she would ever have. When Brinks sank to his knees Bushy managed to rise above the observer role, which had been his sole contribution to the operation so far, by grabbing Brinks by the arm picking him up and pulling him into the parking lot to escape the tornadic fury of Jill's rage. Bushy threw Brinks arm over his shoulder, and the two made a run for it in the manner of a couple guys trying to win a three legged race. Jill spotted a beer bottle on the ground by the curb. She picked it up and sent it twirling through the air and bouncing off Brinks's head with a satisfyingly loud hollow thud, which elicited a moan from Brinks and caused the pair to pick up their awkward pace. She turned back to Jack. "Those guys were in here the other day asking questions about you and your uncle. The things they were asking, I'm pretty sure they were cops."

"Yeah I know. I appreciate the effort, but I had it handled." Jack's smile made it impossible to hide the fact that he was amused and impressed by the display.

"Oh, sorry, I should have known. Just kind of freaked there when I saw them talking to you."

"It's cool. That was pretty entertaining actually." Jack's smile broadened. "Kind of hot seeing you get all bad ass too." He winked at her.

"Oh, well then." She pretended to blush. "Maybe you could buy a girl a beer?"

"Least I could do," said Jack.

Chapter 27

It had been over an hour since the waitresses at the Buzzsaw ushered the last of the drunks out of the bar and locked the doors so they could wipe down the tables, empty the ashtrays, take out the trash, put the chairs up on the tables, sweep and mop the floors and, finally, go home. Tracy still sat in the parking lot chopping up lines of meth on a Dixie Chicks CD case in her Jeep. All of the other patrons were gone. When she saw the waitresses heading to their cars and the head bartender locking the front doors, she knew it was time to go. Leaning over the passenger seat, where the CD case lay, she snorted a line up her right nostril. Then she switched the rolled up dollar bill to the other nostril and hoovered up the other one. She sat up, wiping her nose and started the Jeep.

As she pulled out from under the islands of light cast by the parking lot lamps and into the abyss of the dark moonless night, she flipped the headlights on and fumbled around the ashtray for a half a joint she'd left there earlier. She found it, lit it and inhaled deeply. Her meth-fueled heart beat against her chest like a wild animal trying to escape a box. There would be no sleep tonight. She was way too wired to go home. Maybe her cousins were still up. She had over a sixteenth of meth left. Even if they weren't up, they'd be down for getting out of bed to get wired. Jack would for sure. Jimbo would too. If he were there, which he most likely wouldn't be on the account of the cops looking for him and all. When she could hold her breath no longer, she exhaled a cloud of smoke, took a couple of big breaths, then took another hit and held it.

Even if Jack and Jimbo weren't there, Jay would get up happy to see her. When she asked him if he wanted to get wired, he would give her the lecture. The one about how she should stick to the hippie highs, the holy highs, weed, hallucinogenic and, of course, whiskey. Then, when he figured his big cousin duty was done, he'd say, "Well, I might as well try a line. See if it's any good." After that, he'd be in for the whole ride, matching her line for line till it was all gone.

Just as she was about to take another hit, she saw the dreaded cherry colored lights that no pot smoking drunk driver wants to see in their rearview. "Fuck!" she said, crushing out the joint. She shoved it, along with the baggy of meth, down the front of her pants. She quickly lit a cigarette and rolled down the windows hoping the combination of ventilation and tobacco smoke would sufficiently dilute the pot smell. Hopefully it was one of the local guys. If so, she would likely get a warning at most. But what if it was a state boy? Unlikely, but if it was, he wouldn't care who her cousins were.

She took a deep breath, unsuccessfully willing her rabid heartbeat to slow, at least a little, and pulled over. Looking at the cop car in her rearview, all she could make out were the headlights and the cherries. Not enough to tell whether it was local or a state trooper. The driver's side door of the cop car opened. The cop got out. When he stepped into the light cast by his own headlights, she saw that it was Larose. A wave of relief flooded over her. She never thought she would be happy to see that asshole, but it beat getting arrested. He'd probably just hit on her for a few minutes, she'd tell him to fuck off, and she'd be on her way. "What the fuck do you want?" she asked as he approached her door.

"I need you to exit the vehicle now." His tone was all business. Was it possible he didn't recognize her?

"Why?" she asked.

"Exit the vehicle now!" He yanked open her door, grabbed her arm and yanked her out of the car.

Chapter 28

"What the fuck was going through your pea sized brains? That's what I'd like to know." Franks asked. Jill had briefed him by phone of the events that had taken place at the Buzzsaw. Franks called the agents and told them to report to his motel room immediately and they now stood before him, John Deere cap, rebel belt buckle and all, enduring his wrath.

Before either could muster an answer to his question, the motel room door flew open and Jill came stomping in. "What the fuck is your problem?" she screamed at Brinks.

Brinks, temporarily cowered by Frank's anger, became enraged by Jill's. "You're my fucking problem cunt! You haven't done shit to close this investigation since you started, and just as we were about to crack the whole damn thing wide open, you blew it because you couldn't stand to see me do, so easily, what you couldn't!"

Jill looked at Franks and laughed in a way that was void of humor. "Are you listening to this shit?"

"Look bitch!" continued Brinks. "Jack McCray was just about to make a sale to me, that's right, to me. And it would have taken me and Bushy about ten minutes of questioning, after we busted him, before he would have signed a full confession to everything, including the murders, and agreed to testify against his uncle and probably even give up the location of his father!"

"It's not possible," Jill shook her head. "It's not possible you could have passed the F.B.I. I.Q. test. You think if you bought a few grams of pot off Jack McCray he would give you his entire family. Not that it would have mattered, because he never would have fallen for that dog and pony show you were putting on, he would have led your dumb ass out into the woods, killed you where you stood and buried you where you fell."

"What the fuck ever." Brinks turned to Franks. "This is the problem with letting a twat be in charge, no balls."

And, with that, Jill snapped, and for the second time Brinks's own balls felt the full fury of the tip of Jill's cowboy boot. Once again, Brinks crumbled from the pain, but this time, before Jill could follow up on the attack, Franks threw his arms around her and pulled her, with considerable effort, toward the door. Brinks managed to gather enough of his wits to pull his pistol from its shoulder holster and aim it at Jill, while Bushy handled the situation in much the same way he handled the situation at the Buzzsaw, which is to say he stood off to the side, wide eyed and motionless. "I want them gone Franks! They are off this case!" screamed Jill.

"I'll handle this Jill." Franks got the door open and shoved her out before blocking the doorway with his body so she couldn't get back in. "Just go to your room and cool off. I'll be over in a few minutes." Stepping back, he closed the door and locked it. When he turned around he saw Brinks still sitting on the floor holding the pistol in both hands pointing it at the door. "For Christ sake put the weapon away."

"Is she gone?"

"I locked the door, I think you're safe."

Brinks rose to his feet, and, only after looking out the window and satisfying himself that Jill was gone, put the weapon back in its holster. "She can't keep hitting me Franks. I'm serious. I want to press charges."

"Shut the fuck up."

"Fuck you man, I don't have to take this shit."

"O.K." Franks threw his hands up. "You're right."

Brinks looked at him knowing it couldn't be this easy. "I'm serious Franks."

"Go ahead then." Franks held out his cellphone. "Go on and call it in. Tell them you were interfering with a Federal investigation and after you put that investigation in jeopardy, a hundred and ten pound woman beat the shit out of you." He continued to hold out the phone. Brinks made no move to take it. After a few seconds Franks put the phone back in his pocket. "Then, if there is any chance that your career isn't ruined, and you don't kill yourself out of shame, know that I'm going to dedicate the rest of my career to ruining you, you little pissant."

"Well she said she was going to kick us off the investigation, so that's probably going to fuck up our careers anyway." The hostility in Brinks's voice given way to whining.

"Look, no one is getting kicked off the investigation." Franks's own voice softened. "I'm going to talk to her and smooth this over. You will stay with the team and we will leave all this out of the reports. In return, you will sit in your motel room, keep your god damn mouths shut and do what you're told. When this is done, we will all go our separate ways. Do you understand?" Brinks shrugged his shoulders. "I want to hear you say it."

"Yeah O.K., fine," said Brinks.

Franks turned to Bushy who continued to stare blankly. Franks snapped his fingers in front of the agent's face.

"Yeah, I mean yes sir, I understand," said Bushy.

"Good," said Franks. "Now go back to your motel rooms and, for God's sake, stay away from Jill." The two left his room and Franks watched them through the blinds walk down to their own room and enter. He grabbed the bottle of Smirnoff and the bottle of orange juice from the little cooler he had set on top of the dresser, walked over to the door that connected his room to Jill's, took a deep breath and knocked on the door.

"It's open," came Jill's voice from the other side

Franks walked into her room. She was sitting in the chair and appeared much calmer. From the pungent aroma coming from the bathroom, he could guess why. He wasn't the least bit bothered by this, on the contrary, he was glad she was stoned, it would cool her rage. He took the two plastic cups sitting on the table next to her and poured them each a screwdriver. She took hers and gulped half of it down before speaking. "You said this is my case. I want them off it Franks, out of here."

"This is your first case as lead Jill. We don't know how it's going to turn out yet. You kick them two retards off the team, and things go bad, they'll be right there in the brass's ear telling them how you fucked everything up." Franks took a sip and let that sink in. "On the other hand, if we keep them on the team out of the way, mind you, but on the team, we've got something on them, something we can hold over their heads." He took another sip and studied Jill. She didn't look happy, but she wasn't arguing. "I'm just saying, sometimes loyalty can be born out of less than ideal circumstances."

Jill downed the rest of her screwdriver and handed the empty cup to Franks. "More please." Franks refilled her cup, and she drank half of it before responding to his point. "O.K. Fine. But you're going to have to keep them in line, I don't want to have to deal with them at all."

"That's not a problem." Franks finished his own screwdriver and set the empty cup down and rubbed his hands together. "So, kind of smells like a party in here."

Jill's eyes narrowed. "You really want to give me any shit about that now? Believe me I only used it for medicinal purposes, calms my nerves better than a Xanax."

"Not giving you any shit about it." Franks smiled. "Actually I was wondering if you had any more."

Chapter 29

Jay decided to hike out with Jack to Jimbo's camp and have supper with him. They packed up two rucksacks with frozen steaks and some potatoes in zip lock baggies. Jack had already humped out a small barbecue pit and big bottle of whiskey days earlier, but they decide to play it safe, and each added a bottle of whiskey to their rucksacks. Jack also put a little surprise in his.

It was about a two-hour hike to the campsite. They took their time moving through the woods, stopping here and there to smoke a joint or check some plants. When they finally strolled into camp they tossed off their rucksacks and sat on the ground. "What y'all bring me?" asked Jimbo digging into their rucksacks and pulling out the zip lock baggies. "Jackpot!" he said. "I'm so ready for something sides canned goods and squirrel." Jack grabbed Jimbo's bottle of whiskey, took a swig and handed it to Jay. Jimbo gathered some sticks, stuck them in the barbecue pit and set them on fire. As they started to burn, he lit a hog leg joint and sat down across from Jay and Jack. Jay had been thinking he might hump it back home after supper, but sitting there getting high, he decided to spend the night. At home he had to sleep lightly, wondering if every sound was a cartel death squad come to kill him. But out here, deep in the woods, he could sleep deep and easy. No one would find him out here unless by accident. It occurred to him that he could stay out here and outwait the cartel if he wanted to. Just stay out here, take care of the plants, and go into town when they needed to get supplies or sell some weed, maybe kill the occasional cartel soldier just to let them know they hadn't won. That might work, but Jay knew there was no way he was going to do that. He would not surrender his home unless they killed him first, which seemed to be a strong possible outcome to this situation, more possible every day he failed to come up with a plan on how to deal with them.

The day wore on, and their mood grew lighter and easier with thoughts of the cartel and Federal agents lost in the free flow of whiskey, clouds of pot smoke and the seclusion of the deep Missouri woods. They feasted, drank, smoked, and feasted some more. The shadows expanded like an inkblot till the night swallowed the woods making them even more cut off and secure from the threats of the outside world. They built up the fire and made a pile of dry sticks to keep it fed through the night, then they each took a seat around it. The light from the flames danced across their faces as they all three stared into the fire in that semi-hypnotized way that campfires at night seem to lull people into.

Jack decide it was time for his surprise. "So you know that place out on Morning Glory, the one they use to say was a nudist colony, then they said it was some kind of L.S.D. religious cult?"

"I remember it," said Jimbo. "All kinds of nutty rumors about that place. Most of them bullshit I'm sure."

Jack took one last hit off the cigarette he was smoking and flicked the butt into the fire. He took a swig off the whiskey jug and passed it to his uncle. "Yeah," he said wiping his mouth. "That's what I always figured. But these two old boys I went to school with, they get it in their heads that these people are sitting on an ass load of acid, so they decide to go in there and jack them strong arm style. They bust in right through the front door, guns drawn." Jack noticed both his dad and his uncle were leaning forward suddenly interested. He took his time uncapping the whiskey and taking a swig so as to raise the level of dramatic tension.

"So," said Jimbo. "What happened?"

Jack held a finger up as he took the extra-long swig. He put the bottle down and wiped his mouth. "God damn! I love whiskey." He suppressed a smile when his dad rolled his eyes and shook his head. "So where was I?"

"They busted in, guns drawn," said Jay.

"Oh yeah, so they bust in, guns drawn, and there's like a dozen people gathered around a table dressed from head to toe in green. There's a crucifix and candles on the table, and the head priest dude is handing out shot glasses that he's filling with this thick brown sludge. So, anyway, come to find out that there ain't no acid. All they got is this sludge, which apparently is an even more powerful psychedelic than acid. It's called," he snapped his fingers several times, "what the fuck is it called?"

"Ayahuasca," said Jay.

"That's right! Ayahuasca. You know about this stuff?"

Jay had heard of it before. He was a longtime fan of hallucinogens and had tried most of them but had never been able to acquire ayahuasca. "I have," he said. "It's this substance South American shamans make out of plants they get out of the jungle. It's supposed to have d.m.t. and some other stuff in it."

"D.m.t.!" said Jimbo. "I've heard of that."

"Right, d.m.t.," said Jack. "Anyway, apparently there were a couple of religions that used this stuff as a sacrament. Some of these religions opened branches in the U.S. and the courts ruled that they could bring this stuff into the country and legally use it as part of their religious ceremony."

Jay knew about these religions. He had researched ayahuasca online and found out about the various religions that could use them legally and was surprised to find one nearby. The Sacred Forest of Divine Sunlight, it was called. He figured the religious angle was a racket so they could sell d.m.t. without fear of law enforcement. But this didn't turn out to be the case. When Jay approached the priest of this local religious chapter, he offered him a generous sum for a sample, but the priest flatly refused. He invited Jay to participate in one of their ceremonies where he would get an equal portion of the sacrament and it would cost him nothing, though donations were appreciated. The religious angle wasn't a con after all, it was sincere. As much as Jay wanted to try the hallucinogen, he couldn't bring himself to participate in organized religion. "So cut to it," he said to Jack. "You got some of this stuff or what?"

Jack nodded his head and smiled. "Yep. Traded some bud for it." He pulled a large silver thermos from his ruck sack. "If we like it, they got more."

"Some guy's jacked some trippy shit and traded you some for bud," said Jimbo. "See how quick and easy you could have told that story? Why you always got to draw shit out?"

"Fuck off," said Jack. "So." He held up the thermos. "You guys down?"

"I'm in," said Jay. He'd wanted to try this stuff for some time. And that it was being presented to him now, the first time in a long time he could let his guard down, made it seem meant to be.

"You know I'll try anything once," said Jimbo with a shrug of his shoulders.

"All right then." Jack rubbed his hands together. "Let's do this." He took the cup off the top of the thermos, unscrewed the cap and poured some in the cup. "I don't know how much of this stuff we are supposed to take, so we'll start with a cup a piece and give it a while, then if we don't feel nothing, we'll drink more." He looked at the other two, Jay nodded his head and Jimbo shrugged his shoulders again. "O.K. then. Here it goes." He raised the cup to his lips, paused, lowered it, took a deep breath, closed his eyes, raised it to his lips again and gulped it down. "FUUUUUUUUUCK!" he said lowering the cup.

"What's it taste like?" asked Jimbo.

"Kind of like," Jack thought about it, "two parts turpentine, and one part rancid chocolate milk." He refilled the cup and passed it to Jimbo who slammed it with no ceremony or hesitation.

"Yeah," said Jimbo tossing the cup back to Jack. "I kind of like the taste."

"You're a god damned liar," said Jack. He refilled the cup and handed it to Jay.

Jay looked down at the thick brown sludge in the cup. He tipped the cup to his lips and chugged it down. It left a thick residue in his mouth, but overall it wasn't as bad as he'd expected. He handed the cup back to Jack.

"So how long does it take this stuff to kick in?" asked Jimbo.

"Not sure," said Jack.

"I think it takes a while," said Jay. "Like an hour or so. Maybe longer. Might as well smoke weed while we wait."

"Always a good plan," said Jack. He pulled a fat joint from his cigarette pack and lit it. Jimbo reached for the whiskey bottle.

"I wouldn't do that," said Jay. "I've heard this stuff can have a purging effect."

Jimbo paused in his reach for the whiskey. "What does that mean?"

"It can make you puke and have the shits."

"The shits? You might have shared that little nugget of info with us before we drank it." Jimbo grabbed the bottle and took a swig anyway.

They smoked the joint, put wood on the fire and made small talk, eventually lapsing into silence waiting for the drug to take effect. About an hour later, Jack broke the silence. "I don't feel shit. Do you guys?" Jay shook his head.

"I feel a little drunk," said Jimbo. "Little stoned too."

"I guess I feel a little, a little—" Jack stopped speaking, mid-sentence, and leaned forward, cheeks bulging. Jay turned his head, knowing what was coming but was unable to escape the sound of Jack vomiting up the brown sludge onto the dirt in front of him.

"Thar she blows!" yelled Jimbo.

Jay looked back at Jack when he stopped retching and saw a thick strand of brown saliva connecting his lip to the ground. "Jesus," said Jay looking away again. He'd seen men shot, burned, beaten, even blown to bits without flinching, but the sight, sound and smell of someone else puking still made him sick to his stomach every time.

"Fuck me!" Jack said, wiping his mouth. "That was like uncontrollable, and—" He felt a sudden alarming burning in his intestines and his butt cheeks clenched instinctively. "I got to take a shit."

"Go out in the fucking woods and do that!" yelled Jay.

"Uh, yeah, that's what I was planning." He jumped up and started to head off into the woods in an awkward butt cheeks clenched trot. After a few feet, he stopped, trotted back, grabbed Jimbo's roll of toilet paper and disappeared into the woods. He was tempted to let loose his bowels as soon as he was out of sight of the camp but made himself go farther to guarantee the smell wouldn't drift back to camp. When he felt he could hold it in no longer, he stopped, pulled down his pants and before he had even fully squatted, the brown sludge exploded from his backside with twice the fury it had erupted from his mouth minutes before. When the squirting subsided, he pulled a handful of toilet paper from the roll but paused when he felt another rumbling deep in his intestines followed by another ass eruption of brown sludge. He stayed squatted for several minutes till his legs started to tire, then he cleaned himself up, stood up and pulled up his pants.

He decided to stay out in the woods for a bit and smoke a cigarette just to make sure the squirts and puking were done. He walked about twenty feet deeper into the woods to put sufficient distance between himself and the smelly brown ass discharge. When he found a small clearing where he could look up at the night sky he stopped and gazed upwards. Looking up at the stars, he almost felt he might be starting to trip, but when he looked down at the forest floor everything looked normal. He felt nothing. After all the puking and squirting, he still wasn't tripping. He pulled his cigarette pack from his pocket and got out a smoke. He put the pack back into his pocket and pulled out his lighter, but it caught on his belt and he fumbled it to the ground. He reached down to pick up the lighter, and that's when it started. His arm stretched out to an impossible length even after his elbow locked and his arm was straight, it continued to stretch in an elastic-like fashion all the way to the ground, which was suddenly hundreds of feet below him. He grabbed the lighter and yanked his hand back. Like a stretched rubber band released from one end, it snapped back to its original size. Jack quickly looked around as if to see if there was someone else who could verify what just happened, but, of course, there was no one there. He must be tripping. He looked around at the trees then up again at the night sky. Nothing. No tracers, no hallucinations, nothing. He shook his head then lit his cigarette. He took a drag off the cigarette and stared at the lighter in his hand for a few seconds. He extended the hand holding the lighter out in front of him. It happened again. When the lighter was at arm's length, the arm continued to stretch until the hand holding the lighter was far off in the distance. "Whoa!" he said out loud. He stretched out the other arm and observed the same phenomena with the hand holding the cigarette joining the lighter hundreds of feet away at the end of his suddenly pencil thin stretched out arms. He brought the lighter back, and again his arm snapped back to normal. Then he brought the cigarette back. This time it seemed to happen in slow motion. The cigarette cherry grew from a tiny glowing speck to a flaming comet heading straight for him. As it neared, it continued to grow till it was no longer a comet but a giant burning sun on a collision course with the earth, the impact of which would surely reduce the entire planet to a charred ball. When Jack figured it must be seconds from impact he let out a yell, dropped the cigarette and lighter, stumbled backwards and fell on his ass shielding his face and head with his arms in preparation for the world ending hellfire that surely was about to envelope everything. But as he sat there, eyes closed against the expected flames, nothing happened. He heard nothing but crickets, felt nothing but a gentle breeze. He opened his eyes and lowered his arms. Nothing. Nothing but an ordinary peaceful night in the woods. Not only were the trees not in flames, the earth not punctuated with a giant crater from the impact, no mushroom cloud of debris blooming in the sky, but nothing looked the least bit unusual as he would expect if he were tripping. "Holy fuck!" he said.

Back at camp, Jay peered at the fire with an increased awareness as if truly seeing it for the first time. He wasn't so much looking at it as he was looking into it. There was something there he hadn't noticed before. Something in the flames? No, that wasn't it. It was something behind the flames. He noticed that the flames weren't constant like he thought they were before. There was a sort of high frequency blinking to them, like they were there then, for a fraction of a second, they weren't, then they were back again. They were rapidly blinking in and out of existence and it occurred to him that everything was doing this but doing it too rapidly to be noticed. In some faded corner of his mind, that continued to fade every second, he was aware of Jimbo becoming agitated, standing up, sitting back down again and looking around.

"Did you hear that?" asked Jimbo. He stared into the woods perfectly still then grabbed his shotgun and took off at a sprint into the woods.

In the back of Jay's mind, a voice told him he should be

concerned about what Jimbo was doing, but the voice seemed distant and he had no interest in listening to it. Instead, he continued staring into the fire, focusing his attention on the moments when the flames flickered out of existence. As he focused on these moments, they expanded lasting longer and longer till he could see that these moments in between were actually a doorway to another place and, he thought, another time. Despite the fact that he made no attempt to move from the spot where he was seated, he felt his perspective of the fire getting closer and closer till the flickering flames were directly in front of his face. Then he was in the fire. He was in the fire looking out. Only the scene he was looking out at was not his campsite. He was looking out from a different fire in a cave. In the dim light he saw beings in this cave who were looking back at him, aware of his presence. They were human, but not entirely. They seemed something more, or maybe it was less than human. There was something simian and primitive about them, but also something else alien and futuristic. Was this sometime in the distant past or the distant future? As soon as the question appeared in his mind, so did the answer. It was both. Human civilization was a circle, and like all circles, the beginning and the end were the same point, and these future primitives were that point.

These beings jumped up from their seated positions around the fire as if they had been waiting for him and moved to the cave wall. In the reflected firelight that splashed across the cave wall, he saw the beings scratching out equations with chalk-like stones. These equations included numbers, letters and symbols he didn't recognize. The beings were frantic, clearly in a hurry to finish the equation, though they occasionally stopped to argue about one part or another. He could hear none of their words and was fairly sure he wouldn't be able to understand them if he did. Eventually, when a ten foot by ten foot section of the cave wall was covered by the long complex equation, they dropped their chalk stones and fell to their knees, looking into the fire which he looked out from. Their mouths moved, but he heard no words. They repeatedly pointed at the alien hieroglyphic equation, emphasizing its importance. He grasped that the equation was of importance but could discern no meaning beyond that.

He heard a distant thunder that he realized was coming from the campfire back in the Missouri woods. When he heard it a few more times, he recognized it as gunfire. The future primitives seemed to sense that he was pulling away and they all pointed at the equation. He was torn between the growing sense of danger back at his campsite and what they were trying to communicate to him through the scratchings on the cave wall. He glanced over the entire equation from beginning to end. It held no meaning for him. He considered trying to memorize it and translate it later, but it was too long. No matter how important their message was, their attempt to communicate it to him was a failure.

With this realization, he was back at his campsite. The fire he stared into was now nothing but an ordinary fire. He couldn't shake the feeling that he had just failed at something big. Jimbo came bursting out of the woods, hurdling a fallen tree and dropping behind it flat on the ground where he curled into a ball and clutched the shotgun in a death grip. Jay grabbed his own rifle, dropped to his belly and low crawled over next to Jimbo, taking cover behind the fallen tree. "What are we dealing with?" asked Jay hoping it was cartel and not the Feds.

Jimbo looked at his brother. "Jay! Jesus Christ! I ain't never seen nothing like it. There's a fucking dragon in the woods!"

Jay relaxed. He sat up leaning against the fallen tree, laying down his rifle and pulling out his cigarette pack. He started to reach for a cigarette then noticed the joint he had in there and pulled it out instead. "You want to run that by me again there Jimbo."

"I know how it sounds man. But I saw it with my own eyes. A fucking dragon! It was as big as a building, and it breathed white fire. Right over that hill, everything is on fire! I shot it in the face, and that just pissed it off, he damn near killed me, I barely got away!"

"Relax man." Jay lit the joint and took a big hit. "Take a hit off this, maybe it'll chill you out."

"Smoke a joint? I really don't think it's the best time to smoke a joint, did you not hear what I just told you? You need to duck down behind this tree. If that thing sticks its head over the hill and sees you, we're done. Well done, as in dragon fucking barbecue."

"It's just the ayahuasca. There is no dragon."

"I'm telling you I saw it. And I ain't even tripping."

"Think about it," said Jay still holding out the joint. "You took one of the most powerful hallucinogens on the planet, and then you saw a dragon. Let that marinate in your mind for a minute."

"But I'm not tripping." He looked toward the campfire and considered his brother's words. "Am I tripping?" He turned back to Jay. "Fuck I'm tripping!" He laughed and took the joint. "That's a fucking relief. I ain't scared of no man alive, but I ain't trying to fuck with no dragons." He took a drag off the joint and handed it back to Jay. "Where's Jack?"

"Last I remember seeing him he was heading out in the woods to take a shit," said Jay hitting the joint.

"How long ago was that?"

Jay thought about that. How long had he spent in that cave? He had no idea. He'd lost all concept of time. And even if he had a sense of how long he'd been there, he wasn't sure time was the same over there as it was here, or for that matter, if time was real at all. "I don't know," he finally answered. "How long were you in the woods?"

"I don't know."

"Should we go find him?"

"I guess so."

It took some effort, but Jay finally convinced Jimbo they should leave the guns at camp. He figured the odds of running into the Feds or the cartel out here in the middle of the night was significantly lower than the odds of Jimbo shooting Jack because he thought he was a dragon. They walked out into the woods in the direction that Jack had went, zigzagging in progressively wider arcs to cover more ground. Finally Jay threw off all caution and yelled out Jack's name.

"You sure that's a good idea?" asked Jimbo. Jay explained the unlikelihood of any of their enemies being out there this late. "I guess so." Jimbo nodded slowly. Jay suspected that his concern was not the Feds or cartel but the possibility of the dragon reappearing. Eventually Jack answered, and they found him sitting on the ground with his legs and arms wrapped around the base of a tree. "So what the fuck you doing there, son?" asked Jimbo.

"Can't stand up," said Jack. "Every time I try, the earth just sort of drops out from beneath me. I mean my feet stay attached to it, but my legs stretch out real long and—I can't explain it, I just can't stand up that's all."

"It's just the ayahuasca," said Jay. "We saw some stuff too. It's pretty much wore off now though. Why don't you just try standing?"

"I ain't doing it."

"Just try it nice and slow. We'll hold your arms, make sure you don't fly away or whatever."

Jay and Jimbo each grabbed one of his arms and pulled him up. He resisted at first, then shifted his feet beneath him and stood up. Once he was fully vertical, he looked at the ground. It was a normal distance away. He stretched out his arm. Normal. "Whew!" he said. "That was some freaky ass shit, I'm here to tell you." They all stood there silently for a few seconds, each man reliving his individual experience in his head. "You know," said Jack. "We didn't even drink half of that stuff." There's still plenty left." Jimbo and Jay looked at him. "Sooooo," he continued. "You guys want to do some more?"

"I'm down," Jimbo said without hesitation, surprising Jay.

Jay looked at him. "Really? After all that? You want to— seriously?" He shrugged his shoulders. "Fuck it. Let's do it."

Chapter 30

After the devastation at the bar, Julio found a vacant house out the woods that he could buy dirt cheap and it became the cartel's new headquarters. After everyone and everything had been moved, Julio went back to the bar to do a sweep and make sure nothing incriminating was left behind. Hector didn't bother clearing anything with Julio, so when Julio returned to the house, he knew nothing of the deputy taking Tracy. Hector was gone when Julio walked into the living room. He noticed the deputy sitting on the sofa. Larose gave him an affable nod. Julio made no attempt to return the gesture. "What the fuck is that dipshit doing here?" he asked Santiago in a tone that gave no caution to the possibility of Larose overhearing.

"He's with us now I guess," said Santiago. "He brought the McCrays' cousin to Hector."

"What? She's here?"

"Yeah, she's tied up in there," Santiago pointed toward one of the bedroom doors. "Hector had to run, where I have no idea, but said no one should fuck her till he gets back. He wants to go first. Is this what we're about now Julio?"

"Is she in there alone?"

"Right now she is."

"I'm going in there. Watch the door and make sure no one goes in before I come out. Be ready to back me up."

Julio walked in and stood in front of the girl. She had to be scared but she did a good job of hiding it. He saw nothing in her eyes but hate. "Listen carefully to what I say. I am going to take that gag off your mouth. I'm going to untie you. I'm going to give you your keys." He scooped her car keys off the dresser. "I'm going to walk you to your car. You're not going to sass anybody. You're not going to try any of your tough country-girl shit. You're just going to get in your car and go home."

Her eyes narrowed, but she nodded her head slightly.

"You're not going to try anything stupid?"

She barely shook her head from side to side.

"Because, and I can't stress this enough, the only way you don't go safely home is if you do something stupid. If you be cool, you will be on your way home in a few minutes. Do you understand the words that are coming out of my mouth?"

She nodded her head a little more emphatically.

He ripped the tape off her mouth, went behind her and took a couple minutes untying the knots. He held out the keys to her car. She held out her hand and he dropped the keys into it. "Now I'm going to take you by the arm and walk you to the car. Don't look at anyone and definitely don't say anything to anyone even if they say something to you. If anyone tries to stop us, let me handle them. O.K.?"

She nodded, "O.K." It may have been desperation but there was something in his voice she trusted.

"Let's go." He took her arm and walked her out of the room. All the men in the living room area watched them walk to the door but nobody said a word or moved to stop them. They made it out the front door with no problem. But in the parking lot, in front of her car, Paco was checking the oil in Hector's car. Paco was the one man Julio knew absolutely for sure was loyal to Hector till the end. The last person, short of Hector

167

himself, which he wanted to deal with at that moment. But there was no way to get Tracy to her car without passing him.

Paco looked over his shoulder when he heard their footsteps. He turned to face them wiping his hands on his shirt. "What's this?"

"Change of plans. We're letting the little senorita go."

"Is that right? And who made that call?"

"I did."

"Did Hector sign off on that?"

"Thing is bro, Hector doesn't run things north of the border. I do. And I'm making a judgment call."

"I don't think so." Paco stepped in front of them.

Julio pushed Tracy to the side. "Oh, you in charge now Paco? I'm just a little bitch so you and Hector just going to come to my house and take over? Is that how you thought it would work?"

They both stood still and silent. It's impossible to say which of them went for their gun first or even which shot first. Paco went for a head shot and only managed to graze Julio's ear. Julio wisely went for dead center of the body. He put a hole in Paco's chest. Paco's eyes opened wide and he looked down at his chest. When he started to raise his gun again, Julio gave him three more to the chest. The pistol slipped from Paco's fingers clanging to the pavement. He dropped to his knees then fell over backwards.

Julio turned around to see that all the men had come out of the house. They all had their guns out, but none pointed them at Julio. He looked at the faces of men he came out of Mexico with, and had fought alongside with, in so many American cities for so long. It was time to reassert himself as their leader. "We've come too far!" he yelled. "We've shed too much blood and lost too many brothers to let Hector or a piece of shit like that," he pointed his pistol at Paco and fired two more rounds into his body, "to push us to the side! We've fought bigger battles than the one we are in now and we didn't have to rape and murder women then, we don't need to start now. We've come this far together. I'm asking you to stick with me now." He scanned their faces. None of them said a word. A few nodded their heads. But the real answer was in their eyes. They were with him.

He turned to Tracy. "Go," he said.

Chapter 31

Larose burst through the door of his double wide mobile home and ran towards his bedroom, stepping on his cat, banging his knee and cursing along the way. His girlfriend, Beth, who was lying on the sofa watching a Jerry Springer episode while eating Oreo cookies out of the package, sat up quickly. "Jesus Christ, baby, you scared the shit out me! What's wrong?"

"Pack! Pack your shit now, we got to get the fuck out of here!" he yelled from the bedroom where he had pulled a suitcase out of the closet and was stuffing it haphazardly with random clothes.

She came running into the bedroom. "What happened?" Her front teeth were almost completely black from the Oreos.

"Pack! Pack your shit now. I called that Fed Franks on the way here. He'll be here soon with an ass-load of other Feds. We're going to go into that witness protection program thing." He paused suddenly. "Fuck I should have told them to meet us somewhere else. What if they don't get here on time?" He ran over to the window and peeked out the blinds. Then he ran to the closet, pulled out a twelve-gauge and a box of shells and started loading.

"Baby you're scaring me. Tell me—"

"You should be fucking scared! Now pack your shit or I swear to fucking God I'll leave you behind." Her lip started to quiver then the dam broke and she started bawling. Larose rolled his eyes. "Baby I'm sorry, but you got to hurry." She continued to bawl. He grabbed her by the shoulders and shook her. "God damn it I ain't got no time for this shit!" He raised his hand to hit her, she covered her face, but before his hand came down, they heard a car door slam outside. He let go of her, grabbed the shotgun and peeked out of the blinds again. "It's Franks. Pack now." Her bawling eased to sobs and she nodded her head.

He ran to the door and opened it before Franks had a chance to knock. "You came by yourself? What the fuck?"

"Calm down." Franks stepped inside, and Larose closed the door behind him. "I couldn't understand a fucking word you said on the phone. Now tell me what's going on."

"Gotta go!" Larose went back to the bedroom where Beth was packing and resumed his own frantic packing. Franks followed him in. Larose spewed words as fast as he could spit them from his mouth. "They're probably on their way, you should have brought more agents, you got to give me witness protection, I can give you everybody, I can give you Jimbo McCray, I can give you all the McCrays, they're all a bunch of fucking animals, dope dealing, murder, all kinds of twisted shit. And the cartel! The Diaz cartel, they're here and they're worse than the fucking McCrays They're—"

"O.K. stop for a minute," said Franks.

Larose stopped talking and packing.

"Now take a deep breath, and tell me specifically who are you afraid of right now?"

"The McCrays."

"Why?"

"Their cousin."

"What about their cousin?"

"They got this cousin, cute little piece of ass named Tracy, anyway they took her!"

"Who took her?"

"The fucking Mexicans!"

"The cartel took the McCrays' cousin?"

"Yeah! But then one of them pussed out and let her go. I know that little bitch is going to run straight to the McCrays and tell them everything, and the first thing them fuckers will wanna do is come after me. That little prick Jack don't like me anyway."

"Wait a minute. If the cartel took the McCrays' cousin, then why would the McCrays come after you? Were you working with the cartel?" Larose went momentarily silent. He hadn't put in enough thought about the story he'd give to the Feds.

"Who are the cartel?" asked Beth who had stopped packing and stood there following the conversation.

"Jesus Christ!" He grabbed her by the arm, marched her to the bedroom door and shoved her out into the living room slamming the door behind her. He turned back to Franks. "They made me." He sounded unsure at first but gained more confidence as he continued. "That's right. They made me. At gunpoint! I barely made it out of there alive. That's why we got to get out of here, they could be here any minute."

"I thought it was the McCrays you were worried about."

"The McCrays, the cartel they're all after me. Fuller is with them. I'm the only honest cop in the mix and the only guy that stood up to them." He started really liking the sound of his own story, he imagined them someday making a movie about him. "Look, I'll tell you everything later, right now we got to blow leave. Oh shit! I almost forgot." He tossed his shotgun on the bed, dropped to the floor and reached under the bed. He had inherited a box of war medals and old coins when his father died. He rushed the coins to a coin dealer the very day he got them and was disappointed when told they were worth only a few hundred dollars. But he convinced himself that if he just saved them long enough they would make him rich in his old age. He patted around under the bed but felt nothing. He stuck his head under the bed and waited a few seconds for his eyes to adjust to the darkness. He saw a couple sizable dust bunnies, an errant flip-flop, a dried up pizza crust and an empty beer can. "Christ Beth, don't you never clean up under the god damned bed!" He pulled his head out from under the bed and looked up to see Franks pointing the shotgun he'd left on the bed at his face. "What are—" were the only words he could get out before Franks pulled the trigger and his brains and blood were soaking into the carpet.

Franks pumped the shotgun sending a shell flying onto the bed. He exited the bedroom to see Beth running for the back door. He raised the shotgun, but she was out the door before he could pull the trigger. As he ran for the back door, he saw her through the window running down the porch steps. He stepped out onto the porch and blasted her in the back before she could round the corner. She stumbled, fell, got up, stumbled a few more steps and fell again face first. When she tried to get up again, Franks pumped another round in her and she went down for good. Franks looked around. Nobody in sight. Even if someone heard the shots, nobody out here would think twice about a couple of shotgun blasts. He scratched his chin, wondering what to do with the bodies. To start with, he decided to drag her body into the house, out of sight, and go from there.

Chapter 32

Tracy headed straight for her cousins' house after Julio let her go. She sat smoking a joint with Jay as she recounted her ordeal. "I ain't gonna lie Cuz, I was scared, wasn't gonna let them fucks know it, but I was."

"And they just let you go?" He passed her the joint.

She took a big hit then broke into a coughing jag. She took another big hit and managed to hold it. "It was only one of them that decided to let me go. I got the feeling he didn't like that they took me. One guy tried to stop us and he straight up blew him away on the spot. He was the one that talked to you that night at the Buzzsaw."

"The one that got shot or the one that let you go?"

"The one that let me go. I think I heard someone call him —"

"Julio?"

"Yeah, that was it. Julio." She passed the joint back to him. "So what are we going to do now?"

"Now, we get, you, out of Dodge till all this is over."

"Fuck you! I ain't no pussy and I ain't running from these assholes. It's Scarface time bitches." She stood up on her chair. "Say ello to my little friend!" She pumped an imaginary M203 grenade launcher and fired an imaginary grenade complete with sound effects.

Jay shook his head. "You done, Tony Montana?"

"That's all I got for now." She sat back down on her chair. "But I ain't running, so you can forget about that right now."

"Can't believe you're turning down an all-expense paid vacation to the one, the only, Las Vegas."

Her eyes lit up. "Well, since you put it that way, can I bring someone?"

"Fine. One other person. But they got to be ready to go tomorrow morning. Because tomorrow, me or Jack are going to take you to that travel agent in St. louis that I used when I went to Vegas. We'll book you a two week package to start with, I'll even give you spending, gambling and food money. You call me right before the two weeks are up and I'll either tell you to come home or, if necessary, extend your vacation."

Chapter 33

Agent Franks insisted that Hector drive several hours north to meet him. He was understandably paranoid about being seen with Hector, and saying too much on the phone was out of the question. Miguel drove while Hector sat in the back seat staring out the window. The first half hour of scenery was mostly woods. Hector enjoyed that. So much green. After about an hour, the foothills of the Ozarks gave way to flatland and the woods became farming fields. Field after field. The tall crops on both sides of the road made Hector feel oddly claustrophobic. No wonder these people were so good at growing marijuana.

When Hector turned his gaze from the fields to the interior of the car he grew bored and his mood soured. Just as he was about to ask how much further, the series of fields was mercifully interrupted by the welcome sight of something man-made. A gas station/truck stop/diner.

"Is this it?" asked Hector. "Please tell me it is."

"This is it boss." Miguel pulled into the parking lot.

"Thank Christ!" Hector was opening the door before the car had fully stopped. When he got out, he slammed the door and stretched out his arms, back and legs. His ass felt numb from sitting for so long.

Pushing through the diner door, he saw Franks sitting at a booth in the corner and made his way over to him. As soon as he slid into the booth, the waitress was there with a pot of coffee. She filled the cup sitting in front of Franks, then turned to Hector.

"Coffee, sir?"

When he looked up, he saw the waitress recoil from the sight of his scarred face, taped-up ear and broken teeth. He made a mental note to come back here when all this was over and kill the cunt. "Please," said Hector turning over the coffee cup in front of him.

She filled the cup then set two menus down in front of them. "I'll give ya'll a minute to decide then come back for your order."

After she left, Hector picked up the sugar jar and poured half of it into his coffee. "So, what is so important that you had to drag me all the way out here to the, how you say, children of the corn country?"

Franks took a sip of coffee and glanced around to assure no one was in earshot. "You had some Barney Fife, Deputy Larose help you kidnap a McCray cousin?"

"So." Hector shrugged his shoulders.

"So, he wanted to turn on you, he was going to testify, name names including yours in exchange for witness protection. By a stroke of luck he called me instead of somebody else."

"What did you do?"

"I dealt with him."

"When you say you dealt with him—"

"I mean I, dealt, with him as in he won't be talking to anybody about anything."

Hector nodded. "Good. You should be happy. I was starting to wonder what good you are. You finally proved yourself not to be a completely useless asshole. Just an asshole. Is that all you brought me here for?"

"Also there's a brother. James McCray, a.k.a. Jimbo. He busted out of the penitentiary, killed six guards single handedly, severely wounded another. These god damned Irish fucks, they're like cockroaches, they—" He was cut short when the waitress returned.

"Ready to order yet sweeties?"

"Yes," said Hector opening the menu for the first time. "I'll have two full stacks of blueberry pancakes, three, no, four scrambled eggs, four fried eggs sunny side up, a side of ham, a side of pork sausage, a side of bacon, oh, and make the sausage patties not links, I don't like links, an order of hash browns, an order of french toast, a bowl of Lucky Charms, a breakfast burrito, a glass of milk, a glass of orange juice, a diet Coke, a regular Coke and an iced tea. Unsweetened of course. Trying to watch my calories."

The waitress finished writing then shook out her hand. "Expecting more people I assume?"

"No," said Hector. "Why do you ask?"

"No reason." She shrugged. "I love a man with an appetite." She winked, evidently having got past the battered face enough to flirt for a tip. She turned to Franks.

"Just the coffee." He waited till she was on her way back to the kitchen before he continued. "So this fuck, Jimbo, he's probably coming back here if he's not here already."

"So what," Hector said with a dismissive wave of his hand. "Two heel-bee-lees, three heel-bee-lees, what's the difference?"

"It ain't the fucking hillbilly I'm worried about!" Franks caught himself yelling, and looked around. A couple of heads turned their way, but turned quickly back to their breakfasts when they saw Hector. Franks took a deep breath then continued, "These new Feds, the ones that come looking for Jimbo McCray, I won't have any authority over. Maybe I can slow them down a bit but I can't keep a lid on this much longer."

Hector sipped his coffee. He glared at Franks over the rim of the cup. He set the cup down. "So what the fuck do you want from me?"

"I'll tell you what I want." Franks glared back at Hector's angry eyes. "I want you to wrap things up, one way or another. Either kill these guys or give up on them and let us bust them. But end it now."

Hector took another sip of coffee. "I will deal with the McCrays when and how I want. You will figure out a way to deal with the new Feds for as long as it takes. Or—" he stared at Franks while taking another sip. When he set the coffee cup down he continued, "I'll just kill the McCrays, kill the new Feds, kill your Feds and anyone else that gets in my way. Then, of course, I'll kill you. Because you'll no longer be of any use to me." Another sip of coffee. "Then I'll by another American pig, one who knows how to do what he's told." Another sip. "Any questions?"

Franks Jaw tightened. "No. I think I got your point."

"Good," said Hector standing up. "I've got to go. You don't mind getting the check do you?" Hector smiled.

Franks took a deep breath. "Sure, my pleasure."

"And be sure to eat all the food. It would be a waste if you didn't." Another smile.

"Yeah right," said Franks.

"I said, eat all the food." This time Hector didn't smile.

"Fine, whatever," said Franks.

Hector turned and headed for the door. The smile returned to his lips.

Chapter 34

While Jack drove down the highway, Tracy held the aluminum foil under his face while waving the zippo lighter beneath it. A straw dangled from Jack's lips at a downward angle. He sucked in the wisps of white smoke as they floated up from the burning meth. When he could inhale no more, she passed the foil and lighter to Suzie in the back seat. She pulled the straw from between Jack's lips and passed it back as well. Suzie finished up what was left in the foil.

"If you guys are good on that for now, I'm gonna fire up a hooter," said Tracy. She didn't smoke meth, only snorted it. It didn't hit you as quickly, but when it did hit, it hit harder.

"Do it to it," said Jack drumming his thumbs on the steering wheel. She pulled a hog leg joint from her cigarette pack and lit it. She passed it to Jack, noticing how furiously he was grinding his teeth.

"First thing I wanna do when we get checked in," said Suzie, "is get us tickets to that 'Thunder Down Under' show."

"What the fuck is that?" asked Jack.

Tracy smiled. "It's a bunch of male strippers from, like, Australia or something."

"Shit," said Jack. "You don't need to go to Vegas to get a bunch of guys to shake their junk in your face. You could get that right here at the Buzzsaw any Friday night, and for free too." He took a hit off the hog leg and passed it back to Suzie.

"No thank you," Suzie said taking the hog leg. "I've had my fill of small-town rednecks. I'm interested in meeting more cultured men of the world."

Jack laughed. "Right, because having a guy shake is junk in your face that's a high culture activity right?"

"Fuck off," she passed the joint back up to Tracy.

"Why don't you two just fuck already and get it over with," said Tracy taking the joint.

"Been there, done that," deadpanned Jack.

Suzie punched him in the arm. "Shut up! God, why do you have to be such an asshole?"

Jack waited at the airport till they got on the plane and the plane took off. He made his way back to the car, grinding his teeth the whole way. He was already jonesing for more meth, but the rest of what they had brought was on its way to Vegas nestled securely in Tracy's crotch. When he got back to the car, he programmed the address Jay had copied from the file into the GPS then pulled out of the airport parking lot. After leaving Lambert airport, which rested on the edge of the St. Louis area, he ventured farther into the core of the city, where stoplights and stop signs grew more frequent and the overall character of the city became more desperate and hostile. The farther he ventured, the more the city seemed to close in around him squeezing him in a fist of concrete and steel. There was so little green. Very few trees and only occasional patches of grass. He couldn't wait to get back to the woods.

When the GPS showed him getting close he started looking at the numbers on the side of the buildings. He saw a car down the road pull up to the curb and a man run up to it, lean in the window and make some sort of transaction before the car pulled off. The man who ran up to the car looked Mexican. This had to be the place.

He pulled over and scoped out the scene. There was the guy running up to the car, Jack guessed he was selling crack, and there was another guy standing not too far from him, leaning against a post. He must be there as a lookout for cops and a backup if someone tries to jack the other guy. There most likely were more men in the house. They probably traded off in shifts. Any guy out selling crack on the street would be low level, of course. But that didn't matter. This was about sending a message.

He pulled the 9 mm. out from under his seat, flipped off the safety and chambered a round. He took a deep breath then exhaled. "Showtime," he said. He wedged the 9 between the passenger seat and the center console, then pulled up to the curb.

The Mexican sauntered up to the car and leaned in the passenger side window. "What up homey?" You want twenties or tens?"

"Can I see how big the twenties are?" The Mexican rolled his eyes then gave a quick glance to the left and the right. Satisfied there were no unwanted eyes on him, he dug around in his pocket, leaned farther into the car and extended his upside down fist in front of Jack. When he opened his hand, Jack looked down to see a dozen or so little white rocks each individually packaged up in the torn-off corners of plastic baggies. "These are twenties?" asked Jack."

"Yeah homey! Best deal you're gonna get in the city. Now you buying, white boy, or just wasting my time?"

"All right, all right man. I'll take," he paused, considering, "all of it." Jack grabbed the pistol and brought it up quick, smacking it into the back of the Mexicans hand and sending the crack rocks flying. As the man tried to pull himself out of the window, Jack gave him a bullet in the forehead to take with him. Before the Mexican's body even hit the pavement, Jack twisted around in his seat and aimed out the rear window at the other man. Seeing his buddy go down, that man went for his own gun. Jack fired twice, shattering the rear window and dropping the man before he could get a shot off. Jack swung the 9 back around and aimed it out the passenger window at the apartment's front door. It took a good ten seconds before the front door opened and two men came charging out one with a shotgun, the other with an A-K. Jack emptied his clip and sent them both stumbling face first onto the sidewalk. He popped the empty clip from the 9, slammed in a loaded one, chambered a round, put the car in park, shut off the engine and got out. He ran up the steps to the apartment's front door, pausing to stuff the pistol under his belt and pick up the A-K the man dropped. He stepped over the bodies and into the house. Just as he crossed the threshold, two men came barreling down the staircase that led upstairs. Jack raised the A-K waist high and squeezed the trigger, holding it down long enough to fill the stale apartment air with the oddly satisfying smell of gunpowder and the echoes of rapid gunfire. An avalanche of dead bodies and cartwheeling assault rifles came tumbling down the staircase. The echoes faded and gave way to the thumping of footsteps from above. There was still someone upstairs running across the room, maybe to escape out of a window, maybe to get a weapon. Jack pointed the rifle at the ceiling and followed the thumping. When he felt he had the timing down he squeezed the trigger sending a burst of rounds into the room upstairs. He heard a couple more clumsy uneven steps followed by a heavy thud. He smiled.

He noticed that there was a girl sitting on the sofa. A thick white girl, blond hair pulled into tight cornrows, hoop earrings, tight tube top, short shorts. Maybe she was a hooker, maybe she was just trying to look tough, but she clearly wasn't feeling tough now. She held her palms up, "Please don't kill me!" She closed her eyes.

Jack pushed the barrel of the rifle past her hands and pressed the tip of the muzzle against her face. "Where is it?" he asked.

He wasn't entirely sure what "it" was, but he knew a dope house like this had to have either drugs or money, maybe both.

"I don't know what the fuck you're talking about." She kept her eyes tightly closed as if that could offer some degree of protection. "They don't tell me shit!"

"To bad for you bitch." He pushed the barrel a little harder against her face. That was all it took.

"O.K., O.K." She opened her eyes. "It's in the kitchen." She pointed down the short hallway.

"Show me, now!"

The girl got up and walked quickly down the hall with Jack following. She stopped by the sink and opened the cupboard door beneath it. "Back there in the back."

Jack looked where she was pointing. In the very back past the sink pipes the wall had a square of drywall that didn't quite match the rest. "Move," he said. When she stepped out of the way, he squatted, took the butt of the rifle and smashed it into the square of drywall, easily smashing through. He reached through the hole and groped around till his hand found a paper grocery bag. He pulled it out. It was full of money, different denominations, but mostly hundreds. He stood up. "Well, I guess that'll do then. You have a nice day ma'am." He brushed past her carrying the bag in one hand and the assault rifle in the other.

Outside, as he was coming down the steps to his car, he noticed several black teenagers standing across the street watching. As he approached they broke and ran, all except one, the oldest, who looked to be about seventeen or so. He stood his ground showing neither fear nor aggression. Though he knew he should be getting on his way, Jack couldn't resist walking past the car and approaching him. He stopped about five feet from him. "I killed them fucks and took their money." He shook the bag. "Cause lions like you and me don't go hungry while jackals like them eat, know what I mean? You can have this." Jack tossed the A-K to him. He barely got his hands up in time to catch it. "And I'll take all of this." Jack opened the bag and showed him the money before turning his back and walking to his car. He stopped right by the driver side door. "That is, of course, unless you're lion enough to take it from me."

The teenager's eyes focused on the bag, then the A-K in his hands then back at the bag. He considered the crevice between where he was and where he wanted to be. It was deep enough to be his death but seemed narrow enough that if he just had the guts to jump. His eyes narrowed and his resolve hardened. His finger found the trigger. His heartbeat accelerated. He couldn't have been more than a second or two from action when his eyes moved from the bag of money to the window of Jack's car. In that window he saw Jack's reflection staring straight at him. Jack's fingers tapped on the butt of his pistol. The most unsettling part was the grin on Jack's face. The kid threw the A-K onto the ground and took off at a sprint.

Jack turned and watched him run. "Fucking pussy!" he yelled. "You ain't no lion!" He opened the door and climbed behind the wheel. Sirens screamed from a couple streets over as he pulled away. Before he even got around the corner, the first police car rounded the same corner from the opposite direction and had to come to a screeching halt not to hit him. "Jesus Christ!" Jack yelled out the window. "There's a bunch of Mexicans back there killing each other!"

The cop took in Jack's white face and panicked demeanor and dismissed him as a threat. "Just get off the street sir, and stay out of the way!" The cop hit the gas and continued on to the crack house.

Jack laughed and headed for the highway. Several more police cruisers passed him, lights flashing, sirens screaming. Jack made a few quick turns down side streets in case anyone tried to follow. When he figured the coast was clear, he programmed the GPS for home. He was nervous all the way to the highway, which seemed to take forever to get to. Police were everywhere, but none gave him a second look. A wave of relief rolled over him when he finally rolled up the on-ramp to southbound highway 55. On the highway, he resisted the urge to rush and held the vehicle to the speed limit. He started feeling safe when he was out of the city limits but made himself continue another half hour before he risked stopping. When the buildings became less frequent and patches of woods began dotting the landscape, the last tension drained from his mood, and he began to think about getting high again. The jones of coming off the meth, which had been temporarily replaced by the adrenaline dump that accompanies bursts of violence, returned full force.

He decided to make a quick stop at a gas station just off the highway. When he parked on the side of the gas station, the first thing he did was collect up the crack rocks. Eight of them on the front passenger seat alone, two more on the front floor, a few made it all the way to the back seat and he managed to fish one more out from between the seat and the console. Looking down at them all in the palm of his hand, a tingling anticipation danced over his body. He pulled the cellophane off his cigarette pack, dumped the rocks in it and stashed it, along with the 9, under the seat.

With the pistol and crack secured out of sight, he headed into the gas station. He ventured down the few aisles they had, seeing if there was anything that might come in handy. In the end he opted for the aluminum can solution. It worked better for weed than crack but it would suffice.

Back in the car, he gave the parking lot a quick scan for cops. He popped the top of the aluminum coke can, took a drink and poured the rest out the window. He dented the side of the can, took his pocket knife out, poked a few small holes into the dent, and then poked a big hole in the side of the can for a power hit. He lit a cigarette. After a few hits, when the cigarette had a nice long ash, he flicked the ash on top of the small holes. He loaded a rock onto the ash, put his lighter to it and took a hit. It took a few seconds then, BAM, there it was. That instantaneous full body wire that comes from smoking crack. For a good minute after the first hit, he was superman, the meth jones a distant memory. Before the feeling could even start to wear off, he took another hit. It was like a lightning bolt, shot through the pipe past his lips, all the way down to the tips of his toes and back up to his brain not missing a single nerve or cell along the way.

After he finished that rock, he loaded the pipe again and lined the rest of the rocks up on the passenger seat next to him so he could load the pipe and smoke as he drove. He took a hit off the second rock, then pulled out of the gas station and got back on the highway. He wouldn't have to stop again till he got home.

Chapter 35

Jimbo poured some whiskey into the pot of chili sitting atop the crackling fire. The chili was nothing special, just canned, but the whiskey would give it character. Jack had brought a pillow case full of various canned goods to the campsite. Without refrigeration, canned goods were about all the food he could keep except for a bag of barbecue potato chips, a package of Oreos, a jar of Jiffy peanut butter and a loaf of wheat bread. Every time Jack came out to the camp he brought some comfort item to make the campsite a little homier. A battery powered radio, an air mattress, a pile of *Playboy* magazines, a lawn chair, a little foldout table, a couple plastic jugs of drinking water, and, of course, a bottle of whiskey, bag of weed and a carton of Camels.

Jimbo was completely content. After years in prison, sleeping outside under the stars was hardly a sacrifice. It was a little lonely. But, come harvest time, even company wouldn't be a problem. His brother and son, along with some handpicked laborers that would certainly include some free-spirited hippie chicks, would move out to the woods to pull the plants. There would, out there among the pot plants, spring up a little off-the-grid society perfect for the likes of

Jimbo McCray. Periods of bossless work punctuated by periods of smoking pot, drinking whiskey and fucking. The thought of it brought a smile to his face. But after that, would come winter. Then he would have to make some tough choices about where to go. But that was awhile off. And there was always a fair chance that he'd be dead by then anyway, so why stress on it now.

The chili started to bubble up sufficiently enough to pull it off the fire. He set it on the little fold out table and sat down on the lawn chair. He considered letting the chili cool a bit, but a growl from his stomach settled that debate. He scooped up a spoonful, blew on it a few times and shoved it in his mouth. Could have been a bit spicier. He made a mental note to tell Jack to bring out some Jalapenos next time he saw him. Still, it beat the hell out of prison chow.

As he was about to dip in for his second bite, he heard something. It was far off. Somewhere to the right, he thought. A small sound. A snapping twig, the crunching of leaves. Most likely just wildlife. Maybe even something as simple as a falling branch. Just ignore it, he thought, it's nothing. But he couldn't. He took the bowl of chili and zipped it into his tent, to keep the insects away. He cursed himself for lighting a fire during the daytime. If the Feds were out here looking for him the smoke may have led them right to him. He grabbed a plastic jug of drinking water, unscrewed the cap then dumped it onto the fire. The burning wood hissed, popped and spit up some steam before dying out altogether. He dropped the jug and grabbed the shotgun from the tree it was leaning against. He took a few steps in the direction he thought the sound came from but stopped. He looked down at the shotgun he was carrying, then turned around and went back to the tent, unzipped the flap, put the shotgun in, pulled out the .308 and zipped the tent back up.

He set off in the direction he thought the sound had come from. He walked far. He saw nothing. To play it safe he walked further still. Then further. Then, as he was about to head back and eat his now cold chili, he saw it. A doe, twenty yards off, chewing on some leaves. He raised the rifle and sighted in the deer. Before he could pull the trigger, the doe bounced over a hill and out of sight. He was downwind from it so he was sure it didn't smell him, and from the lack of urgency in the way it bounced over the hill, he didn't think it saw him either. The thrill of the hunt and promise of fresh venison made him forget all about the chili back in his tent. He decided to track the deer. He reached the top of the hill and looked down. There it was again. It hadn't gone far at all. Easily in range. He pointed the rifle. As he started to squeeze the trigger, the silence was shattered by the rat-a-tat-tat of automatic gunfire.

Jimbo dropped flat to the ground and swung the rifle toward the direction of the shots. Two men holding Uzis. He sighted one of them in, but when they both raised their Uzis again, he saw that they weren't shooting at him. They were shooting at the deer. They were as oblivious to his presence as the deer was. Both men held down their triggers and emptied their clips. Bullets zipped all around the deer as it ran, but none hit their target, and the deer disappeared into the woods.

One of the men said something in Spanish, and they both laughed. The dark skin, Uzis and city boy clothes were enough of a clue, but hearing them speak Spanish left no doubt. They were cartel. Considering their empty clips and their cluelessness to his presence, he could kill them both easier than he could have killed the doe. Watching them through the scope, he considered doing just that. It was tempting. But he was curious. Where did they come from? This was far from the old bar they had set up shop in. What were they doing all the way out here? Where they looking for him? He doubted it. If they were they wouldn't be joking around and shooting at the deer. Were they looking for the plants? It was possible.

When they turned and started walking away from him he decided not to kill them. At least not yet. He would keep that idea in his back pocket. They weren't out of the woods yet. Not literally or figuratively. But for now he wanted to follow them, see where they came from. He followed easily, at a safe distance. They were loud and clumsy. In less than a half an hour, they popped out of the woods and into someone's yard.

Jimbo crept to the edge of the wood line and looked out at the yard they were crossing. He realized where he was. It was the old Miller place. It had been empty for years but not now. He dropped back down on the ground and studied the property through the scope of his rifle. It was a hive of activity. The porch was full of men, with more steadily coming out of and going into the house. The front yard was infested with tents, as well as the side yards and, he suspected, they were most likely in back as well. There were countless men gathered around various tents, sleeping in them, walking around them. Christ, he thought. How many of them were there? More than there was before. That was for sure. They must have moved out here. The two men he'd been following made their way up to the porch. One of them said something to the men on the porch and then mimed shooting his Uzi. They all laughed.

How many could I kill if I decided to attack right now, he wondered. He thought about it, letting the idea stew in the violent juices of his mind. A lot. That was the short answer. He figured he could pop three right off the bat before any of them could even think about reacting. Then they would panic, run for cover, which would mean going into the house or behind it. They would bottleneck at the front door. That's when the orgy of killing could really begin. All bunched up, stuck there by the door, he'd be able to drop them as fast as he could pull the trigger. After that they would hold up in the house for a while. He could just stay there and wait. How long would it take? A half an hour? An hour? Two? Sooner or later a couple of them would poke their heads out. What choice did they have? They couldn't call the law or stay in the house forever or pinpoint his position in the wood line to return fire. He wouldn't shoot. Not right when they came out. He'd let them get confident. Let them come out of the house. At some point a few would try to cross the yard, come where they figure he had been hiding. He'd just lay there quietly. Let the flies land on the web.

The idea excited him. He wanted to play it out. But he couldn't. There was one undeniable problem. Ammo. The rifle was fully loaded, but he didn't bring any extra ammo with him. It would work just like he envisioned it till they bottlenecked at the front door. At that point, he'd aim at those fish in a barrel, start to pull his trigger, they'd start to fall, then he'd run out of ammo and it would all be over. And, despite the fact that several of them would be dead, it would ultimately be a wasted opportunity. Right now they thought this location was safe. That gave him the element of surprise. He couldn't burn that advantage without extracting maximum bloodshed for it.

A man came out on the porch holding a coffee cup. By the way he carried himself and the way the others reacted to him, he must be the head enchilada. Jimbo put the scopes crosshairs between the man's eyes. "Next time buddy," he said quietly. "Next time." He tore his eyes from the scope, stood up and retreated back into the thick of the woods.

Chapter 36

Jay climbed the porch steps, he noticed the curtains briefly flip when Jack peeked out the window. When he entered the door, Jack was just sitting back down on the sofa. He recognized the chick sitting next to him, Carly was her name. Back in their coke dealing days she was always good for a blowjob for one good size line. The years had been cruel to her. Her head was crowned with long, stringy black hair that looked like it hadn't been washed in a good while. She had the unnatural concentration camp thinness of a meth head, which gave her face that sunken in quality of a skull spray painted flesh color. She wore a bikini top and skintight jeans. Her body somehow had the appearance of being thin and flabby at the same time. Popeye sat in the corner watching them with disinterest. His head raised momentarily when he saw Jay, his ears standing up, his nub of a tail giving a little wiggle, then his head dropped back to the floor and he resumed relaxation mode. Jack picked up his homemade crack pipe off the coffee table, and Jay noticed the remaining crack rocks spread across the table. Jack took a long hit off the pipe, then set it back down before exhaling a cloud of white smoke. Carly tried to pick up the pipe but put it back down quickly. "Fuck that's hot," she said sticking the tips of her fingers in her mouth.

"Told you to let it cool after each hit," said Jack.

"I take it your trip went well," said Jay sitting on the armrest of the chair across from them.

Jack nodded. "Message was delivered and received. After which, our friends no longer needed this product here." He gestured at the crack in front of him. "So I took it off their hands. This is Carly by the way."

"Howdy," she said picking up the pipe and loading it. Jay gave her a nod. He wanted more details on Jack's trip but didn't want to say too much in front of her. "Fuck!" she yelled throwing the pipe back down. She'd managed to get a hit but burned both her fingers and her lips.

"Didn't I just tell you to let it cool?" said Jack. He turned to Jay. "You want a hit?"

"Fuck no." Jay didn't really care for any of the speed type drugs, but crack above all else he hated. The reason he didn't like speed in general was because of the landing, that is to say the harshness of the comedown, the ruthless jones that grabbed him by the jugular. The crack jones came on within minutes of each hit. The first and only time he tried it was with his brother, who never met a high he didn't like, and a couple of other guys. He remembered that first hit, remembered thinking this is as good as it gets. And then he passed the pipe. As the next man put fire to rock and the small white pebble began to bubble, the rush started to subside. By the time the pipe had made its way around the small circle of men smoking, he had a full on jones and had to resist the urge to yank the pipe from the last man and rip a hit off it, blasting him away from the sharp talons of the jones. When it did get back around to him, of course, it was hot. But it was unthinkable to wait the several excruciating minutes it would take to cool. He remembered feeling his lip burning as he took the fourth hit but being unable to pull away from it until he got a full hit. He had a blister on his lip when it was over, a blister that had an embarrassing resemblance to something herpes related. Then, when it was over, he remembered getting down on his hands and knees and spending twenty frantic minutes looking through the carpet for any flakes of crack that might have fallen. It was one of the few moments in his life he felt like a weak man. He never smoked crack again and only snorted coke a handful of times. The fact that he didn't like using it contributed considerably to his success in selling it.

"Do you have any meth?"

"What?" Jay asked, shaking off the bad memories and returning to the present moment.

"Do you have any meth?" asked Carly. "I prefer it to this nigger crack shit."

"No," said Jay.

"Ya'll supposed to be big time, and you ain't got no meth."

"Sorry to disappoint you," said Jay.

She shrugged her shoulders then slowly spread her legs. "I'd do just about anything for some meth." She picked a beer bottle up off the coffee table and raised it to her lips. Looking directly into Jay's eyes she flicked her tongue out and twirled it around the neck of the beer bottle.

The faint sound of a car pulling up drifted in from the open window. Jack dropped the pipe, grabbed the shotgun that was leaning on the side of the sofa, tossed it to Jay and then grabbed his .45 from the coffee table. As they both ran to the front window, Carly took the opportunity to grab the pipe and finish off the rock Jack had loaded. When Jay looked out the window he smiled, seeing Jill climb out of her car. "It's Megan," he said to Jack. "Why don't you take Carly and the crack back to your room?"

Hearing this, Carly dropped the pipe and jumped up from the sofa. "What?! You think that uppity chink bitch is too good to be subjected to my company! You think she's better than me!? You think you're better than me!? Fuck all y'all, you ain't no better than me!"

Jay took a deep breath and looked at Jack. "I got this," said Jack. "By the way," he whispered barely loud enough for Jay to hear. "There's somewhere around eighteen grand in a paper bag under the kitchen sink. I figure we can use it to fund Cousin Tracy's trip, split what's left over three ways, you, me and Dad." He walked back to the coffee table, scooped up the rest of the crack and the pipe. "You do want you want," he told Carly. "But I'll be back in my room with the rest of the rocks. You're more than welcome to join me if you want." As he headed back to his room, she turned back to Jay who had already turned his back on her and was looking out the window. She flipped a middle finger to his back, then stormed off after Jack.

Jay opened the front door just as Jill was climbing the porch steps. "Tell me something," he said. "Do you just get prettier every day or is it just every day you see me? Cause if it's just every day you see me, then it must have something to do with me."

She smiled stepping onto the porch. "Actually, I think it's your weed. I was wondering if you could help a girl out." She pulled a wad of bills from her purse and waved them at him.

"I was just about to fire one up myself." He pushed the door open for her, and they walked in.

She sat down on the other side of the kitchen table, facing the front door and the window. This annoyed Jay a bit because, with his back to the window, it would be much more difficult to keep an eye on the road. Of course he couldn't explain any of this to her without telling her more than he wanted her to know. Popeye came into the kitchen, saw Jill, went straight to her and put his head on her lap. "Hey baby!" She stroked his head. "How's he doing?" she asked Jay.

Jay was returning from the living room with the weed tray. "Right as rain," he said taking a seat across from her. He sprinkled some weed onto a rolling paper and twisted a joint. Jill scratched Popeye behind the ears, scrunched up his face and kissed him on the nose. Jay handed the joint across the table. "You wanna do the honors?"

"Thank you sir." She fired it up, took a long drag and handed it back to Jay. Leaning back in her chair, she held the hit as long as she could before exhaling the pungent smoke toward the ceiling where it gathered in a lazily rolling cloud. Already she felt the THC working inside her, melting away tension and stress she didn't even realize was there until it started to dissipate. She looked down from the ceiling to see Jay passing the joint back to her while holding his own hit. She took another big drag and realized that by the time she exhaled it, she would already be high. "I said it before and I'll say it again, you boys sure do grow some good bud."

"Well shucks, thank you ma'am."

"So, how much of this stuff can a hard working waitress get for say, a hundred bucks?" She spread out five twenties on the table.

"Well," said Jay. "Lucky for you, we got us a special going today. All smoking hot, drop dead gorgeous waitresses get their first bag free." He shoved a few plump buds into a plastic baggie that was laying on the tray and tossed it to her.

"Alright," she said as she shoved the bag into her purse. She knew there was more to this generosity than just flirting. He didn't totally trust her yet, didn't want to risk a sales bust for such a small amount of money. As the joint was passed back and forth, thoughts of evidence and her investigation morphed into random fractured thoughts of memories of music lyrics, childhood conversations, then the memory of the taste of the hot buttery pancakes she ate last time she was here. The muffled sound of Carly screaming, about God only knows what, drifted in from the other room. Jill glanced in the direction of the shouts then back at Jay. "Got company?" she asked.

"Jack's entertaining." Jay felt irritated at Carly's presence in his house and wondered how long she'd be there.

"Is this a bad time? Maybe I should come back?"

"Fuck no! She's just here to see Jack. Probably won't even come out of his room."

As if on cue, Jay heard Jack's door open and Carly came out

into the kitchen. The skin-tight jeans were gone revealing purple panties and stick thin pale legs with several dark bruises. "Howdy," said Jill. Carly gave her a look like she'd just bit into a lemon and a barely perceptible nod before turning to the fridge, opening it and getting out a beer. Jay was grateful when she unscrewed the cap and took a drink without doing her freaky tongue thing.

"You want a beer?" Jay asked.

"Sure," said Jill.

Not surprisingly, Carly made no move to get her one despite the fact that she was standing right next to the fridge. Jay got up, took two beers from the fridge, opened them, handed one to Jill and took a swig from the other. Jack came out of the room, jaw twitching as it tended to when he was wired. "Sup girl!" he said to Jill.

"How's it going Jack." She got up and gave him a hug. Jay noted with a pang of jealously that she didn't hug him. His pang of jealously was nothing compared to what Carly must be feeling if the way her forearm flexed as she squeezed the beer bottle was any indication.

"So," said Jack. "You smoke rock?"

"No thanks. Your bomb ass weed is all I need." She offered the joint to Jack who took it.

"It is good shit ain't it?" Jack asked taking a hit.

"I do believe it's the best I ever smoked," said Jill.

"I've had better," said Carly taking the joint from Jack's lips and sitting down in the chair Jill had just got up from.

Jack turned to Jay. "This rock is pretty good shit. You sure you don't want to try a hit just for old—"

"Answer is still no," said Jay.

"Oh. Right," said Jack. "Well, I'm about due for another hit. Good to see you again darlin."

"You too Jack," said Jill.

Jack headed back to his room. For a painfully long, quiet few seconds it seemed like Carly was going to stay. But it had been a few minutes since her last hit of crack, and the knowledge that Jack was in there getting ready to fire up another hit proved too strong of a pull. She looked at Jay, shot Jill one final dirty look, then headed back to Jack's room taking her beer and their joint with her.

"Well," said Jill. "She seemed nice."

"Uh, O.K. If you say so," said Jay. "You want to smoke another joint?"

"I'll roll the next one," she said. "Least I could do. But first, is there any chance you got any more of that pancake batter?"

Chapter 37

Hector burst out of the room where Tracy had been held. "Where is she? Where is the bitch? Where is she!?"

"Take it easy," said Julio. His voice was calm but insistent. "There has been a change of plans. I decided to go in a different direction. I let her go."

"You let her go? You let her go!" Hector noticed someone was missing. "Where's Paco?"

"Paco was under the false impression that you were running things and objected to my change of plans. Then he got carried away and decided to emphasize his point by going for his gun. He's buried out back."

"You let the bitch go, and you killed Paco." He nodded his head.

"That is correct." Julio stood up. "We haven't put the shovels away yet. We're not going to have to dig another hole are we Hector?"

Hector looked at the pistol tucked under Julio's belt, then at the men standing silently around Julio eyeballing Hector. It was a mistake not bringing more of his own men up from Tijuana. It was a mistake he could fix. But he needed time. "I don't think that will be necessary."

Julio waited a few seconds for Hector to make a move, but Hector stood motionless. "We value your input Hector. And you're welcome to stay." Julio's hand inched, almost imperceptibly, closer to the butt of his pistol. "But you'll need to understand that I'm the boss."

Hector didn't take the bait. "Understood. So since you didn't like my plan, boss, what's yours?"

Julio leaned back in his chair. He'd been prepared to kill Hector, and on some level still thought he should, but hadn't been prepared for Hector to fall in line so easy. And he'd not prepared for the next step. "Just do what you're told Hector. I'll let you know what you need to know when you need to know."

"O.K. boss," said Hector. "I am confident that under your leadership, we will wrap this up in no time."

"I am the boss," said Julio.

"That's what I said, boss." Hector smiled.

Chapter 38

Shultz had an agent surveilling the Buzzsaw, even though he didn't think there was much of a chance that Jimbo McCray would show up there. When the agent notified him that Jay and Jack had showed up, he decided to put in a personal appearance at the bar, see if he could get under their skin. He also wanted to confront the waitress who, he decided after a little investigating, was most likely the undercover agent that Franks had told him about.

He pulled up outside and surveyed the parking lot. He spotted his agent sitting in a car. He made no move to acknowledge him. When he entered the bar, he spotted Jay and Jack. They sat at a table, their backs against the opposite wall of the front door he had just entered. They were devouring a plate of wings. Jay noticed him right away. He stared at him for a few seconds then went back to his wings. He whispered to Jack. Jack looked up and flipped Shultz a hot sauce covered middle finger before returning to his wings. On the wall next to the door was a bulletin board where locals would post notices of cars for sale, or the location of a flea market, or babysitting services. Shultz pulled the thumbtacks out of a swap meet advertisement, letting it fall to the floor before replacing it with a wanted poster of Jimbo McCray. He walked around the bar with a copy of the same poster, asking the patrons if they've seen this man. They would glance at the poster, glance at the McCrays, then shake their heads. He didn't expect them to tell him anything. It was all about annoying the McCrays. Eventually, he took a seat next to the door, and, as he had hoped, Jill came over to his table. "What can I get you?" she asked.

"How are the wings?" he asked staring at the McCrays.

"Haven't had any complaints."

"Maybe I'll just start with a rum and Coke, Miss, or, should I say," he looked at her for the first time, "agent?"

She met his gaze with a perfect poker face. He could see why she was working undercover. "Look," she said. "I'll call you tomorrow, we'll meet and talk. Right now it's not safe."

"No, I don't guess it is." He turned back to the McCrays. "Not for you anyway. Course, since you're not giving me the professional courtesy of respecting my investigation, I don't really see why I should extend you said courtesy."

"I'm going to help you. But right now my cover is the best thing either of us have going for us. It gets blown, both of our investigations are fucked."

"Well then, why don't you go get my rum and Coke before someone gets suspicious?" She turned and headed to the bar. He continued to stare at the McCrays. They ignored him. After finishing their wings, they proceeded to drink.

Out in the parking lot, the agent on surveillance paid no attention to the van full of Mexicans that pulled up, just as the Mexicans paid no attention to the agent. The Mexican in the driver's seat, Luis, turned to the four in the back. They were all armed with Uzis. "The Chevy pick-up truck two spaces over," he pointed toward the passenger side. "That's theirs. We'll get them when they come out of the bar, before they get to their truck. Hopefully they'll be drunk. I'll give the signal, then we jump out and let them have it. Any questions?" No one responded. "Get comfortable. We could be here for a while." He set a small camera on the dashboard, pointing it at the bar's door. He put another one next to it, pointing it out the passenger window towards the McCrays' truck. He went to the back of the van, with the others, and turned on the monitor that both cameras were connected to. A split screen flickered to life. Half the screen showed the front door, and the other half showed the truck. Anyone outside, who looked at the van, would most likely assume it was empty. The cameras were small enough to pass for radar detectors.

That didn't stop Jack from getting suspicious. About every hour, he would go over to the jukebox, located right next to the window, and peek out the blinds. He noticed the van. He didn't see anyone in it. He didn't recognize it. It was still there an hour later. When it was still there an hour after that, he mentioned it to Jay. "There's about a dozen people in here, and I know them all," he said. "I don't recall any of them driving a white van."

"Could be a carpool thing," said Jay. "Some folks met up here, got in another car and left the van behind."

"You really think that's it?"

"No."

"Me neither," said Jack looking around. "I could go out the back door, climb up on the roof, pop a few rounds through their windshield. If there is someone in the back, that ought to shake em up a bit. I could even take a liquor bottle, make up a Molotov cocktail, see if I can hit the van from the roof. Set that fucker on fire, and we'll see real quick if there is anyone in there."

"If they were smart, they would have put a sniper out back covering that back door." Jay signaled the waitress. He had hoped Jill would be serving his table, but this wasn't her section and it was the only table he would sit at because he could see the whole room, and, most importantly, anyone coming in the front door. The waitress looked his way and he held up two fingers and pointed toward their empty glasses. "I don't think they did though. They think like thugs not soldiers. But I'm not sure enough to bet your life on it. Besides, we can't do shit as long as that Fed asshole is eyeballing us," he nodded at Shultz who was still glaring at them after four rum and Cokes. "Let's just keep an eye on them for now. Let me think about it for a while." Another hour went by. The McCrays drank a few more whiskeys, Shultz drank a few more rum and Cokes. Jack made another trip to the jukebox. The van was still there.

Shultz noticed that their conversation grew more serious, though he couldn't hear them. At one point he was sure Jay McCray nodded in his direction. He must be getting to them. He decided to stay and stare at them till they left. Maybe even follow them home. But the prospect of driving down that god-awful road again, especially drunk, dissuaded him of that particular plan. Sitting there and staring at them would do for now. Except, he had to piss. Back in the day, on stakeout, he would sit all night hitting a bottle and only have to piss once, maybe twice. But that was just booze. This was booze and soda. He felt better blaming it on the soda as opposed to his advanced age. When he got up, he didn't make a beeline for the bathroom but, instead, headed straight for the McCrays. He walked with purpose as if fueled by violent intent. Let's see them ignore me now, he thought. When he was a few tables away, they finally looked up. He turned, with a satisfied grin, and headed for the restroom.

Jay watched the Fed go. The waitress set down their double shots of whiskey. "Can I borrow your pen?" He asked the waitress.

"Sure, hun." She handed him the pen from her apron pocket. He jotted something down on a napkin and handed the pen back.

"Thank you," he said.

"No sweat." She moved on to another table.

Jay looked at the bathroom door. No sign of Shultz. He

looked over at the table Shultz had been sitting at. Jill was just setting a fresh drink on it. When she went back into the kitchen, Jay got up, walked over to the table and dropped the napkin next to the drink. When he returned to his chair, he sat down, smiled at Jack and slammed his double shot.

"So what was that?" asked Jack before slamming his own.

"'All warfare is based on deception.' That's Sun Tzu."

"As usual, I have no idea what you're talking about, but I can't wait to find out." He caught the eye of the waitress and held up two fingers.

Shultz came out of the bathroom. "All right, here he comes," said Jay. "Be cool, keep ignoring him just like we were before." He pulled two cigarettes out of his pack and handed one to Jack. They both lit up.

Shultz went back to his table and sat down. Again, he aimed his death stare at the McCrays. Again they ignored him. He saw his fresh drink and, with his bladder freshly emptied, took a couple big swallows. When he set the glass down, he saw the napkin. He picked it up and read:

Jimbo McCray just pulled up outside in a white van. He's waiting for his brother and son. As soon as they see he's here, they'll all leave. You better hurry.

He looked around for the waitress. Was the note from her? She was nowhere to be seen. Of course, if she did write it, she wouldn't want to be seen talking to him right before he busted Jimbo McCray, would she? In fact, it could be from anyone in the bar. None of them would want to be seen talking to him. He looked over at the McCrays. They were still ignoring him. Good. He got up and slipped out the front door. He squinted his eyes and let his vision adjust to the bright sun. There was the white van. He didn't see anyone in the driver's seat. But he didn't expect to. If McCray was in the van, he would be in the back where he couldn't be seen. The windows were tinted. Suspicious. No way he could see all the way into the back of the van without getting right up to it. He pulled out his phone and texted his second in command to get the team over to the Buzzsaw. But, it would take the better part of the hour for them to get there.

Inside the van, the men were getting restless. "Luis, I got to piss man. How about I go into the bar, take a piss and make sure they're still in there. "

"Nobody's leaving the van." Luis was looking at the man who just came out of the bar. He seemed to be staring their way.

"Well, I've got to piss, what do you want me to do?"

"Piss in one of the jugs."

They'd brought three plastic jugs of water in case they got thirsty. "All right. I'll use this one with the pink cap that we already drank out of. Everyone remember if you get thirsty, I warned you." He unscrewed the cap. There was no way he could hit that small of a hole, so he got on his knees and stuck the tip of his dick into the hole and let it flow. "If they don't come soon, we're going to have to get some food. We should have brought some. Can we order a pizza Luis?" As he turned his upper torso to face Luis, his dick popped out of the jug, and urine shot all over the man next to him.

"Jesus Christ!" yelled the man scrambling, along with the other men, to escape the yellow stream.

Shultz couldn't hear the ruckus, but when they started jumping around, he noticed the van bounce slightly. That was enough to convince him. He pulled his .45 and waved over the agent that was on surveillance. The agent saw Shultz waving him over and noticed he had his weapon drawn. He pulled his own weapon, exited the car and headed over to Shultz. He held his weapon down by his side but flipped off the safety. "What's up sir?" he asked when he reached him.

"I got intel that Jimbo McCray is in that white van." Shultz nodded toward the van. "The rest of the team is on their way, but we can't wait for them. His brother and son could come out of this bar any second. We need to move now. Are you with me?"

"I'm with you sir."

"Good man. Stay with me and stay low." They both crouched, holding their weapons in both hands, ready for action and began to advance on the van.

"Come on," said Jay. "You're going to want to see this." Jay led Jack over to the window. The blinds were down, so you couldn't see without walking right up to the window and peeking between the slats. Jay positioned Jack a few feet in front of the window. "Just stand right there." Jay stepped up to the window and peeked through.

Back in the van, things were getting heated.

"I didn't do it on purpose!"

"You fucking pissed on me pendejo!"

"I told you it was an accident. What the fuck do you want from me?"

When the two Feds moved into the range of the camera, Luis saw them and the guns they carried. "Shut the fuck up!" he said. "We got two gunmen moving in!" The argument was quickly forgotten as safeties were flipped to fire and rounds were chambered.

"Is it them?"

"No, it's someone else."

"Who?"

"I don't know."

"Cops?"

"The local cops are working for us."

"Fucking Feds? Shit! I got warrants here and in Mexico."

"It doesn't matter who the fuck it is." Luis put his hand on the door handle. "Somebody rolls up on us, they get dealt with. We let them get close, when I open this door, we blast the fuckers."

"Wait for it," said Jay. He wrapped the cord to the blinds around his hand. "Wait for it." The Feds rounded the side of the van. "And, enjoy!" Jay pulled the cord raising the blinds just in time for Jack to see the van door open.

When the van door opened, the bullets flew. The cartel had the superior firepower, but the Feds were more accurate. They were trained to aim for the center of the body, but, at this close range, it was nothing but headshots. The agent that had been on stakeout dropped two of them right off the bat before one of the Uzis spit a couple dozen rounds into his chest, shredding his heart and lungs. He fell back against the truck behind him and slid down it. He was dead before his butt hit the ground. Shultz got one before two bullets caught him in the shoulder and one grazed his neck. He dropped to the ground and rolled under a truck. One of the Mexicans dropped to his stomach and pointed his weapon at Shultz. Shultz put a round in his eye before he could pull the trigger. Luis and Shultz were the only two left alive. Luis had enough. He made a run for the driver's side of the van. Shultz aimed for his legs, the only part visible from under the truck. The first shot hit the ground. The next one shattered his ankle, bringing him down. They both aimed. Luis pulled his trigger first. Nothing but a click. The downside of a weapon that fires 600 rounds per minute is that you run out of ammo quickly. Shultz emptied his magazine into the prone Mexican.

Chapter 39

Jill stormed through the doors separating her room from Franks's without knocking. "What the fuck Franks! He almost blew my cover! I thought you were going to talk to him."

"Calm down," he said standing up and reaching for his pair of pants sitting on the bed. He was sitting in the chair in his boxers eating from a bag of Cool Ranch Doritos and sipping from a screwdriver when she burst in. He got his right leg in but his left leg caught and he stumbled a few steps before righting himself and pulling his pants up. "I said I would take care of him," he said zipping and buttoning.

"He didn't sound like he was taken care of Franks. Did you tell him I saw Jimbo McCray?"

"I didn't think it was the right time to give him that particular nugget of information."

"Jesus Christ!"

"Jill if I had told him you saw Jimbo McCray, he would have been all over you."

"He's all over me now Franks! At least tell me you warned him about the cartel." The guilty look of a German Shepard that just got caught going through the trash was the only response she got. "Oh, FUCK ME!" she threw her hand up and grabbed two fistfuls of hair.

"Jill—"

"Franks, they shot him! And killed one of his guys, right outside the bar!"

"Jill, I said I would take care of him and I'm going to. Just trust me. I got you."

The front door to the motel room flew open and Shultz came stomping through. His left arm was in a sling, his jaw clenched, his eyes on fire as he made a straight line right for Franks.

Franks put his hands up as if a gun was pointed at him. "Now let's just take it easy, we—"

When Shultz closed the distance between them, he cut off Franks's words with a right cross to the nose that put him on his ass. Franks's hands went to his nose, blood pouring through his fingers. Jill sat down in the chair, her own anger at Franks stifling any urge to intervene on his behalf. Shultz bent over thrusting is face into Franks's suddenly blurry vision. "This bullshit ends now! You are going to answer my questions and if you hesitate or I think you're lying I will skull-fuck you to death."

"No!" said Franks holding one hand over his broken nose and the other in a "stop there," gesture toward Shultz. He rose to his feet, tilting too far in one direction then the other before righting himself. Spurts of blood poured aggressively through his fingers with each word. "We can work this out!" Shultz's bug-eyed glare of hatred held them in a tense pause that lasted an eternity of several seconds. Then Shultz took a breath, shifted his gaze from Franks to the wall. He leaned back against the dresser, which Franks took as welcome digression. "Jesus," Franks said stumbling back to the bathroom.

"First things first. Jimbo McCray?" Shultz continued to stare at the wall, but Jill knew he was speaking to her.

"He's here," she said. "Or, at least, he was. He was at the house the day you came out. Ran out the backdoor while you were pulling up the road."

Shultz closed his eyes, shook his head and pounded his clenched fist against the dresser. "Fuck!" When he opened his eyes he looked right at Jill. "Did you know about the cartel?"

"Yes." She didn't hesitate, glad to no longer have to hide it. "I mean I had no idea about what was going to happen at the bar, but we were aware the cartel was beefing with the McCrays. One of our own was undercover with the cartel when he was murdered by the McCrays along with several other cartel gunmen."

"Jesus Christ!" said Shultz. "So now these puss-bags have killed two Feds."

"Well, technically, your agent was killed by the cartel." She regretted saying it before Shultz turned his angry gaze toward her.

"Look," said Franks coming out of the bathroom with wads of toilet paper stuffed up his nostrils to stem the flow. "It was my fault. I didn't realize how much our investigations would overlap. Blame this on me."

"I do fucking blame this on you," said Shultz.

"As well you should, as well you should." The ends of the tissue stuffed in his nose began to drip red drops on the front of his shirt as well as the carpet. "But the best way out of this is for all of us to work together."

"No! Fuck that. You had your chance to work with me, you blew it. Now, you work *for* me. I'm getting the McCrays and the cartel and you're going to help me. When it's over you can have the collar for everyone but Jimbo, but make no mistake, I'm the one that has to tell my agent's pregnant wife that I got her husband killed, that means I'm in charge now." Franks nodded profusely. Shultz turned to Jill. She gave a single assenting nod.

Chapter 40

Julio called the sheriff for the eighth time and for the eighth time got voicemail. He hung up the phone without leaving a message and, only with considerable effort, put it in his pocket instead of throwing it across the room. Santiago stood across from him in the room that had become his makeshift office. "We've overcome bigger obstacles than this before. We'll overcome this one, you know we will," said Santiago. Julio gave him a look that Santiago couldn't quite decipher. When it became clear Julio wasn't going to answer, Santiago continued, "In the end it's just three men we are talking about here. It's not an army. We kill three men, our problems here are over. It's just three white—"

"Don't!" said Julio standing up. "I don't want to hear one more person tell me it's just three white boys. Let's review these three white boys. Jay McCray came into the bar, massively outnumbered, knocked Hector's teeth out then left while the rest of us jumped for cover. His brother breezed out of a maximum security prison like he was checking out of a fucking bad motel, the nephew, the runt of the bunch, walked into one of our crack houses, by himself, killed everybody and stole my *god damned money!*" He punctuated the statement by kicking over the chair. "I hear the chatter of these superstitious peasants," he nodded toward the door to the living room where the rest of the cartel soldiers were. "That they aren't human. They are white demons spawned from the gringo forest."

"Julio!" shouted a man from the other room. "We got company!" Julio went into the living room and over to the window along with everyone else. Two large buses pulled up in front of the house.

"Now what fresh hell is this," said Julio.

"Oh, didn't I tell you?" asked Hector joining him at the window. "I invited some amigos to join the fiesta." He patted Julio on the back and walked outside followed by Julio and everyone else.

The bus doors swung open and men poured out. The first man off saw Hector. His face lit up. "Hector!"

"Amigo!" yelled Hector. The two men embraced, clapping each other on the back. Every man that got off the bus greeted Hector like a long lost brother. By the time the bus emptied, Hector had three times as many people behind him as Julio did. Hector smiled at Julio. "I sent for them the day we lost Paco. While I explained that you were the boss, unfortunately, your uncle is getting older and gets confused. Through some sort of mistake, all these men have been ordered to be loyal to me." Hector smiled. "To kill and die for me. But no worries. Since I am as loyal to you as a brother, you only need to give me your orders and I'll see they are done. Besides I'm sure the sheriff has killed them by now. Have you heard from him yet?"

Chapter 41

Jill sat in Franks's motel room and took one of the customary plastic cups of vodka Franks handed her before taking a sip from his own. "So I got to thinking," said Franks. "It struck me odd when you told me Jack was smoking crack. Not only have the McCrays, or anyone else in these parts, messed with coke since meth became king, but these backwoods cracker types, back when they did mess with coke, tended to keep to the powder form. Crack was always more of an urban thing. So I dug into it, and it turns out the day before you saw Jack smoking crack, there were several murders and a robbery at a crack house in South St. Louis. And here is the good part, the crack house belonged to the cartel."

"Holy shit! They went all the way to St. Louis. Took the fight to the cartel."

"That's what I'm thinking."

"I think you're right," said Jill.

"These guys got balls, got to give them that."

"That they do."

"So," Franks took a sip of his screwdriver before continuing "if you can connect Jack—I'm guessing he was the one to do it— to these murders maybe we can get him to roll over on his uncle?"

Jill raised an eyebrow and gave him half a smile. "These guys aren't rolling over on anybody, especially each other. But you know that. Don't you?"

Franks smiled and put his hands up. "O.K. Cards on the table. You get enough evidence for an arrest warrant on Jack, we go in heavy when he's with his uncle, they of course resist and are both killed in the resulting firefight, game over, mission accomplished, we all go home."

"Right." Jill slowly nodded her head. "Still, we got nothing so far beyond circumstantial. Certainly not enough for an arrest warrant."

"Any chance any of the crack is left?"

Jill laughed. "Not likely. Jack is as big a junkie as his father was. The crack is long gone and he's probably balls deep in a meth binge by now. Besides, even if there was any crack left, what would that prove?"

"Well, if you could get Jack's gun, maybe ballistics—"

"Come on. We can't count on them being that stupid. Whatever gun he used is most likely long gone by now. Let's just face it. We got nothing but a theory. Unless there was a witness."

"There may be witnesses, but none that will talk." They both fell into silence, sipping their screwdrivers. Franks cautiously broke the silence. "If they trust you, you might be able to get them to talk about it. Of course that would only be of value if you were wearing a wire."

"These guys are still a long way from trusting me enough to blurt out that they murdered a bunch of Mexicans." She slammed the rest of her screwdriver. "A wire would be an unnecessary risk."

"Well, Shultz is going to wire up the house, anyway. You know they talk about this shit in the privacy of their home, so that might be enough."

"How does he think he's going to get the wires in the house?"

Franks shrugged his shoulders. "Maybe bring them in

for questioning or bogus charges, wire the house while they're in custody. That would be my guess."

"Fuck Franks! If they find the wires they're going to think it was me!"

Again Franks shrugged. "I don't know what to tell you Jill."

"Fuck!" She scooped up the bottle of vodka from the dresser and headed back to her room without another word.

Chapter 42

Jay had been lying down trying to nap when he heard the knock on the door. He wasn't too worried. He doubted the cartel would knock. Still, he approached the door with shotgun in hand just in case. When he looked through the peephole he saw the asshole Fed that was in the shootout at the Buzzsaw. Another agent was standing by the car in his driveway.

"Open up McCray," said Shultz. "I know you're in there. I'll give you thirty seconds to come out, then I'm coming in."

Jay looked through the slats in the blinds. They came to arrest him with only two agents? Jay understood as soon as the question popped into his mind. They couldn't really have anything on him. This asshole was just pissed about the shootout. He blamed Jay. But he couldn't make any charges stick. If he'd come with the sizable crew he'd come with last time, he figured Jay or Jack would just surrender without resistance. And he wanted him to resist. He was hoping, if they saw just two agents, they would try to get away or resist. And then he would have an excuse to kill them. Jay set the shotgun down, took Popeye, who stood at attention next to him, and put him in the bathroom and closed the door. Cops loved to shoot dogs. He then returned to the front door and opened it. "Can I help you?" he asked.

Shultz grabbed his arm, and Jay let himself be pulled out onto the porch. "Put your hands on the wall and spread your legs." Jay assumed the position. Shultz kicked his feet farther apart and patted him down. "You the only one here?"

"Yep."

"Too bad. I was really hoping the rest of your white trash family would be here."

"You're lucky they're not. They ain't as docile as I am."

Shultz pulled his pistol with impressive speed and put it to Jay's head. "What did you say shithead? Say it again."

"What am I being arrested for?"

"Interfering with a Federal investigation, resisting arrest, maybe some other stuff, the day is early. Or maybe you'll resist arrest so much I got to put you down now. I lost an agent because of you, and I either will send you to the pen for it or I will kill you, know that."

"Then you might as well kill me now, because you charge me with this bullshit, and I'll walk. And you know it."

Shultz held the pistol to Jay's head for a while considering doing just that. Eventually he put his pistol back in its holster and put Jay in the back of the car.

Chapter 43

Lucy sat at her desk glad to finally be alone in the office. Since Fuller and Larose had disappeared, the F.B.I. had pretty much taken over the station, coming and going as they please. They were uninterested in the disappearance of the two local cops. Their consensus seemed to be that the locals were dirty and on the McCray payroll, which Lucy figured was true, and were possibly working with the cartel as well, which Lucy thought was possible, and with the F.B.I on the scene they got scared and ran before their corruption was discovered, which Lucy doubted. Lucy was regulated to staying in her corner and handling local business, which admittedly wasn't much. She should be investigating the missing sheriff and deputy, but the F.B.I. forbade her from going near the McCrays or the cartel. She looked up when the front door opened and saw Franks coming in.

"How you doing Deputy?" he said.

"Hanging in there," she replied. She didn't like any of the Feds, but Franks was better than most, being merely condescending as opposed to completely dismissive.

"Anything new?" he asked sitting on the edge of her desk.

"They brought Jay McCray in."

"No shit!" Franks stood up suddenly interested.

"No shit. He's back in the holding cell."

"What are they charging him with?"

Lucy shrugged her shoulders. "Nothing I guess. They told me to hold him for a couple of hours, then kick him to the curb. I really don't get how you Feds do things."

"Yeah, well join the club." Franks looked back toward the cell and scratched his chin. "Look, Lucy, why don't you let me take care of him. We've imposed on you enough. Let me lighten your load."

"Oh, gee whiz, aren't you sweet. You don't have to do that for me, you guys are so busy, what with all you're doing to find the sheriff and all." Her voice dripped with sarcasm. She knew he was up to something. She didn't really care, she just wanted him to know she knew. When he stared at her without responding, she relented. "Fine." She threw him the keys. "Do your thing."

"Thank you Lucy. You're the best." He went through the door that separated the office area and the holding cells, whistling all the way back to the rear cell where Jay was sitting. He still had his hands cuffed behind his back. "How the hell you doing Mr. McCray."

"I want to talk to a lawyer," deadpanned Jay.

"No need for that. We're not going to hold you." He unlocked the cell and opened the door. Jay stood up, walked out of the cell and turned around so Franks could take off the cuffs. "No," said Franks. "We're going to leave those on for now." Jay looked at him. "Sorry, it's not that I don't trust you, it's just that, well, yeah I don't trust you. I'll uncuff you when I drop you off." Jay made no response and Franks led him away from the cells and back into the office area. "Have a nice day Lucy," said Fanks holding Jay by the arm and walking him to the front door.

When they were outside, Franks put Jay in the backseat of his car leaving the cuffs on him. He walked around to the back of the car and opened the trunk. He pulled out a taser gun and put it in his jacket pocket. He made a quick phone call then closed the trunk, got in the car and pulled out of the police station parking lot.

The ride was quiet. Franks didn't engage in his usual banter. He occasionally glanced at Jay in the rearview, but Jay was unreadable, looking neither at ease nor panicked. They rode until the pavement changed to dirt. Only when Franks passed the road that led to the McCray house did he bother to speak. "I just need to make one quick stop then I'll drop you off at your place. Won't take long. You don't mind do you?" He looked at Jay in the rearview. Jay stared back at him and said nothing. Jay showed no sign of concern. But Franks knew he was likely a little suspicious, and that belief was confirmed seconds after he turned his eyes back on the road.

Franks was in his own car, which, unlike a squad car, had no barrier between the front and back. Jay scooted down in the back seat and shot his legs up over the front seat, one on each side of Franks's head. He folded his right leg over so his calf slipped under Franks chin against his throat. He folded his left leg over his right ankle to leverage his right calf into an effective choke. Franks slammed the brakes, causing the car to slide sideways and come to a stop. For one terrifying moment, Franks couldn't breathe. Then he managed to turn his neck enough to free up his windpipe and his panic eased, though only slightly. His next instinct was to go for his pistol, then he remembered the taser. He took the taser in his right hand and used his left hand to pull up Jay's pant leg so as to be able to sink the darts into skin. He put the taser against Jay's leg and pulled the trigger. Jay's legs went slack. Frank turned around reloaded the taser gun and gave him another shot for good measure.

Chapter 44

"It doesn't look good," said Jimbo.

"You think the cartel is in there, lying in wait for us or something?" asked Jack. The two of them stood on the edge of the wood line with their rifles, looking toward the house. The front door was open, and, despite the fact that it was starting to get dark, there were no lights on in the house.

"I doubt it. They wouldn't want to leave it look so suspicious, if it was a trap. Still, doesn't look good."

"So, we going to check it out or what?"

Jimbo nodded. "I don't see no other choice. You?"

"Nope." Without another word, Jack started sprinting toward the house.

"Fuck," said Jimbo before following. Jack was running full speed, and there was no way Jimbo could keep up with him. He thought about yelling for him to slow down, but if it was a trap, yelling would give them away, and Jack most likely wouldn't listen to him anyway. Damn adrenaline junky. Jimbo was a good forty feet from the house when Jack went in the front door. By the time Jimbo was climbing the porch steps, Jack had cleared every room, turned on every light and was getting a beer out of the fridge. Popeye stood next to him. His nub of a tail wiggled when he saw Jimbo.

"House is empty," said Jack as Jimbo walked in the front door. "No sign of a struggle either. Popeye was closed up in the bathroom." JImbo looked like he was about to say something, but he was breathing too hard. He pulled a chair from the kitchen table and sat down laying his rifle across his legs. "God damn, how old are you?" asked Jack before taking a swig of beer. Jimbo again looked like he was going to say something then settled for holding up a middle finger. As his breathing started to slow, he held his hand out for the beer, and Jack passed it to him. Jack laid his shotgun on the table and sat down across from his dad. "So, you think they got him?"

"It's weird," said Jimbo. He was still breathing hard but had recovered enough to speak. "I can't imagine they could just come in here and take him without a struggle. But he wouldn't just leave the door open and wouldn't disappear for this long, with everything that's going on, without letting us know where he is. So, I don't know how, but I think they got him. The good news is, if they killed him, I expect they would have left the body for us to find. He's probably still alive."

"I can't believe they could have took him alive."

"I hear you, but I think that's what happened."

"Why do you think they didn't just kill him?" Jack took the beer back and finished it off.

Jimbo shrugged his shoulders. "Maybe to hold him as bait, hoping we would come and get him. Most likely, they just want the satisfaction of torturing him before they kill him."

"Well then, if he's still alive, we go after him right?"

"Right."

"Except we don't know where they are. They left that old bar they were staying in."

"I think I know where they are. Spotted a couple when I was tracking a deer. Followed them back to the old Miller place. It's where they took Tracy."

"Alright then," said Jack standing up. He'd been waiting to go heads up with the cartel since they came, and now it was finally time. "Let's do this!"

"First," said Jimbo standing up, "we're going to need a lot more ammo."

Chapter 45

When Jay returned to consciousness he was tied to a chair in a kitchen. He didn't recognize the place, but he recognized Hector. "Hola gringo. Welcome to mi casa. What's a matter? You don't seem happy to be here. You don't like the house? No that's not it. You don't like me, do you? Why? Why don't you like me gringo?"

"It's your smell." Jay smiled. "That's right. We were talking about it before. Me, my brother and nephew. About how you fuckers all got this certain stink about you. What the fuck is that? It occurred to me, I've smelt that stink before. But where? We couldn't place it. We tried to think of all the worst fucking stenches we could remember: cat shit, rotten eggs, dead animals. But no. You grease balls smell worse than any of that. And then it hit me. There was this time the three of us me, my brother and nephew, closed down the bar, it was like two in the morning, and we're on our way home. We smoked a hog leg joint, of our weed now, not that grass clipping shit you people grow. So, we got a mad case of the munchies and decide to stop off at this cheap all night taco place. We get these greasy ass tacos, you know those kind where they just fry the whole damn thing, shell and all. Toxic garbage to put in your body, but fuck, they taste good. Anyway, we ain't home half an hour, and I got to make a run for the can. Gave all three of us explosive diarrhea. Imagine it. You're sitting there on the toilet, diarrhea blasting out of your ass like a fucking water cannon. You finish, get yourself cleaned up, you're coming out of the toilet and the next guy's rushing to get in there, then the next guy, and, after him, you're clinching your ass cheeks waiting to get back in there. Anyway, after about an hour of this, the air in the bathroom gets permeated with that cheap taco diarrhea smell, woooo doggy! I mean to tell you, I thought it was going to peel the paint off the wall. Anyway, that smell, that's you guys." Jay looked around at all the unfriendly faces. The circle had closed in on him. Jay continued, "You grease balls ooze that smell out of your pores. I'm sorry I had to be the one to break it to you, but I'm only telling you what everyone else is thinking whenever they're downwind of you."

The toxic fog of silent hatred hung in the air. Jay made a point of looking at each face he could and smiling at that face. Clapping his hands and bursting into laughter, Hector shattered the silence. "You so funny," he wagged his finger at Jay. "You're incredibly stupid, but you got balls. I've got to give it to you gringo, you've got the balls of a Mexican. At least you got balls for now, I mean. Before the night is over, I will cut them off, but for now, you got balls. Should I cut them off now?" Jay didn't respond. "Don't worry, I'm not going to cut them off right away. When you cut off a man's nuts, he usually goes into shock, and the effects of everything you do to him, after that, is somewhat dulled. Kind of takes the fun out of it. And I intend to have a lot of fun with you, gringo. So, I'll save the balls for last. Where should I start?" Hector lit a cigarette, leaned back in chair, crossed his legs and blew out a few smoke rings. "Maybe a finger?" He shook his head. "No. Tough son of a bitch like you, that wouldn't even make a dent would it? How about an ear? You ever see that Tarantino flick, *Reservoir Dogs*? The one where he cuts off that cop's ear. That could be fun. But no. That causes a lot of cosmetic damage, but there isn't much pain, probably less than with the finger." Hector took a drag off his cigarette. "Do you have any suggestions?"

Jay took a deep breath. "Take my finger, my ear, pour gas on me and set me on fire, better yet cut my nose off, just get the fuck on with it. Because if I have to sit here listening to you drone on and on, smelling your stank ass spic breath another minute, I swear to God I'm going to try to break out of this fucking chair and kill myself."

Hector's lip twitched. He jumped up from his seat, grabbed Jay by the hair and ground out his cigarette on his cheek. Jay didn't flinch or make a sound. When the cigarette was extinguished, Hector dropped the butt onto the floor.

Jay looked up at him. "Is that all you got?" he said.

Hector met his eyes. This was not how this was supposed to work. He tried to think of a cool line like all the American actors say before they do something violent in the movies. He came up with nothing. This arrogant gringo even took the pleasure out of victory. "Fucking pendejo." He grabbed Jay's hair and yanked his head back so he was staring at the ceiling. "You want to fuck with me! You want to fuck with me puta!" With his free hand, he grabbed a fork off the table and held it above Jay's upturned face. "You disrespect me!" The fork came down, lodging in Jay's left eye. Hector slipped his left arm around Jay's head, holding him in a headlock while digging the fork around in his eye. With a grunt, Hector yanked the fork from the eye socket. He held it up so all his men could see it. Jay's blue eyeball was stuck to the fork's tines. One bloody tendril still connected the eyeball to the socket. Hector gave the fork a yank, and the tendril snapped. The entire circle of men backed up, many of them cringed and averted their eyes. He tossed the fork with the eyeball onto the table and looked at Jay. "Talk some shit now! What's the matter gringo? I thought you were a tough guy! I want to hear you talk some shit now!"

Every muscle in Jay's body tensed, his arms strained against the ropes that bound him, his face reddened, his teeth clenched and his lips peeled back like a growling wolf. But still he didn't cry out. A stream of blood jetted out of his eye several feet and landed on the floor with a splat.

"Jesus," said Hector backing up. "He's leaking! Someone find something to wrap that thing up." Nobody made a move. "Am I fucking talking to myself!"

The men exchanged glances, none of them wanting to go near Jay. Finally, one of them left the room and came back with a bed sheet. He walked over to the drawer, fished around in it till he came up with a steak knife. He used it to saw off a long strip from the sheet. He wrapped that sheet around the left side of Jay's face and tied it behind his head. A circle of crimson bloomed and expanded on the portion of the sheet that covered Jay's left eye, or more accurately, where his left eye use to be. Without the ghoulish sight of Jay's empty eye socket blighting their field of vision, the men became less squeamish, and regained a bit of their composure.

Hector sat down and lit another cigarette, letting himself calm down. Enraged screaming was not his usual style. It was not the way the Fonze would have done it. Hector preferred to deliver his violence with a cool, almost disinterested smile. Still, this was the first time he'd felt any satisfaction in the presence of this gringo. His phone rang and he answered. It was Franks. "This better be good," said Hector.

Chapter 46

The wire that was planted when Shultz arrested Jay picked up the conversation between Jimbo and Jack, and despite the fact that they were still light on evidence, the knowledge that the McCrays and the cartel would all be in the same location proved too tempting to resist. They crammed as many agents as they could into each vehicle so as to limit the overall number of vehicles they had to bring. Still, the line of cars and SUVs stretched along the country backroad where they parked them about a half mile from the house. The road was completely blocked by the vehicles, but there was nowhere else to park them. They decided to approach through the woods so their vehicles wouldn't be spotted this time. Doors slammed up and down the line of vehicles as agents got out of their cars and prepared for the raid. Bullet-proof vests were strapped on, guns were loaded, then checked and rechecked, last cigarettes were smoked. A few of the agents stepped off into the woods and emptied their bladders after the long, rough car ride.

Shultz whistled and waved everyone over. They gathered around in a loose circle. "Take a knee boys, take a knee," he said. Jill and Franks stayed off to the side, leaning against their car. The rest of the agents kneeled down around Shultz like they were waiting to be knighted. Satisfied that he had everyone's attention, Shultz continued, "All right, I'm not gonna blow smoke up your ass. I'm not exactly running this operation by the book. We should be calling in backup, swat team, the whole nine yards. But these fucks killed one of ours. I'm not letting someone else come in to settle a score that's ours to settle. Neither the cartel nor the McCrays are an innocent party here. If any of them fucks want mercy from us, then they can throw down their weapons and lay face down on the ground. If they do anything, and I mean anything, other than that, then they are a threat and should be exterminated with extreme prejudice. These are *my* orders, and I'll take any heat that comes from following them. We're going to send a message tonight. A message to scumbags everywhere. You kill one of us and you reap the fucking whirlwind, you bring down the thunder, and *we* are that thunder!" He looked around at the men gathered and saw heads nodding and heard a few "fuck yeahs." "Now, if you don't mind, bow your heads, I'd like to lead us all in a prayer."

Jill looked at Franks and he rolled his eyes. They remained leaning against the car impassively while most of the other agents bowed their heads and closed their eyes.

"Oh holy master, eternal father and eternal God, he who teaches us preservation of justice through might of the sword, please deliver unto your faithful servants the perseverance and strength to defeat your enemies on earth, just as you delivered unto thy child David the perseverance to defeat the giant Goliath. Let us not despair for those of us who perish this night, oh Lord, rather let us celebrate that they lived and died heroes, and if it should be our lot to perish this night, let us do it with courage and honor in a manner that brings maximum destruction to your enemies, for thou art our God, and to thee do we ascribe the glory of any victory we attain, to the Father, the Son and the Holy Ghost, now and forever, and unto ages of ages, amen." The agents murmured their amens and raised their heads to look at Shultz. "All right, everybody tie up whatever loose ends you need to. We move out in fifteen minutes." The agents rose to their feet, shook out their legs and went back to their last minute preparations.

Jill turned to Franks. "I've got a bad feeling about this."

Franks nodded his head. "You should. It has all the makings of a bloodbath clusterfuck, that's for sure." He took a flask from his jacket pocket, unscrewed the cap, took a swig and offered it to Jill.

She shook her head. "I think I'm going to try to talk some sense to him."

"I know for a fact you're smart enough to know you're wasting your time trying to talk sense to, 'onward Christian soldier,' over there. Aren't you?"

Jill bit her lip then slowly nodded her head. "Yeah, I do. I don't think I'll be able to sway him. But I've got too much invested in this not to try. I mean it's bad enough we're going in without gathering more evidence, which I was in a perfect position to get. But to go in there like this. With no backup. If we aren't able to take them, we're looking at, who knows how many more dead agents and maybe no arrests, and if we do make any arrests, the charges will be shaky at best." She threw up her hands. "It'll be a disaster, and I'll be responsible for it all."

"No." Franks shook his head. "Not you. Listen to me, this isn't on you. Shultz took command away from us. Whatever shit storm may come out of this, it's on him. I will not let them hang this on you. I promise, I got your back kiddo."

"I know you do." She forced a quick smile before the frown returned. "But I still have to try."

She found Shultz on the other side of the road, staring into the woods with his hands on his hips. A burning log of a cigar jutted at a slightly upward angle from the corner of his mouth. "Sir, can I get a quick word?" she asked.

"Speak." The cigar moved with the single word answer, which he uttered without looking at her.

"I get that you don't want backup here to—" she paused searching for the right words, "to get in the way. But, if I might make a suggestion, considering how long it would take backup to get way out here, if we were to wait till right before we moved out to call, by the time they got out here, it would be all over, at least it would be all over if things went well. If it wasn't over, then that would mean something went wrong, in which case we would likely need backup."

He continued to stare in the woods, the cherry of the cigar periodically brightening with each puff.

"So," she continued, "if you agree, of course, I could make the call right before we move out."

Still staring out into the woods, he reached up and pulled the cigar from his mouth. "When we move out, you can stay here with the vehicles or follow along at the rear. But do not get in the way. And," he turned to face her, "don't you fucking *dare* call anybody. You're only here as a courtesy, one that I'm not entirely sure I even owe you. Do I make myself clear sweetheart?"

"Crystal," she sighed. He turned back to the woods, and she left him standing there.

When she returned to Franks, he arched his eyebrows in a "well?" type gesture. She shook her head. He didn't think she'd be able to convince Shultz to call for backup, but if she had, it would have been a problem. He'd told Hector how many agents were coming and that there wouldn't be any backup, and Hector put it on him to make *sure* there wasn't any backup. As if he had control over that. But Hector wasn't exactly reasonable. "No dice huh?" he asked.

"Fuck no. He wouldn't even consider it. The arrogant delusional prick thinks he's Patton or something."

"Well." He pulled out his flask and took another shot. "At least you tried. Your conscious can rest assured that you did everything you could."

"Did I?" Her eyes narrowed as she pulled out her cellphone and opened the car door. "Fuck it. I'm calling for backup. You

keep watch. If he comes this way, just tap on the window."
She started to get in the car.

"Wait a minute," said Franks. "You stand guard. If he
wants to get pissed, let him get pissed at me. I told you I
would handle him. I haven't done such a great job of it so
far, but I can do this."

"You don't have to do that."

"If this goes bad and they pin it on me, worst they can
do to me is force me into early retirement, which I'm about
to do anyway." He took her by the arm and pulled her away
from the car. "I'll make the call. You stand guard. Please."

She shrugged her shoulders and put her phone away.
"O.K. then." She turned around to keep an eye out for
Shultz while Franks pulled out his phone and climbed into
the car.

Chapter 47

Hector smiled when he got off the phone with Franks. The cop had finally told him something useful. Hector's main mission here was to put a decisive end to the McCrays, a mission that thus far had proved rather elusive but was finally within reach. But now he had an opportunity to do more. Police could be bought in America just as in Mexico, though they were a little more expensive. But thus far the cartel had failed to instill the fear and respect, which were one and the same, in American law enforcement that they had in Mexico. Now he could send a message to the American pigs and put an end to the McCrays in one night. The pigs wouldn't have been arrogant enough to come in here with the limited numbers they have if their intel was good. But their intel was bad. They didn't know about the reinforcements. And many of these reinforcements were ex-military out of Central America. Police liked to think of themselves as something akin to soldiers, but they weren't. Police, especially American police, were used to having superior numbers, and they were used to people submitting to their authority. This time they would be outnumbered, out gunned and out strategized.

"Geno!" yelled Hector. Hector decided that Geno would become his new Paco.

Geno moved swiftly to Hector's side. "Yes boss?"

"The pigs are on the way. We're going to set up an ambush for them. As they get close to the house, they will either spread out to surround the house or at least split into two groups with one covering the rear, while the rest come in from the front. We need to get them before they do that, while they're still in a group. So we need to set up the ambush several hundred yards that way." Hector pointed in the direction of the road where the police were parked. "We'll cut them to pieces."

"Got it boss. I'll make it happen." He headed off toward the rest of the troops. "Everyone gather around!" he yelled.

Yeah, Hector thought. He will do. He waved Julio over. Julio looked at Geno gathering the men. "What's that about?" he asked as he approached Hector.

"The Feds are on their way," said Hector.

"Are you serious? How do you know?"

"Franks."

"We've got to get out of here," said Julio.

"No. According to Franks they don't have a very sizable force and they've made no arrangement for backup. They don't know about our reinforcements." Hector lit a cigarette.

"So, then what? We are just going to kill them all? American Feds?"

"That's exactly what we are going to do." He paused, exhaling smoke. When Julio made no further protest, Hector continued. "After this, Franks will be burned as a contact. There is no way he will be able to explain being the only lawman to survive the night. He is going to meet us at a prearranged point in the woods. He thinks we are going to pay him off and give him refuge in Mexico. You and I are going to meet him. You are going to kill him. I am going to witness it. The rest of the police should be dead by the time we return. Then we can finish off the McCrays and go our separate ways. Is this expectable to you?" Julio shrugged his shoulders. "Yeah, let's do it then."

They made their way through the dark woods silently and slowly, Julio following behind Hector. Hector frequently stopped and looked around, occasionally retracing his steps and going a different direction. Eventually Hector stopped and sat down on a fallen tree. "I'm pretty sure this is the spot," said Hector lighting another cigarette. Julio leaned against a tree facing Hector. "I like your uncle very much," said Hector looking off into darkness while he spoke. It was a departure from Hector's usual style of the kind of aggressive eye-contact that made you want to look away, which he usually leveled at the people to whom he spoke. "But he is the past. You," he finally looked at Julio, "you are the future. Know that I am aware of this. But you should know, I have my own ambitions. I also intend to be a part of the future. It occurs to me that it would be in both our best interests not to make enemies out of one another."

"I never wanted that. I intended to say as much to you when you came to St. Louis, but then you were such a dick."

"I know. I was sent here to be a dick. Your uncle may be the past, but I have to be loyal. If I weren't loyal to him, could you ever trust me to be loyal to you?"

Julio nodded. "I see your point."

"You like the States? I mean better than Tijuana?"

Julio shrugged. "I mean Mexico is my home, I'll never forget where I came—"

"I'm sure you're very loyal to your homeland, a proud Mexican, but that's not what I'm asking you. When you imagine your future, do you like to think of yourself back there?"

"No," admitted Julio. "I know I'll always return to Mexico to visit, but everything else being equal, I'd prefer to stay in the States."

"Interesting." Hector took a big drag and exhaled. He was looking out in the darkness again. "I use to dream about coming here. But now I can't wait to leave."

"Well, you know that's not surprising considering what you've seen of it so far. You really shouldn't be too quick to judge based on this place. I've been in America for years and nothing I've experienced is anything like this place. Even St. Louis is well below par. You should try the West Coast. You'd like it better."

"Perhaps. That could be, but I really think I'm a better fit south of the border. I am, how you say, 'old school'?"

"Right. Old school, just like my uncle."

"But I think that's the way it should be. Old school boss in Mexico. Someone smart and younger like you in the States. If your uncle did pass, I assume you would want to continue taking the U.S. by storm. Who would you foresee taking over the Tijuana side of things?"

Julio could see where he was going with this. "I haven't thought a lot about it. It would need to be someone old school like you said. But, above all else, it would have to be someone I could trust completely."

"Probably someone from your current crew."

"No, I've got a long way to go in America still. I think I'll need to keep most of my current crew with me. I guess maybe that's something I need—"

"Gringo!" Hector suddenly said looking past Julio. "We were about to give up on you Franks!"

Julio spun around, his eyes searched the darkness. Just when he realized the cop wasn't there, Hector's bullet entered the back of his head at the base of his skull. He collapsed face-first onto the cold ground. Hector grabbed Julio's rifle and pistol, took one last drag off his cigarette, flipped the butt at Julio, then turned and started back to the house.

Chapter 48

Geno surveyed the terrain he had to work with and picked the perfect place to set up the crossfire. The time he'd spent in the jungles of El Salvador had given him instincts for guerilla warfare that made him more formidable in the deep Missouri woodland than anyone on the law's side and only rivaled by the McCrays themselves. He would set up an L-shaped crossfire ambush. The short line of the L, the bottom part, would consist of a line of snipers cutting off the path the police were following to the house. This line would open fire first. The longer side of the L, which would run up the side of the police formation, would wait for the first line to fire then open fire themselves. What separated a good field general from a great one was where they chose to set an ambush like this. The good field general looked for as big a clearing as he could find so as to provide the enemy with as little cover as possible. But the great field general looked for a place that did provide the enemy with spots to take cover. But just the right kind of spots. The spots would provide irresistible cover from the first line's barrage of bullets but would put them right in the line of fire of the second line of snipers. The first barrage would catch them unprepared and take many of them out, to be sure. But this initial burst would catch them on their feet where it would be easy to move. Then they would drop to the ground behind the false protection of apparent cover. When the second line opened up, they would be prone on the ground, dug into their position, a much more difficult place to move from. This would be when the real annihilation would occur. This was what Geno found in the spot where he set up the cartel ambush. This is where they waited.

Chapter 49

Though Shultz had no direct combat experience, there were several members of the team who were directly recruited from the Iraq and Afghanistan wars. But none of these men made any tactical suggestions on the strategy of the raid. Part of this was because they had come to understand that police tactics had as little in common with military tactics as police had in common with soldiers. But a bigger factor was that most of them had bought into Shultz fervor. They really felt like a glorious victory was just waiting for them to come and claim it. The one traditional military tactic Shultz did employ was putting a point man in front to lead the raid. He was deluded enough to think that failure in this endeavor was impossible but not so deluded as to expect no casualties. The point man would almost certainly be the first killed. It was an unavoidable sacrifice he was willing to make. But he saw no reason to sacrifice anyone from his own team when he had Jill's team to choose from. So when he mentioned that he needed one brave man to lead the way to glory on point, his eyes went right past his men and settled on Jill's smaller crew. Brinks sensed what Shultz was thinking and subtly edged himself behind Bushy until he was completely concealed behind the man's larger girth. Shultz also noticed Bushy's considerable mass and decided putting him on point may provide additional cover for the men behind him. "You, son," he pointed at Bushy, "what is your name?"

Bushy stepped forward, chest inflating, "Agent Bushy, sir!"

"Agent Bushy, do you have the stones to be my point man?"

"Sir, yes sir!"

"Out fucking standing! It's bold Christian warriors like you that will keep this country safe from the wolves at our door. When this is over, I will make sure your valor is recognized." And he was sincere in this promise, vowing to himself that he would speak of the young man's valor at his funeral and perhaps even present his family with the folded American flag personally.

As they moved out for the cartel stronghold it was obvious that the placement of a point man was the only valid military tactic Shultz would indulge. Whereas the traditional military tactic would have been to space the rest of the soldiers out single file in a long line, making an ambush more difficult, Shultz had the rest of the men bunched up in a disorganized herd twenty or so feet behind the point man, the mass of bodies making one big target for the snipers waiting ahead. To be fair to Shultz he had no way of knowing that the cartel was aware of their approach and hadn't expected any action till they reached the house.

Jill was toward the rear in the center of the mass, not by choice but because Shultz believed it to be his Christian duty to make sure the weaker sex was as protected as possible in such an endeavor. Brinks, who had no confidence in Shultz's fanatical vision, found a place at the rear off to the side. He would stick as long as things went well so he could add it to his resume, say that he was there when it all went down. But if things went bad he planned on making a break for the woods, doubling back for the cars and worrying about making up a cover story later.

There was no talking as they made their way through the woods. Still their walking was clumsy and loud for what they were about to confront. Weapons were locked and loaded, held at the ready, but since most of the men were in the middle of the herd, they wouldn't be able to return fire without the risk of hitting their own men. Shultz took a position in front, as he felt a leader should, content that Bushy's big frame would provide him with enough cover. He marched straight to the slaughter with complete confidence right up until the moment four bullets ripped into Bushy's chest in quick succession. Bushy, like all the agents, was wearing a bullet-proof vest. But Hector's reinforcements were packing armor-piercing bullets that made the vests irrelevant except for slowing the bullets down a bit. Shultz had just enough time to think that this was not right, they were still at least a half mile from the house, and the cartel shouldn't be this far out in the woods. Then a bullet entered his right eye and his thoughts ended.

Brinks had planned if shooting started to keep his head down and watch how the shootout went, holding his position if it went well, running if it didn't. That was his plan anyway. But Brinks, like a lot of lawmen, derived his confidence from the fact that people submitted to the authority of the badge. When that authority wasn't given that respect, his confidence and bravado dissipated. When he saw Bushy go down, he broke into a sprint for the wood line without firing his weapon. He simply ran to get out of the clearing and into the deeper woods. It was only by pure chance that the side he chose to stand on, and therefore the direction he decided to flee, was the side that the crossfire happened not to be lined up on. Otherwise he would have headed right toward the gunfire. The cartel was so caught up in shooting fish in a barrel that almost none of them paid attention to Brinks. It wasn't until he was twenty feet from the wood line that one sniper sent a couple bullets buzzing past his head like angry hornets. Then he was in the safe cover of the tree line. This safety gave only the slightest relief, so Brinks continued to sprint as deep into the woods as his cardiovascular system would allow, then collapsed behind a tree. When he caught his breath and his heartrate had slowed down slightly, he looked back in the direction from which he ran. No one followed him. Without the threat of imminent death, he allowed himself to consider his situation from a larger viewpoint. He realized that he'd gone far enough into the woods that he would be completely lost if not for the sounds of the gun battle which still raged. Based on that sound he got a sense of the direction he came from and based on that he had a very vague idea of the direction of the cars.

Back at the ambush the cartel continued to fire into the mass of bodies despite the fact that it appeared most of them were already dead. Jill, being almost dead center of the group had actually survived by stacking dead bodies to give herself cover from both sides of the L-shaped ambush. She not only managed to return fire but even dropped two of the cartel gunmen, an incredible feat considering she was fighting assault rifles with a pistol and all her targets were wrapped in darkness and had good cover while she was out in the open except for the less than ideal cover of corpses. She came to the conclusion that she wasn't going to win this firefight. Their bullets could rip right through the bodies that were in front of her. The only protection those bodies really gave her was from being spotted. If they couldn't see her they couldn't aim at her. But if she continued to return fire they would get a fix on her position, particularly since she was the only one shooting back.

She put a hold on fighting back opting instead to employ a possum strategy for survival. She dipped her hand into the wound of one of her fallen colleagues and smeared blood across her face giving the appearance of a mortal wound. She lay on her back and pushed the hand she was holding her pistol with just under the body next to her so if a cartel gunman came walking up on her they wouldn't see it, but she could pull it out and use it if needed.

***

With no more visible resistance, the rate of the gunfire slowed. Concerned about ammo, Geno finally gave the order to cease fire. The men closed in on the pile of dead Feds. At first they approached in a crouch, weapons at the ready. As the totality of their victory became evident, their confidence grew. They stood up straight, cigarettes were lit and jokes were made in the relief of satisfying laughter. After getting their butts kicked by the McCrays since things started, they finally had a victory. Geno gathered the men together. He ordered a detachment to go to the road where the Feds were parked and finish off any agents that stayed with the cars. He also ordered two men to walk around group of fallen agents and make sure they were all dead. "When in doubt," Geno said, "put a round in their head." He took the other men and headed back to the house.

The two that were left, walked around kicking various bodies and occasionally putting an insurance round in a skull. Jill waited. It occurred to her that with their only being two left, maybe trying to put them both down would give her better odds than playing dead. She just worried that even a short exchange of gunfire might sound different enough from the single execution shots to bring the group back. She kept her eyes mostly closed, allowing tiny slits so she could keep an eye on the two men. She started breathing as deeply as possible like a fighter trying to catch up on oxygen between rounds. If she decided to play dead when they came to her, she would have to hold her breath for who knew how long. The two men slowly moved closer and closer kicking and prodding, which on occasion would elicit a moan or a slight movement quickly followed by the loud crack of a shot. She noticed that when they started they were prodding and checking everybody and shooting frequently. But as they progressed they started moving faster, skipping over the more obviously dead bodies. Their shots grew less frequent. They wanted to get back to the house. They were starting to rush. There was a good chance that by the time they got to her they would just skip right over her.

She still hadn't decided if she should fight or stick with her possum and pray strategy. If she were going to fight, she shouldn't wait till one of them was looking at her, she should catch them off guard, but just as this occurred to her, one of the men made a sharp turn in her direction. He passed several bodies and stopped when he was standing directly above her. She stopped breathing. The man stared at her. She waited. He was taking too long, she thought. He wouldn't take this long to look at her if he was going to move on.

"Jesus Christ!" screamed the other gunman. When the man standing over Jill turned he saw one of the fallen agents had half-risen and grabbed the other gunman's rifle. The man standing over Jill aimed his rifle at the agent, but as the agent rose to his feet and wrestled for the other man's rifle he couldn't get a clean shot.

Jill didn't remember deciding to act, she just acted. She pulled her pistol from beneath the corpse next to her, sat up and pumped four rounds into the back of the man standing over her. When he dropped she shifted her aim to the wrestling duo. She had the same problem as the man she just killed. Just when she had a shot, they shifted. She had the impression that the agent was losing the grappling match. The next time her target fell in her pistols sights she pulled the trigger. Just as she did, however, they fell to the ground and the bullet went over them. Jill rose to her feet and raced toward the men. Both men still had a grip on the assault rifle, but the way they fell, the muzzle ended up right under the agent's chin. The cartel gunman saw his chance. He slipped his finger to the trigger and pulled it sending a round up under the man's chin, which exited out the top of his skull. He ripped the rifle from the dead agent's hands and spun around to face Jill, but she was on him and emptied the last of her few rounds into his chest dropping his corpse on top of the agent's.

She walked on over to them putting her pistol in its holster. She picked up the rifle and used it to push the man she just killed off the agent just in case he was still alive. He wasn't. She remembered the detachment heading for the cars and wondered if Franks was still there. She pulled a few magazines from the dead cartel soldier and headed for the cars.

Chapter 50

He heard it clearly. A stick breaking just ahead of him. Off to the right. It could have been a deer, a rabbit or any number of a variety of wildlife. But to Brinks, it could only be a cartel gunman's boot stepping on that stick as he maneuvered to kill Brinks. He raised his 9 mm. and fired it in the direction of the sound. With no visible target, he kept pulling the trigger until the semi-automatic was empty.

A single shot ripped out of the darkness and caught him just above the left eye, disintegrating the bone under the brow. He fell backwards, dropping his now empty and useless weapon, and landing on his butt. Somehow he stayed up in the sitting position as he stared out into the darkness. His mind, tranquilized with shock, tried to decode and process the threat hiding under the blanket of night. Two dark shadows emerged advancing aggressively. He became sure that they were two wolves moving in to finish off their kill and feed. Though it made no sense, he was wondering how the wolves learned to use a gun when the two shapes tore themselves from the blackness and manifested in front of him. He saw not two wolves but two men. When they were standing over him and the moonlight reflected back at him from blue eyes, he saw there was something wolflike there. Their bodies were human, but those eyes were all predator. They would look perfectly natural gazing out of the skulls of wolves. They both scanned the night horizon before Jimbo knelt down, his wolf eyes only inches from Brinks. Jack walked behind Brinks, keeping watch in the direction Brinks had come from.

"You're the McCrays," said Brinks like a man who had just spotted Bigfoot and discovered him to be more terrifying than his legend.

"That we are," said Jimbo.

"How bad is it?" asked Brinks.

Jimbo looked at the side of the man's head. Most of the left side of his skull was gone, revealing a perfect side view of his brain. It was hard to believe he was still conscious. Jimbo spit into the darkness before turning his wolf eyes back on Brinks. "Pretty fucking bad. No scenario possible that involves you living till sunrise. If we wrap up your head and tie you to one of the these trees, slit you open and pull your intestines out just a few inches, there's a good chance one of the black bears that live out here, or a pack of coyotes, will catch your scent, start feeding on you before you're dead. They ain't particular about their food being dead before they commence to eating. Or I could show you mercy, end all this for you real quick. Depends on if you tell me what I want to know." Brinks made no verbal response, but his eyes held nothing but surrender. Jimbo continued, "We heard the shooting. What happened?"

"We were going to raid the cartel house. Never made it. We were still out in the middle of the woods when bullets came flying in from every direction. It was a slaughter. You can't go that way. They'll kill you."

"They'll try maybe." Jack's voice came from behind him. It was calm, but there was something there, a hunger. "Well over a dozen of them, by my count, who got it in their heads they were going to do just that. Now they're buried all over these woods, as dead as you're about to be."

Less than a half hour ago he considered the cartel ambush the most terrifying thing he'd ever encountered. But with Jack's cold words filling his ears and Jimbo's colder wolf eyes filling his vision, he could see the cartel as nothing more than prey for these blue-eyed devils. With the acceptance of his impending death, all clouds of delusion cleared from his mind and he saw with perfect clarity how out of place he was here. These thick woods which existed beyond the farthest edges of cities, suburbs and small towns. These patches of dark green that most people just glanced down at as they flew over from one civilized place to another, or blasted past on the highway as they drove the same journey, these places weren't really a part of the America most people recognized. He didn't belong here. None of them did. Not the F.B.I. or the cartel. This place belonged to the primitives, the bears, the coyotes, and the alpha predators that stood before him, the McCrays. "Shoot me, please, right in the head, you said you would."

"Are there any other pigs coming our way?" asked Jimbo.

"I don't think so," answered Brinks. "I ran when the shooting started. I'm sure no one else made it out alive."

"They got my brother?" Jimbo asked.

"They had him. I'm pretty sure. He's dead or as good as."

Jimbo stayed calm but his eyes turned hostile and drilled into Brinks's eyes in a way that almost hurt Brinks. "You're as good as dead, I wouldn't be so sure about my brother."

"I told you everything. You promised, shoot me in the head. I don't want to be here anymore."

"No I didn't. I don't know I can spare the bullet. I don't know how many Mexicans we still got to kill before the night is over. I promised you I would end it quickly." Jimbo pulled his Bowie knife from the scabbard on his hip. With no skull to protect the entire left side of the brain, Jimbo easily plunged the knife in until the tip popped through and hit the skull on the other side. Then he twisted the blade to make sure the brains were scrambled. As he pulled the knife out, he pried a palm-size piece of brain out with it. It stuck to the blade for a few seconds then slid off, plopping to the ground. To Jimbo's shock, the cop stayed conscious, looked over at the piece of brain on the ground then realized what it was and turned back to Jimbo with a horrified look frozen on his face. The expression remained, but the light in his eyes dimmed. Jimbo pushed his chest lightly with the tip of his knife and he fell over backwards. Jimbo wiped the blade on the dead man's pant leg till it had a clean shimmery gleam and replaced it in its scabbard. He exchanged looks with Jack. Then, without a word, they disappeared into the night continuing on to the cartel house.

Chapter 51

Survival mode. That's what Jill was in now. Gone was any thought of arresting either the McCrays or the cartel tonight. All she could focus on now was getting back to the vehicles, getting Franks, assuming he was still there and alive, and getting out of this clusterfuck alive. Like Brinks, Jill moved off into the woods to conceal her movement. Instead of striking out blindly like Brinks though, she kept the pathway in sight and moved alongside it. She wasn't sure how many cartel soldiers were sent to the vehicles. She was playing dead when Hector sent them, but she knew they had a head start on her. There was a good chance they would do what they had to do, and she might meet them on the way back. Hence she stayed off the path. Despite trying to keep the path in sight, several times she had to move further into the woods to navigate around various obstacles. A couple times she became disoriented and had a difficult time making her way back to where she could see the path again. She was struck by how easy it was to get lost out here at night. That, coupled with the idiotic bunched up formation that made it so easy for the cartel to ambush them and the lack of backup, made it painfully obvious how unprepared they were for this whole endeavor.

She continued this awkward, slow process moving in small increments toward her destination. There was no doubt that if Franks was there she would almost certainly arrive too late to help him, but she suppressed this thought because rushing would almost certainly mean getting lost. Her concern about being late was confirmed by the sound of gunfire coming from the direction of her destination. She put her finger on the trigger of the rifle and picked up the pace. She was able to move much faster because she didn't need to keep looking at the path. Instead she moved toward the sound of the gunfire. And the gunfire lasted awhile. Considering that Franks was alone the shooting went on a ridiculous amount of time. There was no way Franks could be holding them off for that long. Then the sound stopped. The finality of that silence somehow scared her more than the gunshots. She reverted back to her slow plodding, constantly checking the path to make sure she wasn't going astray. Just when she was thinking she might be lost, she noticed a gleam through the trees. Studying it closer she decided it must be the metallic gleam of a vehicle. Throwing out all caution she charged forward. When she burst from the woods she found herself on the dirt road. To the right she saw the cars. Many had been backed up to clear the point where the path met the dirt road. All the tires were flat, which explained why she heard so many gunshots.

"Jill!" She turned and pointed the rifle in the direction of the voice. Franks ducked down behind one of the cars. "Jesus Christ, don't shoot! It's me."

"Franks? I thought for sure you'd be dead."

"Come on now." Franks stood up, came out from behind the car and walked toward her. "Take more than a cartel death squad to kill this cowboy."

"So you hid?" Jill smiled.

"Yeah, I hid up in the woods till they left. What happened with the raid?"

"They ambushed us. Killed everyone. There seemed to be

more of them than there was supposed to be. I played dead. Did you get a call out for backup?"

"No, I couldn't get reception. None of these cars are drivable."

"That's for sure."

"We're going to have to walk out of here."

Jill looked at the way the lead cars had been moved back. "You know they moved these cars back so they could get their cars out. We shouldn't walk on the road. They could be leaving any time. We should go about twenty feet into the woods and follow the roads. It's how I got here from where we were ambushed."

Franks looked down at his dress shoes and dress pants and out at the woods. "You know that will take all night?"

"It would most likely take longer than that to make it back to civilization. But at least we won't get shot."

"No just eaten by a fucking bear."

"Well bears don't have assault rifles." She held up the rifle in her hand. "The cartel does. Besides we only have to make it far enough to get a signal then we can call for some backup."

Franks took a deep breath. "All right then. Let's go."

Chapter 52

Hector left two men to watch Jay when he took the rest outside. The two men kept their distance from Jay, not speaking to him or each other for that matter other than to speculate what was going on outside. Hector told them nothing. They would take turns going to the window and peeking out, always being cautious not to be noticed by Hector. It was when they heard the nearby sound of gunfire that they abandoned all concern over Jay and Hector and both went to the window.

Jay knew this could be his only shot. He pulled his hand trying to free it from the rope. He felt the rope catching against the bone of his thumb. He pulled harder deciding to either get his hand free or break his thumb trying. He strained and strained till the rope cleared his thumb then his hand slipped free. He rose from the chair and advanced on the two men. They both stared out the window oblivious to Jay. One held an assault rifle with both hands at waist level. The other held a pistol in his hand. Jay crept up behind the closest one, the one with the assault rifle, and put his arms around him as if giving him a hug from behind. He grabbed the rifle, put his finger on the trigger, pointed at the man with the pistol and squeezed the trigger. The rifle was a fully automatic and he held the trigger down till the magazine was empty. As the dead man with the pistol slid down the wall, Jay let go of the rifle, wrapped his arms around the man hoisted him up and slammed him down hard on the floor. By the time the man had regained enough of his senses to stand up, Jay had retrieved the dead man's pistol and was pointing it at him. There was a second of eye contact then Jay gave him one in the head and two in the body.

Chapter 53

When Hector emerged from the woods, the shootout with the Feds was over. The men were milling about, celebrating their victory. Geno lit up when he saw Hector. "Hector! Tremendous success my friend! The woods are full of dead American pigs."

Hector nodded. "Of course, I never doubted it with you in charge."

Santiago approached Hector. "Where is Julio?"

"What?" asked Hector.

"I said, where is Julio?"

Hector pulled out a cigarette and took his time packing and lighting it. He didn't like the aggressive way Santiago was questioning him. "He's out there."

"Out where?"

Hector took a drag off his cigarette, exhaled and pointed out towards the woods he'd just emerged from. "Out there. Out in the woods. He didn't make it."

"What do you mean he didn't make it? You mean he's dead?" Santiago's hand was on the butt of his pistol as was Geno's who was following the exchange between the two.

"That's right," said Hector. "There were a couple of cops

out there. I don't know, they must have got separated from the group, anyway they fired on us. I killed them both, but not before they got Julio. I'm sorry."

"There weren't no fucking cops in the woods." Santiago stepped closer to Hector. "Why don't you tell me what really happened?"

Hector dropped his cigarette to the ground and stepped on it. "I'm going to tell you one more time." Hector looked straight at Santiago. There was a tense quiet span of several seconds as the two men stared at each other. Everyone was watching now. Hector drew his pistol and put a bullet in Santiago's head and one in his chest. Santiago dropped with a thud. When Hector looked up from the body on the ground, he saw everyone had their guns drawn. Some of Julio's men began by pointing their guns at him, which caused his own men to point their guns at them, which in turn caused those men to turn their guns from Hector and point them at the men who were targeting them. It was clear which men were on his side and which weren't. But they were all mixed together. Hector cursed himself for not seeing this coming. His mind raced for a solution, something to say to deescalate. He could think of nothing.

He couldn't have said who fired the first shot. But that first shot was the spark to the gasoline. Suddenly everyone seemed to be firing, dying or both. Hector dropped to the ground and rolled under the porch. He pointed his gun out toward the action, but no one noticed him. Hector had witnessed much violence in his life. But it tended to be controlled violence that he himself was the author of. He couldn't remember a shootout this chaotic. The only upside was that it was over quick. In less than a minute, he peeked out from beneath the porch. There were maybe a dozen men left standing. They were all his. When he crawled out from under the porch Geno gave him a nod. "Good job my friend," said Hector. "Your loyalty will not be forgotten.

That goes for the rest of you too." He raised his voice so the rest of the survivors could hear.

"It's an honor," said Geno. "I'll strike down anyone who stands against you. And I promise these McCrays will not find me so easy to—"and that was when Jimbo's bullet shattered the back of his skull before exploding out of his face. The man standing next to him fared no better from Jack's bullet. More McCray bullets followed in quick succession as the already depleted cartel ranks shrank even further from the McCrays firing from the woods.

Hector and four survivors raced up the porch for the perceived safety of the house. When Hector charged through the doorway, he was greeted by the sight of Jay pointing a pistol at him and the men he'd left in the house dead on the floor. He just managed to dive to the left and hit the floor as Jay pulled the trigger. The man behind him caught the bullet. When he went down, Jay let the two men behind him have it. The fourth man took the hint that the house was no longer a safe refuge and retreated back outside, which only extended his life a couple seconds as Jack and Jimbo lit him up from the woodline. Hector was alone. He managed to get to the kitchen table and flip it over for cover. Jay put a few rounds through it, but Hector laid low and the bullets went over his head. Hector reached his hand around the table and popped off a few rounds without aiming.

When Jay heard a window in the back room shatter, he didn't worry. Though there was no way he logically could be sure it wasn't Hector's men, he felt instinctively that it was his brother and nephew. He was right. A few seconds after the sound of the breaking glass, they dove behind the sofa, he'd taken cover behind, landing next to him. "Took you fuckers long enough," said Jay.

"How did you let these dipshits take you?" asked Jimbo.

"Long story. How many are left outside?"

"Looked like they were all dead," said Jack.

"You killed them all?"

"We got a few of them. Most of them killed each other." A

259

few of Hector's bullets tore through the sofa and lodged into the wall behind them. The three of them popped up in unison, put a few rounds into the kitchen table and dropped back to the floor.

"What happened to your eye?" asked Jack noticing the bloody sheet wrapped around Jay's head.

"I think it's laying somewhere over there on the floor. It's all good though. I'm going to look badass with a patch. It does kind of hurt though."

"Well," said Jimbo. "If you're done whining about your little boo-boo, you mind if we go ahead and kill this prick?"

"I would *not* mind that at all," said Jay.

Chapter 54

Julio woke face down on the damp earth in considerable pain. He lifted his head, spit out a mouthful of blood, removed two wet leaves that stuck to his face and sat up. Hector had shot him in the back of the head but the bullet went just under his brain, knocked out his front tooth and exited above his upper lip. The force of the shot knocked him unconscious but it was not a kill shot.

He felt the back of his head. His hair was matted with dried blood and the wound was still oozing. His lip and gums were pouring blood. He looked around for his A.K. It was gone as was the .45 from his shoulder holster. But he still had the .38 in his ankle holster. He pulled it out and the feel of it in his hand gave him hope.

Standing up, he stumbled a bit, found his center of balance and headed for the house stepping over several bodies, some of which he recognized, some he didn't. He climbed the steps of the porch. The front door was open slightly. Looking through the crack, it appeared that the only players left alive were Hector and the McCrays. Hector's back was to Julio. He had the kitchen table turned over and was using it for cover, holding a pistol which he would lift above the top or around the side of the table

261

and fire occasional shots. Because he wouldn't risk putting his head up to aim, the bullets harmlessly went into the wall above the sofa the McCrays were hiding behind.

So that was the standoff Julio saw through the doorway. The logical thing to do would be to just let them shoot it out then deal with the survivors. But Julio didn't want anyone else to kill Hector. Without much thought, he knew what he was going to do. The plan was pretty risky, even crazy. He pushed open the door and stepped into the room, behind Hector but in full view of the McCrays. Raising his pistol, he pointed it at Hector, hoping the McCrays would see this and decide not to put a bullet in him. Every step he grew more confident. When Hector's automatic ran out of ammo and he dropped down to reload, Julio knew it was his chance. He stopped worrying about being sneaky and walked right up to him. Hector ejected the empty clip and was reaching for a new one when he saw Julio. Julio waited till there was recognition in Hector's eyes, wanting him to know who was taking his life. When he saw that recognition, he fired. The first bullet went through Hector's eye and put him on his back. Taking no chances, Julio emptied the rest of the bullets into his body.

He stood looking down at Hector's corpse. When he looked up he saw all three McCrays pointing their weapons at him. He pointed his pistol at Hector's corpse. "That piece of shit is dead. Everybody else," he waved his pistol around at the dead bodies scattered about, "is dead. And now you can kill me. But that won't be the end. Senor Diaz will send more soldiers. And if you kill them, he'll send more and more after that if needed. There is no shortage of gunman in Mexico."

"Ain't no shortage of bullets in America," said Jack.

"Not to mention," Julio continued as blood dripped from the hole in his face, "cops have been killed here. Feds. You're harboring a fugitive who broke out of prison. Even if by some miracle you could survive the cartel, how long do you think you could stay here and dodge the Feds?"

Jay lowered his gun. "I'm sensing you're winding up for a pitch. I'll bite. But it better be a doozy. And drop that pistol first."

He let the pistol slip from his fingers and clunk to the floor. "Senor Diaz wanted this fucker to kill me because he knows I'm the only one who can take the cartel from him. We take out Senor Diaz and a few of his capos, and I am the heir apparent. Cut the head off the snake and what is left *will* be loyal to me. You help me with this coup d'état, and not only do I promise this god-forsaken wilderness will be yours, if you want it, but you will leave Tijuana millionaires."

The McCrays stared at him. Several silent seconds stretched between them. Julio began to regret dropping his gun. Then Jimbo lowered his gun. "So, the four of us drag our sorry asses all the way down to Mexico and kill the kings of the Diaz cartel? That is fucking psycho." Jimbo glanced at his brother then his son then back at Julio. He smiled. "Count me in."

"What about you Jack?" asked Jay.

Jack was the only one still pointing his gun at Julio. "I don't know. You think we can trust this beaner?"

Jay gave Julio a hard prison yard appraisal. "Yeah, I do."

"Well then, I'm in too," said Jack lowering his gun.

"There you go then," said Jay. "Viva la Mexico!"

Things moved fast after that. They wanted to get out of that house. That many dead Feds couldn't go unnoticed for long. Jay and Julio both needed urgent medical care. And plans had to be made to take Tijuana. But that, is another story.

About the Author

Here is what Jesse James Kennedy tells us about himself:

"My nephew was sent to prison a couple of years back and asked me to send him my stories to help him pass the time. After he read the stories I wrote, he asked me to write something longer and I began *Missouri Homegrown*. I sent him chapters as I wrote them and he passed them around to other inmates and a couple of guards and they enjoyed them and asked for more so I kept going. (I left out the chapter on the prison break for obvious reasons.)

"I am 45 years old, did a short stint in the Army, 10th Mountain Division Light Infantry which was part of the inspiration for Jay McCray. After the Army I got a little wild, did a little time, then moved from job to job keeping out of trouble and reading a lot and learning to write. I've known many people similar to my characters though none were quite that violent."

Jesse James Kennedy lives in Missouri, where he is at work on another novel about the McCrays.